PENGUIN C

THE SEBASTOPOL SKETCHES

COUNT LEO NIKOLAYEVICH TOLSTOY was born in 1828 at Yasnaya Polyana in the Tula province, and educated privately. He studied Oriental languages and law at the University of Kazan, then led a life of pleasure until 1851, when he joined an artillery regiment in the Caucasus. He took part in the Crimean war, and after the defence of Sebastopol he wrote *The Sebastopol Sketches* (1855–6), which established his reputation. After a period in St Petersburg and abroad, where he studied educational methods for use in his school for peasant children in Yasnaya, he married Sophie Andreyevna Behrs in 1862. The next fifteen years was a period of great happiness; they had thirteen children, and Tolstoy managed his vast estates in the Volga Steppes, continued his educational projects, cared for his peasants and wrote *War and Peace* (1865–8) and *Anna Karenin* (1874–6). *A Confession* (1879–82) marked an outward change in his life and works; he became an extreme rationalist and moralist, and in a series of pamphlets after 1880 he expressed theories such as rejection of the state and church, indictment of the demands of the flesh and denunciation of private property. His teaching earned him numerous followers in Russia and abroad, but also much opposition, and in 1901 he was excommunicated by the Russian Holy Synod. He died in 1910, in the course of a dramatic flight from home, at the small railway station of Astapovo.

DAVID MCDUFF was born in 1945 and was educated at the University of Edinburgh. His publications comprise a large number of translations of foreign verse and prose, including poems by Joseph Brodsky and Tomas Venclova, as well as contemporary Scandinavian work: *Selected Poems* of Osip Mandelstam; *Complete Poems* of Edith Södergran; and *No I'm Not Afraid* by Irina Ratushinskaya. His first book of verse, *Words in Nature*, appeared in 1972. He has translated a number of nineteenth-century Russian prose works for Penguin Classics. These include Dostoyevsky's *The Brothers Karamazov*, *Crime and Punishment*, *The House of the Dead*, *Poor Folk and Other Stories* and *Uncle's Dream and Other Stories*; Tolstoy's *The Kreutzer Sonata and Other Stories*; and Nikolai Leskov's *Lady Macbeth of Mtsensk*. He has also translated Babel's *Collected Stories* and Bely's *Petersburg* for Penguin Twentieth-Century Classics.

THE SEBASTOPOL SKETCHES

LEO TOLSTOY

Translated with an Introduction and Notes by
DAVID McDUFF

PENGUIN BOOKS

PENGUIN BOOKS

Published by the Penguin Group
Penguin Books Ltd, 27 Wrights Lane, London W8 5TZ, England
Penguin Books USA Inc., 375 Hudson Street, New York, New York 10014, USA
Penguin Books Australia Ltd, Ringwood, Victoria, Australia
Penguin Books Canada Ltd, 10 Alcorn Avenue, Toronto, Ontario, Canada M4V 3B2
Penguin Books (NZ) Ltd, 182–190 Wairau Road, Auckland 10, New Zealand

Penguin Books Ltd, Registered Offices: Harmondsworth, Middlesex, England

'Sebastopol in December' and 'Sebastopol in May' first published 1855;
'Sebastopol in August 1855' first published 1856
This translation first published 1986
7 9 10 8 6

Printed in England by Clays Ltd, St Ives plc
Typeset in 9/11 VIP Bembo

CONTENTS

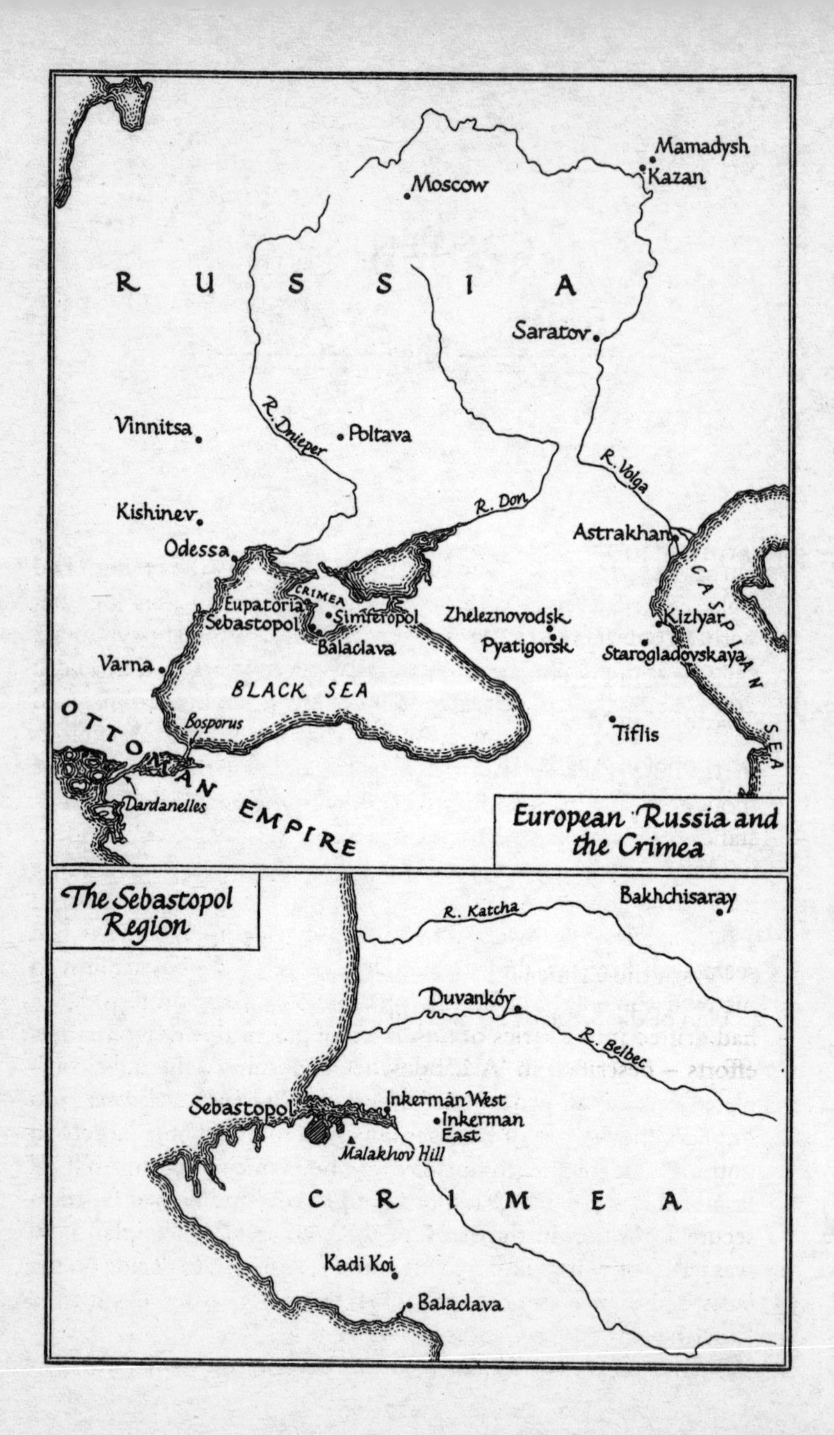
Mamadysh
Kazan
Moscow
RUSSIA
Saratov
Vinnitsa
R. Dnieper
Poltava
R. Volga
R. Don
Kishinev
Odessa
Astrakhan
CRIMEA
CASPIAN SEA
Eupatoria
Sebastopol
Simferopol
Zheleznovodsk
Kizlyar
Pyatigorsk
Balaclava
Starogladovskaya
Varna
BLACK SEA
Bosporus
Tiflis
OTTOMAN EMPIRE
Dardanelles
European Russia and the Crimea
The Sebastopol Region
Bakhchisaray
R. Katcha
Duvankóy
R. Belbec
Sebastopol
Inkerman West
Inkerman East
Malakhov Hill
CRIMEA
Kadi Koi
Balaclava

INTRODUCTION

On 29 April 1851, at the age of twenty-two, the young Leo Tolstoy set out from Yasnaya Polyana for the Caucasus together with his older brother Nikolai, whose battery was stationed there. Nikolai had entered the Russian army seven years earlier, and it was doubtless with a certain amount of envy that Leo had listened to the vivid tales he had to tell of military life and daring exploits in the campaign against the Muslim hill tribes. To Leo, the thought of making a complete break with the established circumstances of his life must have seemed a tempting and attractive one, holding out the best prospect for his future development. Since leaving the University of Kazan's Faculty of Jurisprudence without a degree after less than two years' study, repelled by what had seemed to him the almost total irrelevance of the curriculum to his own concerns and by the 'obstruction' of the professors, he had drifted into a series of unsuccessful practical endeavours. His efforts – described in 'A Landowner's Morning', the only completed part of the pedagogical *Novel of a Russian Landowner* – to improve the welfare of his serfs appeared to have come largely to nothing. He had been unable to find a niche for himself in fashionable society; he had not found a wife; and he had failed to secure a position in the army or the civil service. His plan now was to travel with Nikolai to his battery, and then to decide on the basis of his own impressions whether or not to serve with the Russian army in the Caucasus.

Such a break – it followed in the tradition of earlier Russian writers, such as Marlinsky and Lermontov – seemed to promise Leo Tolstoy the best hope of realizing some of the literary ambitions he secretly nursed. Up to then, his most significant literary achievement had been the keeping of an intimate diary, in which he recorded his personal feelings and formulated rules for the conduct of his life. The diary, which he had begun to write in 1847 at the age of eighteen, was to become his lifelong companion. In it he would sketch and give expression to the inner conflicts and debates that in time would bring many of his fictional characters into being. For the present, however, it was not much more than the place in which he set down his hopes, worries, discontents, resolutions and plans for literary works, such as the 'tale of gypsy life' (8 December 1850), and the 'history of my day' (*istoriya moego dnya*) which was eventually to develop into the three-part novel *Childhood, Boyhood, Youth*.

After making short stops in Moscow and Kazan, in the second half of May the brothers embarked by boat from Saratov down the Volga to Astrakhan; from there they travelled by carriage to Kizlyar, finally reaching the Cossack village of Starogladovskaya, where Nikolai's battery was stationed, on 30 May. The journey made a lasting impression on Tolstoy. Although on reaching Starogladovskaya his first reaction was one of disorientation and bewilderment ('How did I ever end up here? I don't know. Why have I come here? I don't know that, either,' reads the diary entry for 30 May), the wealth of visual impressions he had received – the great flat river, the spectacular mountain scenery, the Circassian tribesmen and their beautiful women who lived like noble savages amid peaks and torrents – was to remain with him to the end of his days, and he later considered this to have been the happiest time of his life. Arrival at the Russian battery did, however, mean that he had to decide whether to join the army or not. It was a decision he put off: for some months he roamed about between Starogladovskaya and the nearby fortified camp of Stary Yurt, where he was based, meditating on his past life and present feelings in extensive diary entries. Yet not all his time was devoted to introspection: the diary contains abundant evidence that the exposure to a radiant, transparent southern nature and to the lives of Cossacks, Tartars, Circassians and other tribesmen was having a profound effect on the development of his personality. His participation as a volunteer, in late June or early July, in a raid on a Chechen village, led by Major-General A. I. Baryatinsky, commander of the left flank of the Caucasian army, seemed unsatisfactory to him at the time ('I didn't act well; unconsciously, I was even afraid of Baryatinsky,' he noted) – yet such activity had the effect of building up his self-confidence. After the raid he was presented to Baryatinsky by Ilya Tolstoy, one of his relatives who was travelling in the Caucasus. Baryatinsky praised the 'young civilian' for his bravery and composure under fire, and recommended him to enlist for active service forthwith. It was, however, another four months before Tolstoy could bring himself to take that step. He set to work on the first part of a novel (*Childhood*), began to study the Tartar language, sketched and read. In the conversations he had, during hunting and woodcarving, with the Cossack tribesman Yepishka (later faithfully portrayed as Yeroshka in *The Cossacks*), he began to come under the influence of a world-outlook that was utterly unlike the Russian, one that valued freedom and bravery above all else and was unfettered by formal religion or institutionalized morality.

At last Tolstoy's life seemed to be opening out in new and unexpected ways: he was living a free and independent existence away from his family, friends and social circle, and he had the latitude he required for writing and creation. Yet this gypsy nomad existence could not continue indefinitely: more and more he was finding it difficult to be a civilian among soldiers; if he were to remain in this land of colour, vitality and adventure, he would have to find some firm rationale for his presence there. The logical next step was for him to take the examination for entrance into the army. On 1 November 1851 Tolstoy and his brother travelled to Tiflis, where the necessary formalities could be completed. After a two-month stay in the city, he passed the examination to become a cadet; now he was a *feyerverker*,* an artillery NCO.

His passing of the examination and subsequent induction into the army were experienced by Tolstoy as the crossing of a moral and spiritual divide. 'Seek out difficult situations,' he had exhorted

* From the German *Feuerwerker*, meaning 'artificer'.

himself in one of the 'rules' contained in his diary of 1850. Filled now with militaristic zeal, he longed to begin his new life as quickly as possible. Sweeping aside official and bureaucratic delays, he used all the influence he could possibly exert in elevated circles in order to have himself assigned at once to his brother's battery, the 4th of the 20th Artillery Brigade, as a fourth-class NCO, thereby making it possible for him to take part in the winter campaign that was already under way. 'With all my strength and with the aid of a cannon I shall assist in destroying the predatory and turbulent Asiatics,' he wrote to his brother Sergei. In a long letter to his aunt, T. A. Yergolskaya, dated 12 January 1852, he portrayed his forthcoming army career as a God-given chance to atone for his faults, the first major test of his character. At the end of this time of danger, discipline and expiation, he would emerge at last as a man worthy of family life:

This is how I picture it to myself. After an unspecified number of years I am at Yasnaya, neither young nor old – my affairs are in order, I have no anxieties, no worries – and you still live at Yasnaya too. You have aged a little, but are still fresh and in good health. We lead the life that we used to lead; I work in the morning, but we see each other almost the whole day; we have dinner; in the evening I read you something that doesn't bore you; then we talk. I tell you of my life in the Caucasus, you talk to me of your memories – of my father and mother; you tell me frightening stories that we once listened to with startled eyes and gaping mouths. We recall people who were dear to us and who are now no more; you will weep, I will do the same; but these tears will be sweet. We will talk of my brothers who will come to see us from time to time, and of dear Marya, who will also spend some months of the year at Yasnaya, which she so loves, with all her children. We won't have any friends – no one will come and bore us and talk gossip. It's a beautiful dream, but it's still not all that I allow myself to dream of. I am married – my wife is a sweet, good, affectionate person; she loves you in the same way as I do. We have children who call you 'grandmama'; you live in the big house, upstairs – the same room that grandmama used to live in; the whole house is as it was in papa's time, and we begin the same life again, only changing roles; you take the role of grandmama, but you are even better; I take the role of papa, but I despair of ever deserving it; my wife, that of mama; the children – our own; Marya – the role of the two aunts, excepting their misfortunes. Even Gasha* will take the role of

* Tolstoy's grandmother's maid.

Praskovya Isayevna.* But we shan't have anyone to take the role that you have played in our family. Never shall we find a soul as beautiful or as affectionate as yours. You will have no successor. There will be three new persons who will appear on the scene from time to time – my brothers – especially the one who will often be with us – Nikolai – an old bachelor, bald, retired from service, as noble as ever.†

During February 1852, Tolstoy took part in fighting against the Chechen tribesmen led by their pugnacious and skilful chieftain Shamil. On 17 and 18 February there were pitched battles on the River Michik, and in one of these an enemy shell hit a wheel of the cannon of which Tolstoy was in charge; miraculously, he escaped with his life. He received two citations for bravery and was on each occasion recommended for the St George Cross. For the rest of 1852 he lived a quiet existence, mostly in Pyatigorsk. For more than a year now he had been working on his novel *Childhood*. In July he sent the manuscript to N. A. Nekrasov, the editor of the *Contemporary*, a literary journal in St Petersburg. Two months later Nekrasov wrote back enthusiastically, offering to publish the novel. Publication took place in October, and although Nekrasov declined to offer a fee for this first work by an unknown author, he led Tolstoy to suppose that the *Contemporary* would pay handsomely for any subsequent works of his it published.

The moral regeneration Tolstoy had hoped to undergo as a result of joining the army was slow to materialize. In particular, he was gambling a great deal at cards, a pastime that was endemic in army life. He justified his gambling to himself and others by representing it as the only chance he had to attempt to make money in order to clear up the troublesome financial affairs of his estate at Yasnaya Polyana. In practice, however, the gambling only made matters worse: he was constantly sending home instructions to Yergolskaya and Sergei to sell off pieces of property to raise money with which to pay off his card debts. With the success of *Childhood*, authorship seemed to offer another possible source of income (during 1852 he completed *The Raid*, a story

* The Tolstoys' housekeeper.

† *Tolstoy's Letters*, 2 vols., translated and edited by R. F. Christian, Athlone (1978).

about his recent military experiences). He began to have serious doubts about whether he should remain in the army or return to Yasnaya Polyana and concern himself exclusively with writing. His health was also debilitated at this period, and he spent much time treating himself at the spas of Zheleznovodsk and Kizlyar. In the end, the pledge he had made to Sergei and his aunt Yergolskaya seems to have been too strong. He remained in the service and during 1853 took part in a further campaign against Shamil, again distinguishing himself for bravery, though again failing to obtain the coveted St George Cross. The campaign was a lengthy one, but during 1853 he managed to undertake a relatively large amount of literary activity including work on *Boyhood* (the continuation of *Childhood*) and some four or five other tales and novels (among them *The Cossacks* and *The Woodfelling*).

Failure to achieve promotion also contributed to Tolstoy's uncertainty about remaining in the service. After two years in the army he was still a cadet, and this had much to do with the delays of the military bureaucracy as well as with his own lack of the necessary official documentation. In July 1853 he wrote to General Baryatinsky complaining about the treatment he had received, and a short time later, against the advice of Sergei and Yergolskaya, he applied for a discharge. Lack of documents meant that this too was delayed, and he then applied instead for military leave.

In the meantime, international political events were about to complicate the situation even further. The vexed question of Russia's relations with her neighbour Turkey, which had been simmering away ever since the signing of the Treaty of Adrianople in 1829, now began to erupt into open hostilities. The closing of the Bosporus and the Dardenelles to the warships of all foreign countries, including Russia, which had followed the conclusion of the international Straits Convention of 1841, proved an intolerable limitation on Russian sovereignty in the area. On 2 July 1853 Tsar Nicholas I sent his troops to occupy Moldavia and Wallachia. Much to his dismay, the British and French promptly sent naval forces to the Dardanelles. At the same time they consulted Austria and Prussia, arriving at a general formula in principle for the solution of the difficulty, which Russia accepted.

However, the actual wording of the formula was, on the advice of the British ambassador, modified in such a way that made it inevitable that Russia would reject it. On 22 October 1853 the British fleet sailed up the Straits, and on the following day Turkey declared war on Russia.

It was now out of the question for Tolstoy to leave the army: all retirement was forbidden until the hostilities were at an end. He decided to follow up his application for leave with one for a transfer to the war zone, seeing in this his best chance of obtaining a speedy promotion. In January 1854 his applications for leave and transfer were approved, and on 2 February he arrived back at Yasnaya Polyana before joining the 5th battery of the 12th Artillery Brigade in active service on the Danube.

In Yasnaya Polyana the news reached Tolstoy that his promotion to the rank of ensign had come through. Together with Nikolai, who had now retired from the army, he went to Moscow and bought a large quantity of military equipment, mostly on his older brother's advice. On 12 March, exhausted after a journey of some 1,400 miles by way of Poltava and Kishinyov, he arrived in Bucharest. While he was there, the Russian armies crossed the Danube and laid siege to Silistria. Tolstoy was assigned to the 3rd battery of the 11th Artillery Brigade, stationed at Oltenitsa, on the outskirts of Bucharest. From Oltenitsa he made frequent trips into the city, where he attended fashionable balls, visited the Grand Opera and the theatre, and continued his medical treatment. At the end of May he rejoined the staff of General Serzhputovsky before the besieged town of Silistria. Here he had his first whiff of 'Turkish powder', and the 'funny sort of pleasure', as he described it, of watching men kill one another. Sitting in the elegant gardens of Mustapha Pasha, breathing the rose-scented air, he admired the view:

> Not to mention the Danube, its islands and its banks, some occupied by us, others by the Turks, you could see the town, the fortress and the little forts of Silistria as though on the palm of your hand. You could hear the cannon fire and rifle shots which continued day and night, and with a field-glass you could make out the Turkish soldiers . . . The spectacle was truly beautiful, especially at night. At night our soldiers usually set about trench work and the Turks threw themselves upon them to stop them;

then you should have seen and heard the rifle fire . . . I amused myself, watch in hand, counting the cannon shots that I heard, and I counted 100 explosions in the space of a minute. And yet, from nearby, all this wasn't at all as frightening as might be supposed. At night, when you could see nothing, it was a question of who would burn the most powder, and at the very most 30 men were killed on both sides by these thousands of cannon shots . . .*

After the lifting of the siege, the Russian army entered Bucharest, and once more the round of theatre-going, gambling and dissipation began. It was at this time that Tolstoy received a flattering letter from Nekrasov, informing him that *Boyhood* had been accepted by the *Contemporary*. Suddenly he decided he had had enough of sitting on the sidelines: he wanted to experience warfare not as a spectator but as a participant. He petitioned Prince Gorchakov, the Russian general who had led the siege of Silistria, to send him anywhere where service was at its most active. Uppermost in his thoughts was the Crimea. Rumours of events there had been filtering through to the Russian forces on the Danube for some time. Tolstoy did not have long to wait: on 19 July the staff left Bucharest for the Russian frontier.

The reasons for the curiously unnecessary conflict that came to be known as the Crimean War lay in the refusal of Nicholas I to countenance the growth of French influence at Constantinople and his desire to restore the dominant position Russia had enjoyed there in 1833. The hostility of France was a foregone conclusion; Nicholas was, however, relying on the support of Prussia, the friendship of Austria and the neutrality of Britain – none of which were forthcoming. Thus instead of an easy war with Turkey alone, he had to fight a complex series of actions against a multiple enemy which included British, French and Sardinian as well as Turkish forces. The Crimean campaign, which followed the siege of Silistria, was the most important of these actions: it was initiated by the British and French forces who on 2 September 1854, after sailing in full view of the Russians, past Sebastopol, the only Russian naval base on the Black Sea, landed at Eupatoria. They met no opposition from the unprepared and disorganized

* *Tolstoy's Letters*, op. cit.

Russians, whose naval commander, Admiral Menshikov, had repeatedly declared his belief that the landing would not take place until 1855.

Tolstoy reached the Russian frontier town of Kishinyov on 9 September, the day after the battle of the Alma, at which the disarray of Russian strategy had led to a costly defeat at the hands of the allies. The staff set up its headquarters at Kishinyov, and it was from there that Tolstoy was informed that he had been promoted to the rank of sub-lieutenant. The news of the landings and the defeat affected him profoundly. Now that the fighting was taking place on Russian soil, he felt directly involved. The town life of Kishinyov, with its balls, intrigues and entertainments, upset him more than the dissipations of Bucharest, and he at once threw himself into a project which he had contemplated even before arriving in Russia. This was the foundation of an army gazette – independent of the official army newspaper *The Russian Veteran* – which would publish articles by officers containing accurate accounts of battles, war stories, reports of heroic deeds, soldiers' songs and articles on artillery and military engineering. The aim of the gazette was to be the improvement of the forces' morale and the education of the common soldiery. Tolstoy intended to fund it from the proceeds of the sale of the large family house at Yasnaya Polyana, which he had recently instructed his brother-in-law to carry out. He wrote requesting the sum of 1,500 roubles to be sent to him. It would, of course, be necessary to obtain official permission to publish such a news-sheet, and Tolstoy prepared a specimen issue (composed largely of articles he had written himself) for presentation to Prince Gorchakov, who forwarded it to the War Minister. Tolstoy appears to have believed that the idea of a 'spontaneous' military publication of this type would have some appeal to the military-minded Nicholas I; yet he must surely have known that the Tsar, who had succeeded to the throne amid the booming of cannon on the Senate Square and the bloody retribution that followed the Decembrist conspiracy of 1825, would never agree to let the officers in his army take matters into their own hands in the way Tolstoy was suggesting. At all events, Tolstoy's request was refused, and when the 1,500 roubles eventually arrived from Yasnaya Polyana he gambled them away at cards in a single night.

This setback did not, however, lessen Tolstoy's desire to put his literary gift to service in the patriotic Russian cause. As news of the Russian victory at Balaclava began to come through, followed by accounts of the defeat at Inkerman on 24 October, the conviction grew within him that he must gain some experience of the fighting at first hand. After Inkerman, at which the Russian force was driven back with a loss of some 10,000 killed and wounded, Tolstoy's diary began to register with clarity the twin strands of his attitude to the war – a fierce and aggressive patriotism, and an equally fierce and aggressive desire that the military authorities and the Russian people as a whole should be apprised of the truth concerning the glaring deficiencies of the Russian military machine. His diary entry for 2 November, written at Odessa, reflected this:

> Since the time the Anglo-French forces landed, we have had three battles with [the enemy] . . . The first, the action fought along the Alma on 8 September, in which the enemy attacked and routed us; the second, Liprandi's* action of 13 September, in which we were the attackers and the eventual victors, and the third, the terrible action led by Dannenberg,† in which we were again the attackers and were once more put to rout. A treasonable, an outrageous action. 10th and 11th divisions attacked the enemy's left flank, turned it and spiked 37 pieces. Then the enemy brought up 6,000 carbines,‡ only 6,000 against our 30 [thousand] strong force. And we retreated, losing some 6,000 brave men. We were compelled to retreat, for because of the impassable state of the roads half of our troops had no artillery at all and, God knows why, there were no sharpshooters either. Terrible slaughter. It will weigh upon the souls of many! Lord, forgive them. The news of this action has made an impact. I have seen old men weeping and sobbing, and young men swearing to kill Dannenberg. Great is the moral strength of the Russian people. Many political truths will come to the surface and develop in this house of tribulation for Russia.

* Commander of the Russian forces at Balaclava.

† Commander of the Russian forces at Inkerman.

‡ The Russian word is *shtutser*, the name given by the Russians to the French Minié rifle, which, with its superior threading and longer range, proved a deadly and devastating weapon.

The sense of ardent love for the fatherland that is arising and flowing from Russia's misfortunes will long leave its trace on her.

After Inkerman, the Russian forces withdrew to Sebastopol, where they were based, and the winter siege began. The tales of the heroic defence of Sebastopol that reached Tolstoy in Kishinyov impelled him to apply at once for a transfer to the besieged town, where he arrived on 7 November 1854.

The most accurate and comprehensive account of the siege area was given by a member of the British force, Captain H. C. Elphinstone, RE, and was published in 1859 as the *Journal of the Operations Conducted by the Corps of Royal Engineers*. Although the topography employed by the British differed in some respects from that used by the Russians, Elphinstone's account still makes the best introduction to the layout of the siege. I have inserted Russian topography where it differs from the British:

An extensive inlet of the sea, called the harbour of Sebastopol, which runs inland to a distance of nearly four miles, divides this fortress into two distinct parts, a north and a south side perfectly separated from each other. The only means of communication between either is 'by boat' across this harbour, or else by making on land a circuit of many miles. This separation of the two sides is not limited to the harbour only, but extends to the ground beyond, for several miles to the eastward; where the wide and swampy valley of the Tchernaya, bounded on each side by lofty and precipitous rocks, renders communication from one side to the other extremely difficult at all times and during the rainy seasons quite impracticable, excepting in one or two places where roads and bridges have been established.

The separation of the two sides is so complete that the force investing the one side would find it impossible to render ready assistance to a force besieging the other; and they would be utterly unable to supply each other with provisions and ammunition. Each would have to act independently and trust exclusively to its own resources.

A complete investment was therefore impracticable without the employment of two separate armies, each having its own base of operations, and each of sufficient strength to compete by itself with the total force of the Russians in the Crimea. Again, the capture of either side by no means necessitated the fall of the other; for neither can be said to have any command over the other, on account of the great distance between them; and in the event of either side falling to the possession of the attacking party, the great basin would still form an almost insurmountable barrier to the further advance of the besiegers; so that to obtain entire possession of Sebastopol two independent attacks, one against the south, the other against the north front, would be requisite . . .*

The principal defences faced the sea, and on that front were of permanent character, very extensive, and armed with powerful batteries. At the entrance to the harbour, on the south side, stood the two forts of the Quarantine Bastion [Quarantine battery] and Alexander [Alexander battery], mounting 60 to 90 guns respectively; the former a closed earthen redoubt, with its guns mounted *en barbette*, commanding the Quarantine Harbour; the latter a permanent work of masonry, casemated, and likewise closed at the gorge by a crenellated wall . . . All these defences towards the sea were of so formidable a character as to nullify one of the great advantages which the possession of a most powerful fleet gave the allies over the Russians; so much so that the co-operation of the fleet in a joint attack with the land forces could not produce any decisive effect upon works of such strength and magnitude . . .

On the land side the works of defence to the south of Sebastopol were at this time [1854] comparatively trifling, but they occupied very commanding positions and were placed on ground which nature had strongly fortified.

A single stone wall (about twelve feet high and six feet thick), crenellated, but quite exposed, surrounded part of the town, and extended partly as a 'bastion trace' and partly as an 'indented line' from the Artillery Bay to the Central Bastion [5th bastion]. A wide and steep ravine, answering the purpose of a huge ditch, ran in front of the line, from the Quarantine to the Central Bastion, and so completely separated it from the ground beyond that all approaches by trenches on that side were subsequently found to be quite impracticable. The wall, along its whole extent, was lined with numerous pieces of artillery, of which those in the most prominent position were of heavy metal. Exclusive of the 56 guns in the Artillery Fort [7th bastion], about 42 pieces of ordnance of various calibres were then in position in the rear of the crenellated wall.

To the south-east of the Central Bastion, but separated from it by a deep ravine, across which a dry stone wall had been hastily constructed, and armed with about 24 field pieces, was an earthen battery, nearly

* 'Like most of the allied military strategists of the time, Elphinstone assumes that any attack on the fortress would be impossible. Such rigid thinking was responsible for the massive bloodshed sustained by the allies during the war – in the end, however, the Russians surrendered the fortress after only one key point had been taken.' See Philip Warner, *The Crimean War, A Reappraisal*, London (1972), from which Elphinstone's account is quoted.

completed, called the Flagstaff Bastion [4th bastion], occupying a very commanding site, and finished with 12 heavy guns.

Such were the works of defence on the west side of Sebastopol. Of these the Flagstaff Bastion formed the key, for it took in reverse all the works to the west of it. But although the possession of this battery might have led to the fall of the town side of the place, it would have been difficult to hold it without at the same time obtaining a footing on the eastern side as the ground and works to the east of the Dockyard Creek in their turn commanded this battery, and took it in reverse.

On the eastern side, which was perfectly separated from the western by deep and precipitous ravines at the head of the Dockyard Creek, were the following works:

1st An earthen battery called from its shape the 'Redan' ['tooth' – the Russians called this the 3rd bastion] which was armed with 17 heavy guns, and at which large working parties were still busily engaged. Immediately in its rear, a dry stone wall, skirting the brow of the hill, branched off in a westerly direction to a place subsequently called the Barrack Battery where at present 10 field pieces were in position to flank the Redan and the ground to the west of it, and in the valley just beneath it, at the head of the Dockyard Creek, about a dozen field pieces, protected by a low stone wall, fully commanded all approaches to the town from the valleys beyond.

2nd The semicircular masonry tower of the Malakoff, mounting 5 heavy guns *en barbette* around which was a circular entrenchment, with a short flank at each end, nearly completed and armed with 10 heavy guns.

3rd A battery called the Little Redan, still incomplete but most probably armed.

4th Adjoining the harbour a considerable-sized stone building in the shape of a cross, which had been converted into a defensible barrack.

Of all these defensive works the Malakoff had the most commanding position, and formed the key of the whole of the south side of the place. It took in reverse all the works on the eastern side, and from its position on an independent high knoll afforded a good site from which to repel assaults at any time. The enemy appeared fully aware of the importance of this site and employed large working parties in strengthening it, and he had even commenced in its rear a dry stone wall, which surrounded part of the Karabelnaja suburb, and answered the purpose of an inner or second line of entrenchment . . .

The centre of the position was occupied by the three main batteries, the

Flagstaff [4th bastion], Redan [3rd bastion] and Malakoff [8th bastion], powerfully armed, nearly all equally salient, and on commanding positions at the extremity of three leading spurs, by which alone an enemy could approach, and over which the garrison had full view for a distance of more than 2,000 yards to their front. The ravines between these ridges, although winding, run directly towards the batteries, and were consequently enfiladed throughout, and commanded by the enemy's guns. Men of war likewise were moored in the dockyard and careening creeks, and at the head of the harbour, with their broadsides bearing on such of the lines of approach as might be taken by the storming parties . . .

An important feature of the defences was the complex and sophisticated system of earthworks devised by the Russian engineer General E. I. Totleben. R. Chodasiewicz, a Pole who was serving with the Russian army, noted:

This war has proved that the best kind of defence against a regular attack consists of earthworks, that can so easily be changed, altered and increased to meet the attacks. The batteries at Sebastopol were at first nothing but earth, loosely thrown up with the shovel, the embrasures were plastered with moistened clay; but when it was discovered that this was not enough, they were faced with stout wicker work. Then fascines were introduced, and finally gabions* were employed. The batteries were frequently found not to bear upon the required point, or the embrasures were not made so as to enable the guns to be pointed in the right direction. Whenever a discovery of this sort was made the whole was changed during the night. If no changes were required, new and more formidable works were added. In this respect Sebastopol offered unexampled advantages in the arsenal, so that there were always guns to mount in these new works. If one of the bastions of Sebastopol were to be taken, and a section made, suppose for instance of the Malakoff, it could then be traced through its different periods of existence, till it became the mass of sandbags and gabions it is at present, with the enormous embrasures firmly revetted with two or three rows of gabions. Then were added the casemates, holes dug in the ground, and covered with enormous ship-timber that was again covered with earth to the thickness of eight or ten feet, and perfectly proof to the heaviest bomb. In these the garrison, and a part of the gunners, could always find shelter; though these casemates eventually caused the loss of the Malakoff, and consequently the whole town. By this means of defence it was possible to concentrate a tremendous fire upon any given

* Wicker baskets filled with earth, for use in fortification.

point of the trenches. The commander of every bastion and every battery had his orders in which direction he was to fire, and what guns. All these arrangements emanated from Totleben.*

Nicholas I had played an important personal role in the development of Russian engineering, and many of the bold and innovative advances in military technology that were successfully tested at Sebastopol were evolved under his patronage and with his encouragement. During the extensive mining operations during the siege, for example, the Russians exploded all their mines by means of electricity, using the Volta galvanic apparatus. Another of Nicholas's interests was artillery, and here too the Russians were certainly equal or even possibly superior to their British and French adversaries. J. S. Curtiss, the author of a study of the Russian army under Nicholas I, writes:

> The Russian artillery had both foot and horse batteries. Somewhat less than half of the foot batteries were field or heavy artillery, with four twelve-pound cannon, of 4·8 inch calibre, and four half-*pud* (18 lb.) howitzers with six-inch bore. The howitzers, with shorter barrels, were for lobbing shells at the enemy and for firing grapeshot at short range. The cannon fired roundshot, shell, and grapeshot at short range. The light batteries, including most of the horse artillery, had 6 lb. cannon (3·76 inch bore) and quarter-*pud* (9 lb.) howitzers. The heavier guns had an extreme range of almost twelve hundred yards, while the lighter ones carried as far as nine hundred yards.†

Like the engineers, the Russian artillery was an elite force. Because of the ineffectiveness of the infantry, who were armed with old-fashioned percussion muskets and made their principal contribution in massed, sustained bayonet charges, the Russian army 'relied heavily on the fire of the artillery to disorganize the foe and prepare the way for the charge of the infantry'.‡ The shells fired by the artillery were essentially identical with the eighteenth-century 'bomb' (the Russian name for them is *bomba*, which Tolstoy uses to refer to any explosive artillery charge,

* Quoted in Warner, op. cit., pp. 135–6.

† J. S. Curtiss, *The Russian Army Under Nicholas I, 1825–55*, Duke University Press, Durham, North Carolina (1965).

‡ ibid.

whether fired from a mortar, a howitzer or a cannon): this was a spherical cast-iron casing containing explosive; there was an aperture in the casing into which a fuse was inserted. The fuse was ignited by the gunpowder in firing, and the shell would explode when it burnt down into the casing. It was possible to time the explosion to coincide with impact, but in general the shells either burst in the air or lay on the ground for some time before going off. The 'splinters', or fragments, of the shell proved as deadly as any sophisticated small-arms fire, and the Russians discharged very large quantities of these projectiles, as did the enemy forces. During the nightly bombardments, the sky would be criss-crossed by the trails of the burning fuses. The Russian earthworks provided effective protection against the enemy shells and round shot, while the sheer volume of the Russian salvoes caused acute problems to the allied forces, who relied mainly on the protection afforded by trenches.

As an artillery officer at Sebastopol, Tolstoy was well placed to observe all sections of Russian army life. He was shocked by some of what he saw. Under Nicholas, the army had grown in size, and in some respects conditions had improved since the reign of Alexander I. The term of service to the colours had been reduced to fifteen years for men with excellent conduct records; the conditions of life in the military colonies had been made at least tolerable; the army's new accounting system had reduced, though by no means eliminated, the corruption that was such an encumbrance upon the enlisted men; the feeding of the soldiers had improved in quality, and medical and hospital provisions had been made more widely available.* Much, however, was still badly wrong with the Russian military machine. The system of serfdom made necessary the retention of a long period of service for a limited number of serfs, making impossible the formation of a citizen army which would provide much-needed reserves of trained men. The average Russian soldier was a peasant automaton, wholly at the mercy of the landowning nobility. He was poorly armed and poorly equipped, and was trained to march in

* At Sebastopol, the hospital provisions organized by N. I. Pirogov were particularly effective.

dense formations in which musketry was a non-essential adjunct to prowess with the bayonet. ('The bullet is a fool, the bayonet is a hero' was one of General Suvorov's maxims, coined during the reign of Catherine II and still current in 1885.) Unthinking obedience was the order of the day. The soldiers still lived under the shadow of the widespread graft that extended throughout the officer class. There were numerous cases of company commanders starving their men by expropriating the money that was allocated for food. Curtiss describes a large number of 'rackets' common in the service. Some of these involved the private's kit:

> At times the wearing-out of the soldier's equipment was a result of the dishonesty of his commander. Instead of insisting on the issue of first-grade materials by the Commissariat, the dishonest colonel could readily obtain second- or third-rate materials, for which he would receive rebates from the Commissariat, as he would sign a statement that he had received goods of the best quality. The Commissariat officials, who had bought the inferior goods from conniving contractors, had collected the full price for first-grade goods from the government, and thus both colonel and Commissariat officers would profit by the acceptance of poor-grade goods. The troop units were by no means innocent in this peculation.*

Another form of corruption (referred to at some length by Tolstoy in the third Sebastopol sketch) involved the provisioning of the horses:

> While the Provision Department might have supplied the regiments with forage, it rarely did so, as the buying and moving of quantities of oats, hay, and straw would have been complicated and difficult. Hence the regiments themselves handled this matter. Twice a year the regimental commanders through the divisional commanders presented the corps commanders with the prices at which they would agree to feed their horses. The corps commander, armed with a price list from the Provision Department, then established the prices for forage. In theory, he could reduce the prices suggested by the colonels to reasonable levels, but in actuality this was rarely done. If the colonels refused to feed their animals at the lowered prices, the task of supplying forage would then fall to the Provision Department, which was extremely reluctant to do this. Hence the corps commander usually accepted the prices suggested by the colonels and merely demanded that they feed their horses well.

* Curtiss, op. cit., p. 216.

The colonels usually set their prices for forage well over the market price – sometimes double the current rate. While they explained that they could not foresee accurately the future price developments and had to protect themselves against sudden price increases, the real reason probably was to obtain extra income. The Provision Department had no reason to object to this system, for it everywhere retained two per cent or more of the sums that it dispensed, and thus it stood to benefit by the high prices approved for the cavalry regiments. The colonels also were satisfied with the amounts they had received. They did not retain all the profits, however, as they had to turn the actual purchase of the forage over to the squadron commanders. The latter demanded as large a share of the gains as possible, while the colonels sought to keep as much as they could. After much bargaining, a satisfactory bargain was struck. The captains, who were usually in grave financial straits, looked on their squadrons as valuable income-properties and sought to recoup their debts and save a nest-egg for old age. The other officers of the regiment, both the majors and the junior officers, had no share in these transactions and remained in financial straits and often had little to do with the affairs of the regiment. The colonels were the chief beneficiaries of this arrangement.

The results of this were unfortunate for the cavalry. The colonels enriched themselves and spent money on the outward aspects of their regiments. At reviews the horses were sleek and fat, the uniforms clean and new, and the regimental band made a good show. The enlisted men replied to questions with loud shouts of satisfaction with their condition. Hence the inspector would thank the colonel for having done well with his regiment. The divisional and corps commanders would sign the books every month, attesting to the fine condition of the regiments, although those who were intelligent must have realized that the situation was not good, for the generals themselves were products of the same system and in their hearts knew that it was a false one.†

All this prompted Tolstoy to write a personal appeal, entitled 'A Note on the Negative Aspects of the Russian Soldier and Officer', to one of the Grand Dukes (the sons of Nicholas I), in which he bitterly attacked the poor conditions of service, the mismanagement and graft he had observed. An army in which a common soldier was flogged for smoking a long-stemmed pipe or daring to protest when his commander was found guilty of stealing from him could hardly be thought to have a sound moral

* Curtiss, op. cit., pp. 216–17.

core, and could not be expected to fight effectively, he argued. In particular, he criticized the low calibre of the average Russian officer:

> The majority of Russian officers are men who are unfit for any type of profession apart from the military one. While they are in the service their main aim is the acquisition of money. The means they employ towards its realization are extortion and oppression. The Russian officer is uneducated, either because he has received no education, or because he has lost it in a sphere where it is useless and even a liability, or because he despises it as of no use in his struggle for success in the service . . . he despises the rank of officer because it exposes him to the influence of people who are coarse and immoral, and involves him in useless and degrading occupations. The nobleman despises army service on the front. In army society the spirit of love for the fatherland, for chivalrous daring, for military honour provokes ridicule; oppression, debauchery and extortion are what command respect.

The 'Note' was never delivered. It seems to typify the strongly negative strand in Tolstoy's ambivalent attitude towards his Sebastopol experience, one which is countered by an equally strong positive strand. The first words of the 'Note', deleted from the final drafts, were significant: 'The Russian armed forces are enormous, and they would be glorious, would be invincible . . .' Notwithstanding all the evidence of weak leadership, poor military and strategic technique, brutality and extortion, Tolstoy was filled with a profound admiration for the heroism of the defenders of Sebastopol. 'The spirit of the troops passes all description,' he wrote to his brother Sergei on 20 November:

> Not even in the time of ancient Greece was there such heroism. As he inspected his troops, Kornilov would say to them, not 'Good health, men,' but 'If you are called on to die, men, will you die?' And the soldiers would cry back: 'We will die, your excellency. Hurrah!' And they shouted this not for the sake of effect, for on every face you could see that they uttered these words not in jest but *in earnest*, and indeed 22,000 men have already fulfilled this promise.
>
> A wounded soldier almost on the point of death told me how on the 24th [the date of the battle of Inkerman] they had taken a French battery but had been given no reinforcements. He was sobbing out loud. A company of sailors nearly mutinied on being told that they were to be

relieved from the battery on which they had held out for thirty days under fire. Soldiers tear the fuses out of shells with their bare hands. Women take water to the men on the bastions. Many of them have been killed or wounded. Priests enter the bastions bearing crosses and recite prayers under fire. On the 24th, in one brigade there were 160 wounded men who refused to leave the battlefront. Extraordinary days!

On 5 December 1854, Tolstoy visited Sebastopol in order to obtain guns for his battery, and this time he was favourably impressed by much of what he saw. 'The presence of Saken* is visible in everything . . . Saken has introduced arrangements for the transportation of the wounded and has had dressing stations put up on all the bastions. It was Saken who made the order concerning the playing of military music.' On the second trip to Sebastopol in January 1855, Tolstoy visited the 4th bastion. As Elphinstone makes clear in the account already quoted, this was a vital point in the defences, a place under constant fire, where many Russian soldiers had lost their lives. In the middle of January he received another transfer to a new battery on the River Belbek, some seven miles from the town. It was here that he began work on a literary description of military life, one which represented a major advance on the efforts he had so far made in connection with the ill-fated gazette and the undelivered 'Note'. The project began when Tolstoy wrote to the editor of the *Contemporary* on 11 January 1855, offering to send articles and stories on military themes, based on his own war experiences. He proposed to supply Nekrasov with sufficient material for between two and five printed sheets every month and, if the editor agreed, to send first of all an article entitled 'A Letter about the Sisters of Mercy', and then 'Memories of the Siege of Silistria', and 'Letter from a Soldier in Sebastopol'. While he waited for a reply, Tolstoy resumed work on *Youth*. On 18 February, Nicholas I died, and for a short time there was some doubt as to whether his successor, Alexander II, would continue the war. He decided to do so, however, and Tolstoy wrote in his diary: 'Great changes await Russia. One must labour and have courage in order to participate in these momentous hours of Russia's life.'

* Baron D. E. Osten-Saken, the commander of the Sebastopol garrison.

On 20 March, Nekrasov's reply arrived. 'He asks me to send military articles,' Tolstoy noted. 'I shall have to write them all myself. I shall describe Sebastopol during various phases of the siege, and the idyll of the officers' life.'

During the winter of 1854–5, the Russian army had opened no major offensive, but had concentrated instead on a series of counter-mining operations directed by Totleben, which resulted in the wrecking of the French mine corridors. After the French had blown up their own mine system and withdrawn to their trenches some distance to the rear, Totleben supervised the seizure of the craters, which were connected into a formidable trench system that held the enemy at bay for many months. During this period, the Russians launched frequent night sorties, usually in detachments of two or three hundred men, although sometimes in much larger numbers. They are described by Curtiss:

> The attacking parties usually had little difficulty in penetrating the enemy trenches, seizing prisoners and driving back working groups. At such times they often levelled the trenches, spiked captured cannon, and sometimes carried off small mortars. These exploits delighted many young daredevils, who rejoiced in the exciting adventures and on occasion made sorties without orders, although this was generally forbidden. Some of these hardy spirits became adepts at taking prisoners, using short pikes, with the points bent into hooks, to catch unwary sentries. Much annoyed at this, the French Gen. Canrobert sent a note of protest to Gen. Adj. Osten-Saken, commander of the Russian garrison, saying that the Russians were using hooks and ropes to capture men and '*que ce ne sont point là des armes courtoises*'.*

Early in 1855 the French command, acting under the advice of General Adolphe Niel, a skilled engineer, transferred the centre of their attack to the Russian left, in particular to the Kornilov bastion on the Malakhov Kurgan (Malakhov Hill – 'Malakoff' is the French spelling of this name) and the Green Hill, or Mamelon Vert, replacing the British in this sector. On 9 February Totleben had laid out a redoubt (the Selenginsk) on the extreme left, near the River Tchernaya; the French had soon realized that this would outflank their approaches to the Malakhov and tried to capture it,

* Curtiss, op. cit., p. 340.

but were repelled by the Russians and sustained considerable losses. The establishment of the Volhynia redoubt 400 paces ahead enfiladed the French batteries and trenches, and thus halted the French advance towards the Malakhov. By the construction, during the night of 28 February, of the Kamchatka lunette, the defenders turned the tables on the allied forces, who now had to build trenches and batteries against the new defences before they could attack the Malakhov.

On 28 March the French and the British began a heavy bombardment of the lunette and the two redoubts. This lasted until 10 April. The Russian command expected an assault, and Tolstoy's battery, like many others, was ordered to Sebastopol. Here he began work on his new war story: 'Our battery arrived yesterday,' he wrote on 2 April. 'I am living in Sebastopol. We have already suffered up to 5,000 losses, but not merely are we holding our own, we are doing so well that this defence ought to clearly demonstrate to the enemy [the impossibility] of his ever taking Sebastopol. In the evening I wrote two pages of "Sebastopol".' On 3 April Tolstoy was sent to the 4th bastion, where he was placed in charge of a battery of guns. There he had to serve a schedule of four days on duty and eight days off, until 15 May. But he relished his time on the bastion. In its casemate, and later in his town billet, he continued to work on *Youth*, and on his war story, as a recreation during lulls in the fighting.

On 19 April the 'lodgments', as the Russians termed the weak entrenchments which had been dug in front of the 5th bastion and the Schwartz redoubt on the Russian right, were stormed by the French. This action entailed heavy casualties on both sides. Tolstoy wrote in his diary: 'Our spirits are falling daily, and the notion that Sebastopol may after all be taken is beginning to manifest itself in much that is happening.' In response to the storming, Totleben insisted that a system of trenches should be constructed on Cemetery Hill, on the far right, from which he eventually planned to attack the entire allied flank. On 9 May Khrulev led a large force to build lodgments on the hill, and on the night of 10 May the French launched a massive assault of sixteen battalions, which took the Russian trenches, but were eventually repelled by Khrulev's counter-attack. It is this assault which forms the backdrop to 'Sebastopol in May', the second sketch in this volume. The lodgments were held, but Prince Gorchakov instructed Khrulev to withdraw his men if the French attacked again in force, since the position would be too costly to defend. When the French did attack, the Russians retreated. In two nights they lost 3,400 men, for no appreciable purpose. The French put their own losses at 2,303, which Napoleon III described as a greater loss than that sustained by the French at Austerlitz.

During May the French reinforced the gains they had made on the Russian right, causing further heavy Russian casualties. At the same time Major-General Pélissier, who had taken over the French command from General Canrobert, pushed the attack on the Russian left, finally opening a two-day cannonade on the Kamchatka lunette and the Selenginsk and Volhynia redoubts at the end of the month. Although the French succeeded in storming the Kamchatka lunette they were beaten back from the Malakhov itself, and the Russian guns inflicted heavy losses on them. The Russians re-took the lunette, but were again driven out by the French reserves. In their fighting, the Russians reported their losses as 2,500, the French estimated theirs at nearly 3,000, and the British lost 500.

On 19 May Tolstoy was transferred – possibly, some have speculated, as a result of official intervention – to another battery on the River Belbek. Saddened and disturbed by the evidence of Russian mismanagement he had observed towards the end of his period of service on the 4th bastion, he began to return once more to his broodings on the poor moral fibre of the Russian soldiers and officers; while they might be capable of acts of great courage and heroism, the troops were inwardly vitiated by a spiritual malaise that seemed to lie at the heart of Russian life, and were certainly inferior to the British and French whom he encountered from time to time during the odd ceasefire. Applying to the Russian army the same somewhat morbid procedures of analysis he was accustomed to bring to bear upon himself, he began to conceive his mission as a military Gogol, exposing *poshlost* and evil wherever they raised their heads. On completing *The Wood-felling*, he began work on a second Sebastopol sketch, entitled 'A

Spring Night in Sebastopol', in which he depicted the life of Russian officers, and also gave a picture of the besieged town by night. This he had attempted to do in early drafts of the first sketch, but had been unsuccessful; the final draft retained only the 'day' episode.

At the end of April, Tolstoy had sent this first episode, 'Sebastopol in December', to the *Contemporary*. In June it was published above the signature 'L. N. T.', together with a note from the editor informing the public of the author's promise to send monthly reports from Sebastopol. The sketch drew instant praise and appreciation from a wide range of public opinion. Here the positive strand of Tolstoy's attitude towards the war was uppermost: he wrote as a Russian patriot, and praised men, officers and generals alike in his brilliant evocation of daily life in the besieged town, and of the heroic spirit of its defence. Alexander II was profoundly moved by the sketch, had it translated into French, and is supposed to have issued a dispatch to the military authorities ordering that 'this young man's life be guarded well'. Turgenev, who read extracts from the sketch that were published in *The Russian Veteran*, was warmly enthusiastic, writing to I. I. Panayev on 27 June: 'May God give us more such articles!' When Turgenev read the sketch in its entirety, he wrote to the same correspondent that 'Tolstoy's article about Sebastopol is a miracle', and that he 'shed a few tears while reading it, and shouted "Hurrah!" '.

On 4 July Tolstoy sent the manuscript of the second sketch to Panayev at the *Contemporary*, together with a letter in which he wrote:

> Although I am convinced that it is incomparably better than the first [sketch], it will not be liked, of that I am certain. I even fear the censor may not agree to pass it at all. In all the passages that seem to me risky, I have provided variants marked with a 'V', or have designated by means of brackets that the relevant passage is to be excluded if it is found to displease the censor. If they try to delete even passages that I have not marked, please on no account publish the piece. If you do, I shall be very upset. I have provided an alternative title ['A Spring Night in Sebastopol] since 'Sebastopol in May' too obviously refers to the action of 10 May, and the *Contemporary* isn't permitted to publish accounts of military actions. I have

substituted for 'Nieprzysiecki'* the name 'Gnilokishkin',† in the eventuality that the censor says it's impossible for an officer to refuse to serve because he has a gumboil – thus these are two different officers. If it proves possible to insert the Polish phrase, please supply a translation in a footnote . . . And could you denote the Russian and French swear-words by means of dots, even without the initial letters if necessary, though these are essential, in my opinion. In general, I hope and trust that you will be so kind as to put up as strong a defence of my story as you can. Since you are better acquainted with the view of the censor, you will be able to set before him a few of the variants that will least upset him and make whatever minor changes that may be necessary in such a way that the overall meaning does not suffer.

On 18 July, Panayev wrote back to Tolstoy stating that in his opinion something would have to be added at the end of the piece if it were to stand any chance of being passed by the censor. The words which were eventually appended to the conclusion of the final chapter were: 'But we were not the ones who started this war, and it was not we who provoked this terrible bloodshed. We are merely defending our native land, our native realm, and we shall continue to defend it to the last drop of blood.' Later in life, Tolstoy claimed that Panayev, and not he, was the author of these words; but although they most certainly clash with the pacifism later assumed by Tolstoy,‡ they are not out of keeping with

* A fictitious Polish name, which Tolstoy nowhere gives in Roman characters, but which is meant to signify 'non-arriver' (it could also mean 'one who has not taken the oath'). In the letter quoted here the name is actually given as 'Napshisetsky' (a transliteration from the Cyrillic – this may, however be a distortion for the sake of the censor). 'The Russian officer corps . . . contained men of several national origins and probably was more heterogeneous than those of most European armies. While this may have been somewhat harmful, because of the friction between the native Russian officers and those of German and Polish origin, this dissension does not seem to have been serious. In fact, the army may have benefited somewhat from the presence of the non-Russians, as some of them were better educated than the mass of Russian officers and probably helped to raise the general level of the military technique of the forces.' (Curtiss, op. cit., p. 211.)

† A fictitious Russian name, meaning 'Rotten-guts'.

‡ To Ye. F. Korsh, Tolstoy later claimed that 'every time I read them, I feel I would rather be given a hundred lashes than see them in print'. The two sentences were dropped from all editions that appeared after 1886.

similar sentiments to be found throughout his letters and diaries of the 1850s.

The manuscript was submitted to the *Contemporary*'s censor, V. Beketov, who passed it for publication with only minor alterations. The sketch was already printed and ready for inclusion in the August 1855 issue of the journal when the censor suddenly demanded that the proofs be sent to the chairman of the Censorship Committee, M. N. Musin-Pushkin, who read the work through with raised eyebrows. 'I am surprised that the editor should have decided even to submit the article,' he wrote on the proofsheet, 'and that the censor should have passed it for the press. Because of the cheap jibes at our brave officers, the brave defenders of Sebastopol, it contains, I instruct it to be banned, and the proofs to be left in the file.' There the matter would probably have ended, had not Alexander II learnt of the existence of a second Sebastopol sketch by the author who had pleased him so much with the first. An order countermanding Musin-Pushkin's decision was received and the sketch was published, albeit in a considerably abridged and altered form,* and without a signature. On 17 September, Tolstoy noted in his diary:

> Yesterday received the news that 'Night' has been disfigured and published. Apparently the *blues* [the police] have their eye on me a fair bit now because of my articles. I wish that Russia could always have such moral writers; but I can't be a sugary one, nor can I write from the empty into the void, without an idea and above all without a purpose. In spite of an initial moment of anger, in which I swore never to take my pen into my hand again, I know that my sole and principal occupation, dominating all my other inclinations and occupations, must be literature. My purpose is literary glory. The good I can accomplish through my writings.

The third and final sketch dates from September 1855, and concerns the last days of the siege of Sebastopol. After the battle of the Tchernaya on 4 August, which ended in the Russians being beaten back with a loss of 8,000 men, including eleven generals,

* The texts used for the present translations of this and the other two sketches are the ones ultimately sanctioned by Tolstoy, and are identical with those contained in volume 2 of L. N. Tolstoy, *Sobranie sochineniy v dvadtsati tomakh*, Moscow (1965).

it seemed inevitable that Sebastopol would fall. Since June, Gorchakov had been preparing for the evacuation of the town:

> The commander also sought to build a bridge across the bay to facilitate the retreat of the troops, although most of the engineers opposed. Lt.-Gen. Bukhmaier, however, agreed to build it. Vast quantities of timber, bought in southern Russia and hauled by enormous lines of wagons, supplied the floats on which the roadway rested, extending some eighteen hundred feet across the bay. This remarkable feat, which probably saved much of the army from capture or annihilation, was not complete until the battle of the Chernaya.*

On 6 August the allies began a general bombardment of the Russian defences, especially the Malakhov. As the Russians began to run out of powder and projectiles, they were practically forced to cease replying to the enemy's fire. On 25 August an officer told headquarters that if the Malakhov were not reinforced it would be stormed the following day. Curtiss gives the following account of the assault:

> By the eve of the assault on 26 August, the Russians in the Malakhov and the 2nd bastion were helpless, with most of the men forced to take refuge in dugouts to escape the deadly mortar shells that the French rained on them. The French would fire heavily for a time and then halt the bombardment for a brief period before resuming in full force. Rockets were sent up as false signals for attack, so that the defenders became confused and ceased to pay much attention to such tricks. On the day of the assault, the allies opened a heavy bombardment in the morning, which then ceased for two hours. Shortly before noon they opened fire again. Promptly at twelve the cannon lengthened their fire and 10,000 French under Gen. MacMahon dashed the forty paces to the Kornilov bastion on the Malakhov. Thousands of others stormed the 2nd bastion, the connecting wall, and the batteries.
>
> In the Kornilov bastion, many of the defenders were eating, others were asleep in dugouts. The guards on duty barely had time to give the warning when the French were upon them. The Russians at once dashed to arms, but, unorganized and leaderless, they were overpowered by the masses of French soldiers, and fighting furiously were pushed to the rear of the redoubt. Several companies of infantry rallied and drove back the French with the bayonet, but fresh forces poured in and once more drove the Russians to the last corner of the bastion.

* Curtiss, op. cit., p. 355.

Elsewhere along the defence line the French also had success, storming the 2nd bastion, the curtain wall, and several of the batteries, and pushed the Russians to the second line. Russian reserves quickly came up, however, and, aided by the fire of steamers, drove them out. The French again attacked and forced the Russians back, but Khrulev with strong reserves appeared and with the regrouped defenders forced the French to retire. They made one more attack, but the Russians beat them off and finally held the 2nd bastion and the nearby batteries. Khrulev then rushed with his troops to the Malakhov to re-take the Kornilov bastion, but too late. The attackers by this time had consolidated their position and held it in strength. In the attempt to regain it, Khrulev was wounded and his men thrown back, but as more Russians came up and penetrated the bastion, 20,000 men were locked in close combat. Other Russian generals came up, with fresh regiments, and the tide of battle ebbed and flowed. Finally, in mid afternoon a tall general led a column of Russians, with drums beating, into the bastion, only to be decimated by the French fire. The French charged and drove the survivors out, never to return. It is almost certain that the efforts of the Russians to re-take this bastion were severely hampered by the fact that Totleben had insisted on closing the rear part (the gorge) of the fortification, so that the Russian reserves had great difficulty in penetrating its walls.

There was heavy fighting on other parts of the defences as well. The British, with 14,000 men, made a belated attack on the 3rd bastion, only to have their troops mowed down during their long advance toward it. Some of them managed to penetrate the salient, but the Russians rallied and drove them out. British reserves charged again, but were beaten back by superior Russian forces and had to give up the attempt. On the Russian right, the French attacked the 5th bastion and adjacent batteries with 8,400 men, but were completely repulsed.

In this day's fighting the Russians lost 12,913 men, while the allies had losses of at least 10,000, and probably considerably more. In all the allies made twelve charges, of which only the one against the Malakhov had success. All the others were repelled. Hence, except for the loss of the Malakhov, 'the honours of this day completely belong to the Russian arms'. The Russian soldiers were convinced that they had won a victory even greater than that in June. After the assault 'soldiers of all ages, when they were getting them ready to amputate a leg or an arm, said with enthusiasm how gladly they agreed to endure this, knowing that they had succeeded in beating off the enemy'. As for the allies, they expected that a long and costly effort would be necessary to complete the capture of the city. Gen. Pélissier even ordered his subordinates to make careful preparations to beat off the renewed attacks that he believed the Russians would make to regain the Malakhov.

Prince Gorchakov, however, realized that it would be almost impossible to recapture the Kornilov bastion and an effort to hold out in the shattered defences would be impossibly costly. Consequently, at five o'clock on the day of the assault, he issued orders for the complete evacuation of the fortress and the city. By seven the troops began to retire across the bay to the northern side, as volunteers who had stayed in the works kept up fire against the enemy to mislead them, while a rear guard manned barricades in the city to hold off the enemy if they pursued. The troops took all night to get across by the floating bridge or by steamers and other boats. All the wounded, except a few hopeless cases, who were left behind, were taken to safety on the northern side. Some confusion developed during the night, which led to the throwing of numerous cannon into the bay. Late at night the rear guard withdrew and volunteers lighted fuses laid to powder magazines, which blew up at various times. Much of the city burned. The remaining ships were burned or sunk. Maj. Delafield, USA, termed it 'a masterly retreat that does great credit to Russian military genius and discipline'.*

In his third sketch, 'Sebastopol in August 1855', Tolstoy gives a detailed, impressionistic account of these events, seen largely through the eyes of the two Kozeltsov brothers. The detail is exact: the older Kozeltsov's regiment, the Podolsk, was one of the ones that suffered heavy losses on the night of 10 May, and so it is perfectly natural that he should have received his wound then. The 5th light battery of the 11th Artillery Brigade, to which the younger Kozeltsov is assigned, really was stationed on the Korabelnaya, where it formed part of the Korabelnaya reserves. There is, however, a discrepancy in the reporting of the sequence of events as experienced by the two brothers. The end of the sketch relates to the evening of 27 August; we must suppose that its beginning takes place during the second half of 25 August. That, at any rate, is how one of the brothers experiences it. After he parts company with his older brother, the younger Kozeltsov spends one night – that of the 26th – in the house of the battery

* Curtiss, op. cit., pp. 357–8. I have quoted Curtiss's description at length, as it supplies a concise chronological framework of the events in Tolstoy's third sketch. In *War and Peace*, Tolstoy would himself supply such factual accounts, though usually with a satirical dig at military strategists and historians in general.

commander, another – that of the 27th – in the casemate of the Malakhov, and is killed on the day of the 27th itself, during the assault. Meanwhile, however, for the older brother only one night has passed: having said farewell to his brother, he sets off for the 5th bastion, where he sits up all night playing cards, is woken by the battle alarm, and is fatally wounded shortly after. Half an hour later he is lying on a stretcher at the dressing station outside the Nicholas Barracks, where a priest tells him that 'victory is ours at all points', even though the French colours are flying from the Malakhov. The reference is clearly to the events of 27 August.

Writing 'Sebastopol in August' appears to have finally convinced Tolstoy that his true vocation was as an author. Increasingly, military service began to seem a hindrance to his future plans, and in October 1855 he acceded to a request from General Kryzhanovsky that he make a collation of the various reports of artillery action on the day of 27 August, and take them as courier to the military authorities in St Petersburg. He reached the northern capital on 21 November, and soon after tendered his resignation from the service. 'Sebastopol in August' appeared in No. 1 of the *Contemporary* for 1856, with the author's full signature – Lev Nikolayevich Tolstoy – given for the first time in his literary career. It marked his emergence as a literary celebrity, and was enthusiastically received. He later remarked, ironically: 'I failed to become a general in the army, but I became one in literature.'

The Sebastopol Sketches, more than *Childhood, Boyhood, Youth*, and more than any of the other literary works composed by the author during his twenties, look forward to the style of the mature Tolstoy, the builder of the multiple, formally complex structures of *War and Peace* and *Anna Karenin*. From a wealth of sense-impressions, pictures, episodes and conversations, Tolstoy re-creates not merely an autobiographical truth, the experience of a first-person narrator, but the spirit and reality of a whole nation. The first sketch,* couched in the form of a guide-book entry, an

* 'Sketch' is only an approximate translation of Tolstoy's own title of story' (*rasskaz*) for each of the three pieces. Given the tenuousness of the plots, however, 'sketch', with its visual, pictorial connotations, seems more apt than 'story' as a description.

informal address to the reader, is a patriotic homily constructed not out of sentiments but out of living and lived actuality – it is one side of a conversation with an interlocutor who is conceived as a citizen among citizens, able to respond in the name of a public, national conscience. In the second sketch, the 'dark' side of human nature – typified as vanity – is viewed in its struggle with higher aspirations, while in the third the note of patriotic dignity is once again struck against a backdrop of everyday human failings, which pale into insignificance beside the strivings of the Russian people and the noble spirit of the defenders of Sebastopol. Nowhere is the style forced or bombastic. The predominant tone of all three sketches is that of a quiet narrative discourse, gently ironic, lyrical, humorous, epic and elegiac by turns. At times, an additional stylistic dimension is attained – that of oratory. As R. F. Christian has noted in relation to *War and Peace*: 'Running through the syntax of Tolstoy's narrative passages is every device of arrangement and balance known to Cicero and Demosthenes (excluding the rhetorical question).'* In the context of the *Sketches*, Tolstoy has sometimes been called the first modern war correspondent; yet at times he sounds much more like a historian of the classical era – as, for example, in the following passage from the first sketch:

> Only now do the stories of the early days of the siege of Sebastopol, when there were no fortifications, no troops, when there was no physical possibility of holding the town and there was nevertheless not the slightest doubt that it would be kept from the enemy – of the days when Kornilov, that hero worthy of ancient Greece, would say as he inspected his troops: 'We will die, men, rather than surrender Sebastopol', and when our Russian soldiers, unversed in phrase-mongering, would answer: 'We will die! Hurrah!' – only now do the stories of those days cease to be a beautiful historic legend and become a reality, a fact. You will suddenly have a clear and vivid awareness that those men you have just seen are the very same heroes who in those difficult days did not allow their spirits to sink but rather felt them rise as they joyfully prepared to die, not for the town but for their native land. Long will Russia bear the imposing traces of this epic of Sebastopol, the hero of which was the Russian people.

The description of war is, however, more 'modern' in tone and expression, and in many respects anticipates the accounts of

* *Tolstoy's 'War and Peace'*, Oxford (1962), p. 152.

military action to be found in *War and Peace*. Christian writes of the second sketch:

> The hero of his story, he says, is truth, and truth is not at all lovely and not at all reconcilable with the military communiqués of war correspondents. The truth is that war is not what people think it is. It is not as people describe it. Everything is unreal. Nobody really knows what is happening or what will happen. In the midst of superhuman bravery and endurance there is vanity, hypocrisy and hankering for decorations. People are afraid in battle and then ashamed of it (e.g. Nikolai Rostov in his first encounter with the enemy); they embellish their account of battle with fictitious stories redounding to their credit (again one thinks of Nikolai). Death in battle is not a noble or romantic thing. And the scene of the death of Praskukhin in 'Sebastopol in May' provides an early glimpse of the technique which is seen in its maturity in those passages of *War and Peace* where Prince Andrei is wounded: the emphasis on the contrast between the simple, outward action of a few seconds and the complex inner life of those few seconds; the flood of reminiscences and questions; the ardent desire to go on living.*

Soviet critics have made much of the 'satirical' elements in the second and third sketches, anxious to portray Tolstoy as an anti-militarist and a pacifist even as early as 1855. That he later became both cannot, of course, be denied; yet the criticism of the Tsarist military organization and of its pampering of human weakness is really very gentle in the *Sketches*. The 'hero' which is 'truth' is ultimately the Russian people as a whole, irrespective of social class, and transcendent in its self-assertion against the forces that threaten it both from without and from within:

> But let us quickly lower the curtain on this deeply depressing scene. Tomorrow, perhaps, even this very day, each one of these men will go proudly and cheerfully to his death, and will die with calm and fortitude; under these conditions, which appal even the most detached of sensibilities and are characterized by a total absence of the human and of any prospect of salvation, the only relief is that of oblivion, the annihilation of consciousness. Buried in each man's soul lies the noble spark that will make a hero of him; but this spark grows weary of burning brightly all the time – when the fateful moment arrives, however, it will leap up like a flame and illuminate great deeds. ('Sebastopol in August 1855')

* ibid., p. 115.

SEBASTOPOL IN DECEMBER

The light of daybreak is just beginning to tint the sky above the Sapun-gora.[1] The dark surface of the sea has already thrown off night's gloom and is waiting for the first ray of sunlight to begin its cheerful sparkling. From the bay comes a steady drift of cold and mist. There is no snow – everything is black – but the sharp morning frost catches at your face and cracks beneath your feet, and only the incessant, far-off rumble of the sea, punctuated every now and again by the booming of the artillery in Sebastopol, breaks into the morning quiet. From nearby ships sounds the hollow chiming of eight bells.

On the North Side,[2] daytime activity is gradually supplanting the tranquillity of night: here, with a clatter of muskets,[3] a detachment of sentries is passing by on its way to relieve the guard; here a private, having clambered from his dugout and washed his bronzed face in icy water, is turning towards the reddening east, rapidly crossing himself and saying his prayers; here a tall, heavy *madzhara* drawn by camels is creaking its way towards the cemetery, where the bloody corpses with which it is piled almost to the brim will be buried. As you approach the quay you are struck by the distinctive smell of coal, beef, manure and damp; thousands of oddly assorted articles – firewood, sides of meat, gabions, sacks of flour, iron bars and the like – lie piled up near the quayside; soldiers of various regiments, some with kitbags and muskets, others without, are milling around here, smoking, shouting abuse at one another or dragging heavy loads

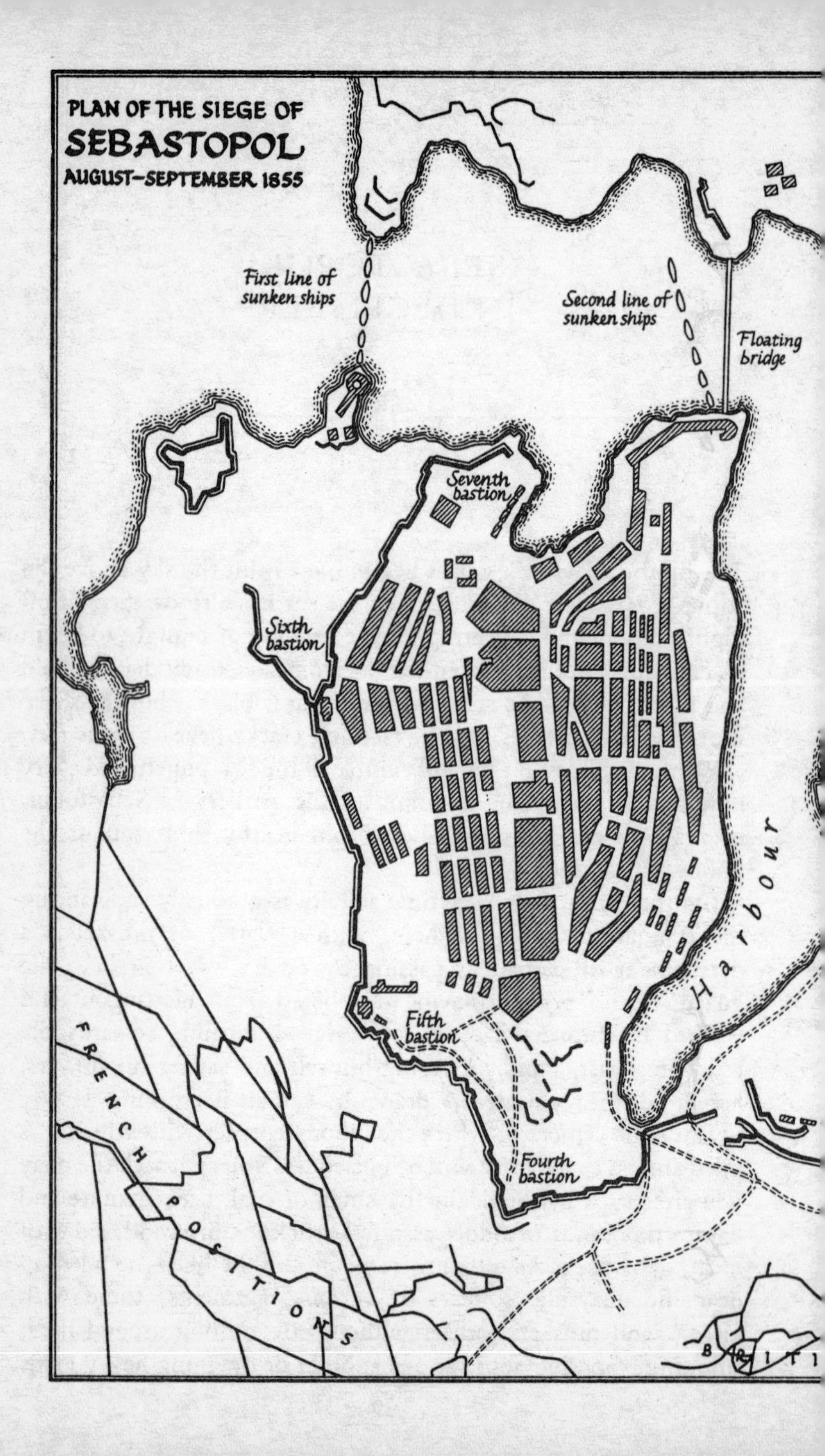
PLAN OF THE SIEGE OF
SEBASTOPOL
AUGUST–SEPTEMBER 1855
First line of sunken ships
Second line of sunken ships
Floating bridge
Seventh bastion
Sixth bastion
Fifth bastion
Fourth bastion
Harbour
FRENCH POSITIONS

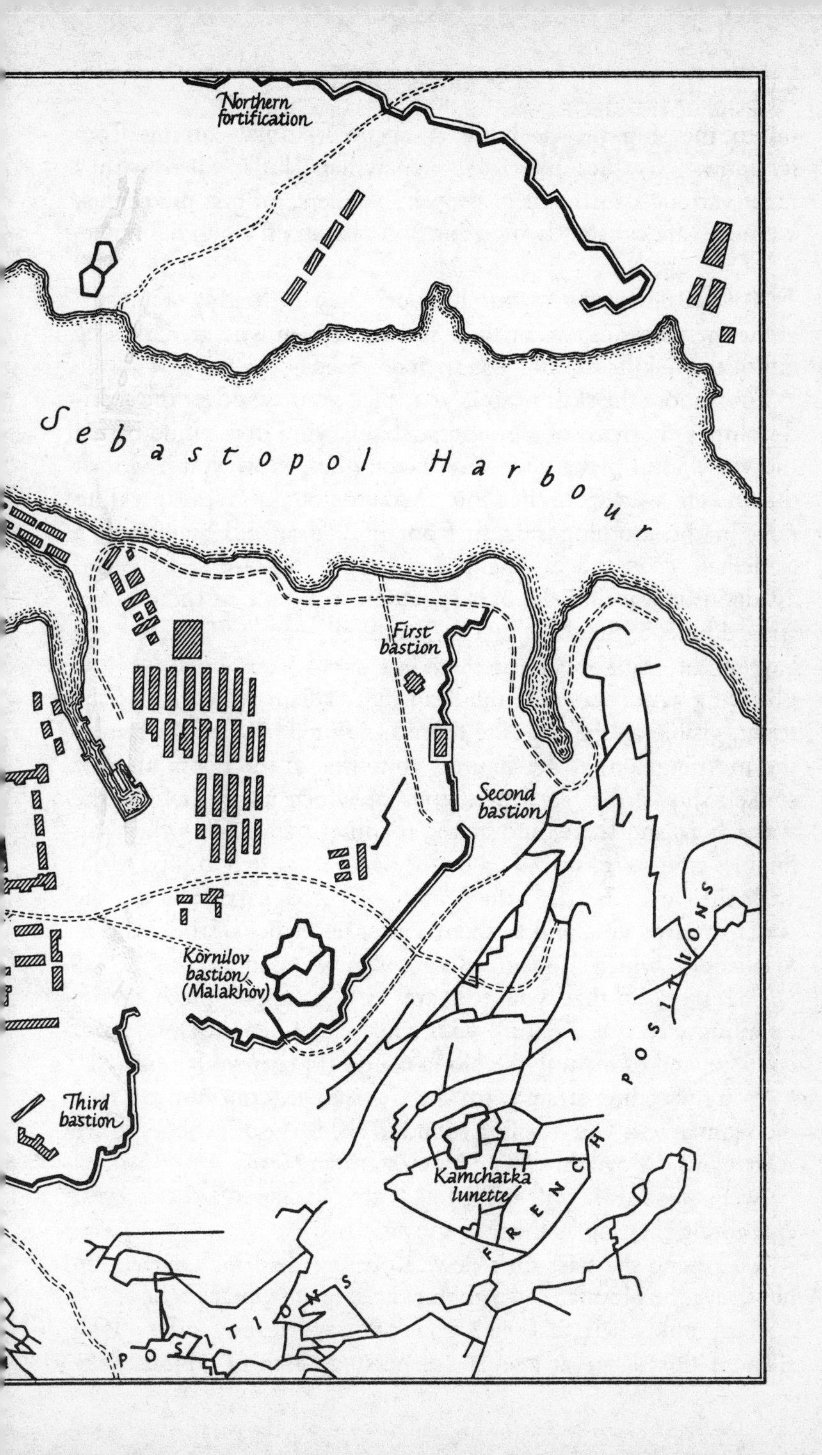
Northern fortification
Sebastopol Harbour
First bastion
Second bastion
Kornilov bastion (Malakhov)
Third bastion
Kamchatka lunette
FRENCH POSITIONS
POSITIONS

on to the ship that is lying at anchor, smoke coming from its funnel, by the landing stage; civilian skiffs, filled with a most various assortment of people – soldiers, sailors, merchants, women – are constantly mooring and casting off along the waterfront.

'To the Grafskaya,[4] your honour? Step right this way, sir,' come the voices of two or three retired seamen who are climbing out of their skiffs to offer you their services.

You choose the skiff nearest you, pick your way over the semi-decomposed carcass of a bay horse that is lying in the mud beside the vessel, and make your way to the tiller. Now you have cast off, and are away from the shore. Around you is the sea, sparkling now in the morning sun; in front of you an old seaman in a camelhair coat and a young, fair-haired boy are silently and assiduously working the oars together. You look at the massive striped hulls of the ships that are scattered near and far across the bay; at the ships' boats moving like small black dots over the glittering azure water; at the beautiful, radiant structures of the town, visible on the opposite shore and tinted pink by the rays of the morning sun; at the spumy white line of the boom and the sunken ships,[5] the black mast-tops of which jut forth from the water here and there; and at the foaming eddies, in which salt bubbles effervesce, stirred up by the oars. You listen to those oars, with their even beat, to the sounds of voices carried across the water towards you, and to the majestic resonance of the firing in Sebastopol, which, it seems to you, is growing in intensity.

The thought that you too are in Sebastopol produces its unfailing effect of imbuing your soul with a sense of pride and courage, and of making the blood course faster in your veins . . .

'You're heading straight for the *Constantine*, your honour,' the old seaman tells you, turning round to check the direction you are steering in. 'Move the tiller a bit to starboard, sir.'

'Well, she still has all her guns,'[6] the fair-haired lad observes, examining the ship as the skiff moves past.

'Of course she has; she's new, Kornilov[7] had his quarters on her,' says the old man, also giving the ship an appraising look.

'Cor, look where that one's gone off!' says the boy, after a long silence, looking up at a small, dispersing cloud of white smoke which has suddenly appeared high above the South Bay, accompanied by the sharp report of an exploding shell.

'That's *him*, he's firing from a new battery today,' says the old man, spitting on his hand indifferently. 'All right, come on, Mishka, let's get ahead of this longboat.' At this, your skiff begins to advance more rapidly over the broad swell of the bay; it really does overtake the heavy longboat, which is loaded with sacks and is being unevenly rowed by some inexperienced soldiers, and finally draws in alongside the Grafskaya landing amid the multitude of assorted vessels that are moored there.

The quayside contains a noisy jostle of soldiers in grey, sailors in black, and women in all sorts of colours. Peasant women are selling rolls, Russian muzhiks with samovars are shouting 'Hot *sbitén*'!',[8] and right here, lying about on the very first steps of the landing, are rusty cannonballs, shells, grapeshot and cast-iron cannon of various calibres. A little further off there is a large, open area strewn with enormous squared beams, gun carriages and the forms of sleeping soldiers; there are horses, waggons, green field guns and ammunition boxes, infantry muskets stacked in criss-cross piles; a constant movement persists of soldiers, sailors, officers, merchants, women and children; carts laden with hay, sacks or barrels come and go; and here and there a Cossack or an officer is passing by on horseback, or a general in his droshky. To the right the street is blocked by a barricade, the embrasures of which are mounted with small cannon; beside them sits a sailor, puffing at his pipe. To the left is a handsome building with Roman numerals carved on its pediment,[9] beneath which soldiers are standing with bloodstained stretchers – everywhere you perceive the unpleasant signs of a military encampment . . .

Your first impression is bound to be a most disagreeable one: the strange intermingling of camp and town life, of handsome town and dirty bivouac is not merely unsightly but gives the sense of an abominable state of chaos; it may even appear to you that everyone is afraid, that all these people are scurrying about with no idea of what to do. But take a closer look at the faces of those who are moving around you, and you will realize that the truth is altogether different. Look, for example, at this convoy soldier on his way to water those three bay horses: so calmly is he humming to himself that it is plain he is not going to be put off his stride by this oddly assorted crowd, which does not even exist as far as he is concerned, but is going to carry out his appointed task, whatever it may be – from watering horses to manhandling a field gun – every bit as calmly, confidently and dispassionately as if this were all taking place somewhere in Tula or Saransk. You will see the same expression written on the face of this immaculately white-gloved officer who is strolling by; of that sailor smoking his pipe on the barricade; of each of those men from the work party who are waiting with a stretcher on the steps of what used to be the Assembly Hall; and of that young unmarried girl who, afraid of muddying her pink dress, is hopping from one stone to another as she crosses the street.

Yes, you are certainly in for a disappointment if this is the first time you have entered Sebastopol. Not on a single face will you read the signs of flurry or dismay, nor even those of enthusiasm, readiness to die, resolve – of that there is none: you will see ordinary, everyday people, going about their ordinary, everyday business, and it is possible that you may end up reproaching yourself for your own excessive zeal, and begin to entertain slight doubts as to the validity of the current notions concerning the defenders of Sebastopol – notions you have gleaned from tales and descriptions of the sights to be seen and the sounds to be heard from the North Side. Before you let such doubts overwhelm you, however, go and observe the defenders of Sebastopol on the defences themselves or, better still, walk straight across to the other side of the street and enter that building which was once Sebastopol's Assembly Hall, but on whose steps soldiers bearing stretchers now stand – there you will see the defenders of Sebastopol and witness spectacles both sad and terrible, noble and comical, but which will astonish and exalt your soul.

As you step inside, you enter the large chamber of the Assembly Hall. No sooner have you opened the door than you are assailed without warning by the sight and smell of about forty or fifty amputees and critically wounded, some of them on camp beds, but most of them lying on the floor. Ignore the sensation that makes you hesitate at the threshold of the chamber – it is not a pleasant sensation – make your way forward and do not be ashamed to have come, as it were, to *observe* the sufferers, do not be embarrassed to go up to them and talk to them: people in distress are glad to see a friendly human face, they are glad to talk about their sufferings and receive a few words of sympathy and affection. Walk down the aisle between the beds and look for someone whose face seems less grim and tortured than the rest, someone you can make up your mind to approach and engage in conversation.

'Where are you wounded?' you ask an old, emaciated soldier, timidly and uncertainly. As he sits on his camp bed he is watching you with a good-natured expression, apparently inviting you to go up and talk to him. I say 'timidly', because it appears that, in addition to a feeling of deep compassion, suffering for some reason inspires a fear of offending those who are enduring it, and also a profound respect for them.

'In the leg,' replies the old man; as he speaks, however, you observe by the folds of his blanket that one of his legs stops short above the knee. 'But I'm off the danger list now, thank God,' he adds.

'When did it happen?'

'Oh, about six weeks ago, your honour.'

'Really? And are you still in pain?'

'No, sir, it doesn't hurt now; only when the weather's bad it feels as though my calf were a bit sore, but otherwise I don't feel a thing.'

'And how did it happen?'

'It was in the 5th bastion,[10] your honour, during the first bombardment:[11] I'd aimed the cannon and started to make for the next embrasure – like this, see – when *he* got me in the leg. It was like falling into a hole in the ground. I looked down, and my leg was gone.'

'You must have been in awful pain when it happened, surely?'

'No, sir, I wasn't, not at all; it just felt as though somebody had shoved something hot into my leg.'

'But later on?'

'I didn't feel anything later on, either; it was only when they started drawing the skin together that I got this kind of burning sensation. The main thing, your honour, is *not to spend too much time thinking about it*; if you don't think about it, it doesn't seem much. Most of a man's troubles come from thinking too much.'

Just then you are approached by a woman in a grey striped dress and a black headscarf; she interrupts your conversation with this man, who turns out to be a sailor,[12] not a soldier, and starts to tell you about him, his sufferings, the desperate plight he was in for four weeks. She tells you how, after he had been wounded, he told the men who were carrying him on a stretcher to stop for a while so he could watch a salvo from one of our batteries, how the Grand Dukes[13] had spoken to him and given him a reward of twenty-five roubles, and how he had told them of his desire to return to the bastion in order to instruct the young men, even though he himself was no good for active service any more. Telling you all this in one breath, the woman looks now at you and now at the sailor who, seemingly oblivious to her words, his face averted, is plucking at a tuft of lint on his pillow; his eyes are gleaming with a peculiar delight.

'This is my wife, your honour!' he remarks, with a look as if to say: 'You'll have to make allowances for her. You know how it is with women – they're always saying stupid things.'

Now you are beginning to see what the defenders of Sebastopol are really like; and for some reason in this man's presence you start to feel ashamed of yourself. There are so many things you would like to say to him in order to express your sympathy and admiration; but you are unable to find any words, or are dissatisfied with the words that do suggest themselves to you – and silently you defer to this man's taciturn and unselfconscious nobility and steadfastness of spirit, his diffidence in the face of his own personal merit.

'Well, may God grant you a speedy recovery,' you say to him as you move on and come to a halt in front of another patient who is lying on the floor in what looks like intolerable agony, apparently waiting for death.

He is a fair-haired man with a bloodless, puffy face. He is lying on his back with his left arm thrown behind him in a position expressive of intense suffering. His parched, open mouth lets out his wheezing breath with difficulty; his blue, pewter-coloured eyes have rolled upwards, and from beneath the blanket, which has become displaced, protrudes what remains of his right arm, swathed in bandages. The cloying smell of dead flesh seems suddenly stronger, and the voracious inner fever that penetrates all the sufferer's limbs seems to penetrate you also.

'What sort of state is he in, is he unconscious?' you ask the woman who is following you and surveying you affectionately, as if you were one of her own.

'No, he still has all his wits about him, but he's in a very poor way now,' she adds in a whisper. 'I tried to get him to drink some tea I made for him today – even though he isn't one of us, you can't but feel sorry for him – but he hardly touched it.'

'How do you feel?' you ask the wounded man.

His pupils stir at the sound of your voice, but he neither sees you nor takes in what you say.

'My h-heart's on fire,' he gasps.

A little further on you come across an old soldier who is changing his underwear. His face and body are a sort of brownish colour, and he is extremely thin, like a skeleton. One of his arms is missing: it has been amputated at the shoulder. He is sitting up cheerfully, he has recovered from the operation; but from his dead, lustreless gaze, his terrible emaciation and the wrinkles on his face you can see that this is a man who has already lived out the best part of his life.

On a bed on the other side of the chamber you will see the pale, tortured, delicate face of a woman, both her cheeks alight with the red glow of fever.

'This is the wife of one of our sailors, sir; she was hit in the leg when a shell landed near her on the fifth,'[14] your guide informs you. 'On her way to the bastion with her husband's dinner, she was, when it happened.'

'So what did they do, amputate?'

'Yes, sir, they sawed off her leg above the knee.'

Now, if you have strong nerves, go through the doorway on the left: that is the room in which wounds are bandaged and operations performed. There you will see surgeons with pale, gloomy physiognomies, their arms soaked in blood up to the elbows, deep in concentration over a bed on which a wounded man is lying under the influence of chloroform, open-eyed as in a delirium, and uttering meaningless words which are occasionally simple and affecting. The surgeons are going about the repugnant but beneficial task of amputation. You will see the sharp, curved knife enter the white, healthy body; you will see the wounded man suddenly regain consciousness with a terrible, harrowing shrieked cursing; you will see the apothecary assistant fling the severed arm into a corner; you will see another wounded man who is lying on a stretcher in the same room and watching the operation on his companion, writhing and groaning less with physical pain than with the psychological agony of apprehension; you will witness fearsome sights that will shake you to the roots of your being; you will see war not as a beautiful, orderly, and gleaming formation, with music and beaten drums, streaming banners and generals on prancing horses, but war in its authentic expression – as blood, suffering and death.

As you emerge from this house of suffering you will not fail to experience a sense of relief; you will breathe the fresh air more deeply and take pleasure in the consciousness of your own health. From the observation of these sufferings you will at the same time, however, derive a sense of your own insignificance, and calmly and without a trace of indecision you will make your way to the bastions . . .

'What do the death and suffering of an insignificant worm such as myself signify, when placed alongside so many deaths and so many sufferings?' you will ask yourself. But the sight of the cloudless sky, the brilliant sun, the beautiful town, the open church and the military personnel moving in all directions will soon restore your mind to its normal condition of frivolity, petty concern and exclusive preoccupation with the present.

Perhaps you will encounter the cortège of some officer's funeral returning from the church with pink coffin, band music and flying gonfalons; perhaps you will hear the sounds of the firing from the bastions, but this will not bring on a recurrence of your previous thoughts; the funeral cortège will seem to you a thoroughly appealing martial spectacle, the sounds of the gunfire thoroughly appealing martial sounds, and with neither will you associate that clear and personally experienced awareness of suffering and death which you had at the dressing station.

Once you have passed the church and the barricade, you reach that part of the town which has the most animated life of its own. The hanging signs of shops and taverns on both sides of the streets; the merchants, the women in bonnets or kerchiefs, the dandified officers – all these things and people will impress you with the strength of mind, the security and self-confidence of the inhabitants.

If you want to listen to the talk of the naval and army officers, go into that tavern on the right: circulating there already, most likely, will be stories about the previous night, about some girl called Fenka, about the action on the 24th,[15] about the exorbitant price and poor quality of the meatballs, and about the death in action of such-and-such or such-and-such a comrade.

'It's damned terrible up at our place!' a tow-haired, clean-shaven naval officer says in a deep voice; he is wearing a green knitted scarf.

'Where's "our place"?' another man asks him.

'The 4th bastion,'[16] replies the young officer. When you hear those words, 'the 4th bastion', you are bound to view the tow-haired young man with heightened interest and even a certain degree of respect. His excessive and undue familiarity, the way he is waving his arms about, his loud laughter and loud voice, which until now seemed to you merely insolent, strike you all of a sudden as an expression of that curiously aggressive state of mind characteristic of certain young men when they have been exposed to danger. You may suppose he is about to say it is the shells and bullets that have been making the day so terrible for him and his men: not a bit of it! It is the mud that has been so terrible. 'You can hardly get to the battery,' he says, pointing to his boots, which are caked knee-deep in mud.

'Yes, and they killed my best gunner, got him right between the eyes,' says another man.

'Who was that? Mityukhin?'

'No . . . Hey, are you ever going to bring me my veal? Blackguards!' he adds, in the direction of the waiter. 'No, it wasn't Mityukhin, it was Abrosimov. He was a plucky lad, too, took part in six sorties.'

At the other end of the table, with plates of meatballs and green peas and a bottle of the vinegary Crimean wine baptized 'Bordeaux' before them, sit two infantry officers: the younger, red-collared one, who has two stars on his greatcoat, is telling the other, a man already advanced in years, with a black collar and no stars, about the battle of the Alma.[17] The young officer has had a bit to drink, and from the pauses in his narrative, the uncertain look on his face which betrays his misgivings as to whether the other man will believe him, and in particular as to whether the role he has played in all this has not been far too important, whether it has not all been far too terrible and extraordinary, it can be seen that he is straying too far from the strict relation of the truth. But you have no time to listen to these stories, which you will continue to hear in every corner of Russia for a long time yet to come: you would prefer to go up to the bastions – especially the 4th bastion, about which you have heard so many different things. Whenever anyone states that he has been in the 4th bastion, he says it with a peculiar pride and satisfaction; if a man says, 'I'm going to the 4th bastion', you are sure to notice that his voice and manner seem slightly agitated or too studiedly indifferent; when one man wishes to poke fun at another, he will say, 'They ought to put you in the 4th bastion'; whenever the men meet a stretcher party and ask, 'Where's he from?', the answer most usually heard is: 'The 4th bastion.' There exist two entirely different attitudes towards this fearsome bastion: those who have never visited it are convinced that it is a certain deathtrap, while those like the tow-haired warrant officer who actually live on it tend to discuss it in terms of whether the terrain there is dry or muddy and whether the dugouts are tolerably warm or freezing cold.

During the half-hour you have spent in the tavern the weather has had time to change: the mist which earlier lay blanketed across the sea has now massed itself into moist, grey, dreary clouds, obscuring the sun; a melancholy drizzle sifts down, wetting the roofs, the pavements and the greatcoats of the soldiers . . .

Passing through another barricade, you emerge from a doorway on the right and proceed up the main street. The houses on both sides of the street beyond this barricade are uninhabited; there are no hanging signs, the doorways are boarded up, the windows have had the glass knocked out of them, in one place the corner of a wall has been removed, in another a roof has been smashed in. These buildings look like old veterans who have experienced every kind of woe and affliction, and they seem to eye you with pride and a certain contempt. Along the way you stumble over cannonballs that lie strewn about in the road here and there, and lose your footing in the water-filled craters dug by shells in the stony soil. You overtake and meet coming towards you detachments of soldiers, Cossack scouts, officers; every once in a while you encounter a woman or a child – this time, however, it is not a woman in a bonnet but a sailor's wife in an old winter jacket and soldier's boots. As you pass further along the street and descend a small slope, what you see around you are not houses but strange heaps of rubble, boards, clay and beams; before you, on top of a steep hill, you can see a black, muddy area traversed by ditches – this is the 4th bastion . . . Here you meet even fewer people; there are no women at all to be seen, soldiers move swiftly about, you encounter patches of blood on the road, and here you are certain to come across four privates bearing a stretcher on which lie a blood-stained greatcoat and a pale, yellowish face. If you ask where the man has been wounded, the stretcher-bearers will reply irritably, without turning in your direction, 'In the leg' or 'In the arm', if the wound is not serious; or, if no head is visible on the stretcher and the man has already died or is gravely wounded, they will grimly refrain from uttering a word.

The whistle, close at hand, of a shell or a cannonball, just at the very moment you start to climb the hill, gives you a nasty sensation. Suddenly you realize, in an entirely new way, the true significance of those sounds of gunfire you heard from the town. Some quiet, happy memory suddenly flickers to life in your brain; you start thinking more about yourself and less about what you observe around you, and are suddenly gripped by an unpleasant sense of indecision. The sight of a soldier glissading downhill over the wet mud, waving his arms and laughing, silences this cowardly voice that has begun to speak within you at the prospect of danger, however, and you find yourself straightening your chest, lifting your head a little higher and clambering up the slippery, clayey hill. You have only managed to climb a little way when the bullets from carbines[18] begin to hum around you, and you may wonder if it might not be more advisable for you to use the trench that runs parallel to the road; but this trench is filled with stinking yellow, watery mud, and you are certain to choose the road, particularly since everyone else seems to be using it. After you have gone a distance of some two hundred yards or so, you will enter a muddy, churned-up area, surrounded on all sides by gabions, earthworks, magazines, dugouts and platforms on which large cast-iron cannon stand beside neat piles of roundshot. It all looks as though it had been thrown together at random, without the slightest purpose, coherence or sense of order. Here, sitting on the battery, is a little group of sailors; here, right in the middle of the open area, sunk half in slime, lies a fractured cannon; here an infantryman, musket in hand, is making his way across the battery, dragging his feet with difficulty through the clinging mud. Wherever you look, in every conceivable corner, there seem to be shell-splinters, unexploded bombs, cannonballs and camp remains, all of them half submerged in watery ooze. You think you hear a cannonball land not far from you; all around you seem to hear the various sounds that bullets make – from the ones that hum like bees to the ones that whistle rapidly by or twang with a noise like a plucked string; you hear the terrible boom of an artillery discharge: it shakes you to the core and inspires you with a profound sense of dread.

'So this is it, the 4th bastion, that dreadful, truly dreadful place,' you think to yourself, experiencing a slight feeling of pride, and an anything-but-slight feeling of suppressed terror. You are, however, in for a disappointment: for this is not yet the 4th bastion proper. This is only the Yazon redoubt[19] – a relatively safe and in no way dreadful place. If you wish to reach the 4th bastion, you must turn to the right along this narrow trench, the one you saw that infantryman plodding along just now, ducking as he went. Here you may meet another stretcher party, a sailor, a soldier with his shovels. Here, perhaps, in the mud, you will see the wires of mines, dugouts so small that only two men can squeeze into them, and even then only if they bend almost double; and here too you will see the Cossack scouts of the Black Sea battalions eating, smoking, changing their boots and in general carrying on with their everyday lives; everywhere you will see the same stinking mud, camp remains and bits of scrap iron of all shapes and sizes. After you have gone another three hundred yards or so you will emerge at another battery; a flat, open area dug with trenches and surrounded by gabions, field guns mounted on platforms, and earthen ramparts. Here you may spot four or five sailors playing cards beneath the parapet; a naval officer, observing that you are a newcomer and, moreover, an inquisitive one, will show you with satisfaction around his domain, pointing out all the things that may be of interest to you. So calmly does this officer roll his yellow-papered cigarette as he sits on a cannon, so calmly does he saunter from one embrasure to another, so calmly, and without the slightest affectation, does he speak to you that, in spite of the bullets that are humming above your head with greater frequency now, you yourself begin to acquire a certain sang-froid and find yourself plying him with questions and listening attentively to his stories. This officer will tell you – but only if you ask him – about the bombardment on the fifth, and about how on his battery that day only one gun was operational and only eight men left out of the entire crew – yet the very next morning, on the sixth, he had all his guns 'blazing';* he will tell you how on the fifth a shell hit the dugout where some sailors were sheltering, killing eleven of them; from one of the embrasures he will point out to you the enemy batteries and trenches, which are no more than seventy or eighty yards away. I fear, however, that when you lean out of the embrasure in order to take a look at the enemy, the humming of the bullets will have the effect of preventing you from seeing anything at all; but if you do manage to see anything, you will find it very difficult to believe that this white stone rampart, which is so close to you and from which white puffs of smoke keep erupting, is in fact the enemy – 'him', as both soldiers and sailors say.

It is even quite possible that, either out of vanity or simply in order to provide himself with some diversion, the naval officer will decide to let off a few rounds while you are there. 'Gunner and crew to the cannon!' he will order, and some fourteen sailors, this one putting his pipe away in his pocket, that one chewing the last remains of his *sukhar'*,[20] will cheerily clatter off at the double

* The naval personnel all say 'blaze', not 'fire'. (Tolstoy's note.)

along the platform to one of the cannon in their hobnailed boots, and start loading it. Take a good look at the faces, the bearing and movements of these men: in every crease of these bronzed, high-cheekboned countenances, in every muscle, in the breadth of these shoulders, in the thickness of these legs clad in their massive boots, in every calm, assured, unhurried movement may be seen those central characteristics that go to make up the Russian's strength – his stubbornness and straightforwardness. As you study these faces you will perceive that the danger, savagery and sufferings of war have added to those central distinguishing features the marks of a conscious sense of dignity and the traces of lofty feelings and thoughts.

All of a sudden the noise of a most fearful explosion startles you out of your wits, delivering a severe jolt not only to your ears but to the whole of your being, making you tremble in every limb. Immediately afterwards you hear the fading whistle of the projectile, and a thick pall of powder smoke enshrouds you, likewise enveloping the platform and the black figures of the sailors moving to and fro on it. You hear the sailors exchanging various opinions on the subject of this discharge of ours; you observe how excited the men are, and watch them give expression to a feeling you for some reason did not expect them to be capable of, one of savage hatred for the enemy and a wish to have revenge on him, a feeling that lurks in the soul of every human being. 'It landed right on that embrasure; looks as though it's killed two of them . . . Yes, they're carrying them away!' you hear them exclaim in high delight. 'That'll make him lose his rag: he'll be sending one over here in a minute,' someone says; and sure enough, a moment or two later you see lightning and smoke ahead of you; the sentry standing on the parapet shouts: 'Ca-a-nnon!', and then a cannonball shrieks past you, slaps into the earth and showers everything around with mud and stones, forming a crater. The battery commander will be very annoyed about this cannonball, he will order a second and a third piece to be loaded, the enemy will start to answer our fire, and you will experience some interesting feelings, and witness some interesting sights and sounds. Once again the sentry will shout 'Cannon!', and you will hear the same shrieking sound, followed by the same slap and showering of earth; or he will shout 'Mortar!', and you will hear the even whistle of a mortar shell, a sound that is quite pleasant and not at all easy to associate with anything very dreadful; you will hear this whistling sound come nearer and nearer in an accelerating crescendo, and then you will see a black sphere and witness the shell's impact against the earth, its palpable, ringing explosion. Then shell-splinters will fly whistling and whining in all directions, stones will rustle through the air, and you will be spattered with mud. You will experience a sensation that is a strange blend of fear and enjoyment. At the moment you know the shell is heading in your direction, you are bound to think it is going to kill you; but a feeling of self-respect will sustain you, and no one will observe the knife that is lacerating your heart. When, however, the shell sails past, leaving you unscathed, you will recover your spirits and be seized, if only for a moment, by a sense of relief that is unutterably pleasant. You will discover a peculiar fascination in this dangerous game of life and death; you will want the shells and cannonballs to land closer and closer to you. But there is the sentry shouting 'Mortar!' in his loud, guttural voice, here again are the whistle, impact and explosion of a shell. This time above the roar of the explosion you are suddenly aware of a man's groans. You arrive by the wounded man's side – covered in blood and dirt, he has a strangely inhuman appearance – just as a stretcher party is coming. He is a sailor, and he has had part of his chest blown away. During these first moments his face can register nothing but terror and the feigned, anticipatory look of suffering[21] that is characteristic of men in his condition; but as the stretcher is brought near him and he lies down on it on his good side, you observe that this expression is replaced by one of exaltation and lofty, unspoken thought: his eyes burn more brightly, his teeth are clenched, he lifts his head with effort; and as he is raised from the ground he makes the stretcher-bearers pause and he says to his companions with difficulty, in a trembling voice: 'Sorry, lads!' It is evident that he wants to add something to this, and that it is something moving, but all he can manage is to repeat the words, 'Sorry, lads!' At this point one of the wounded man's sailor comrades approaches him, places a cap on the head that is raised for him, and calmly, indifferently, swinging his arms, returns to his gun. 'We get seven or eight cases like that every day,' the naval officer informs you, in response to the look of horror on your face, as he yawns and rolls another of his yellow-papered cigarettes . . .

So now you have seen the defenders of Sebastopol on the lines of defence themselves, and you retrace your steps, for some reason paying no attention now to the cannonballs and bullets that continue to whistle across your route all the way back to the demolished theatre, and you walk in a state of calm exaltation. The one central, reassuring conviction you have come away with is that it is quite impossible for Sebastopol ever to be taken by the enemy. Not only that: you are convinced that the strength of the Russian people cannot possibly ever falter, no matter in what part of the world it may be put to the test. This impossibility you have observed, not in that proliferation of traverses, parapets, ingeniously interwoven trenches, mines and artillery-pieces of which you have understood nothing, but in the eyes, words and behaviour – that which is called the spirit – of the defenders of Sebastopol. What they do, they do so straightforwardly, with so little strain or effort, that you are convinced they must be capable of a hundred times as much . . . they could do anything. You realize now that the feeling which drives them has nothing in common with the vain, petty and mindless emotions you yourself have experienced, but is of an altogether different and more powerful nature; it has turned them into men capable of living with as much calm beneath a hail of cannonballs, faced with a hundred chances of death, as people who, like most of us, are faced with only one such chance, and of living in those conditions while putting up with sleeplessness, dirt and ceaseless hard labour. Men will not put up with terrible conditions like these for the sake of a cross or an honour, or because they have been threatened: there must be another, higher motivation. This motivation is a feeling that surfaces only rarely in the Russian, but lies deeply embedded in his soul – a love of his native land. Only now do the stories of the early days of the siege of Sebastopol, when there were no fortifications, no troops, when there was no physical possibility of holding the town and there was nevertheless not the slightest doubt that it would be kept from the enemy – of the days when Kornilov, that hero worthy of ancient Greece, would say as he inspected his troops: 'We will die, men, rather than surrender Sebastopol', and when our Russian soldiers, unversed in phrase-mongering, would answer: 'We will die! Hurrah!' – only now do the stories of those days cease to be a beautiful historic legend and become a reality, a fact. You will suddenly have a clear and vivid awareness that those men you have just seen are the very same heroes who in those difficult days did not allow their spirits to sink but rather felt them rise as they joyfully prepared to die, not for the town but for their native land. Long will Russia bear the imposing traces of this epic of Sebastopol, the hero of which was the Russian people.

Already the day is drawing to a close. Just before it sets, the sun comes out from behind the grey storm-clouds that obscure the sky, and suddenly shines with a crimson light on the purple thunderheads, on the greenish sea bedizened with ships and sailboats and rocked by a broad, even swell, on the white structures of the town, and on the people moving about the streets. The strains of an old waltz that is being played by the regimental band on the Boulevard come floating across the water, together with the booming of the guns from the bastions, which seems strangely to echo them.

Sebastopol
25 April 1855

SEBASTOPOL IN MAY

—I—

Six months have now passed since the first cannonball came hurtling over from the bastions of Sebastopol to churn up the earth on the enemy's works; ever since then, thousands of shells, cannonballs and bullets have been fired from the bastions at the enemy trenches and from those trenches back at the bastions, and the angel of death has hovered ceaselessly above them.

During this time thousands of individual personal vanities have been insulted, thousands have been gratified, and thousands have gone to rest in the arms of death. How many military decorations have been pinned on, how many stripped off, how many St Anne Ribbons and Orders of St Vladimir have been awarded, how many pink coffins and linen palls have gone to the grave! And still the same booming resounds from the bastions, still on clear evenings the French survey, with involuntary trepidation and superstitious dread, the yellowish, churned-up earth of the Sebastopol bastions and the outlines of the Russian sailors moving about on them, and still they count the embrasures from which the cast-iron cannon angrily bristle; still, as before, from the tower on Telegraph Hill a navigational NCO examines through a telescope the brightly coloured figures of the French forces, their batteries, their tents, their columns moving on the Green Hill,[22] and the puffs of smoke that leap up from their trenches; and still, inspired by the same zeal, oddly assorted companies of men with desires that are even more oddly assorted come flocking, struggling their way from different corners of the earth towards this fatal spot.

But the dispute which the diplomats have failed to settle is proving to be even less amenable to settlement by means of gunpowder and human blood.

A strange thought often used to occur to me: what if one of the warring sides were to propose to the other that each should dismiss one soldier from its ranks? That might seem an odd thing to do, but why not try it? Then a second soldier from each side could be told to go, followed by a third, a fourth, and so on, until each army only had one soldier left (this always assuming that the two armies were equal in strength, and that it would be possible to substitute quality for quantity). Finally, if it still appeared that the really complex disputes arising between the rational representatives of rational creatures must be settled by combat, let the fighting be done by these two soldiers: one could lay siege to the town, and the other could defend it.

This argument may seem to be no more than a paradox, yet it is a sound one. For in truth, what difference is there between one Russian fighting one allied representative, and eighty thousand Russians fighting eighty thousand allied representatives? A hundred and thirty-five thousand against a hundred and thirty-five thousand; twenty against twenty; one against one – none of these figures is any more logical than another. Or, it might be argued, the latter figure is by far the most logical, because it represents the most humane suggestion. One of two things appears to be true: either war is madness, or, if men perpetrate this madness, they thereby demonstrate that they are far from being the rational creatures we for some reason commonly suppose them to be.

—2—

In the besieged town of Sebastopol a regimental band was playing next to the pavilion on the Boulevard, and crowds of military men accompanied by women were moving gaily along the paths in holiday mood. A bright spring sun had ascended the morning sky above the English positions, had moved over to the bastions, then to the town and the Nicholas Barracks and, shining with equal joy on all, was now descending towards the far-off, dark blue sea whose even swell gleamed with a silvery sheen.

A tall, slightly stooping infantry officer, pulling on a glove that was, if not immaculately white, at least fairly presentable, emerged from the gate of one of the little seamen's houses on Main Street and, looking reflectively at the ground as he walked, set off up the hill towards the Boulevard. The expression on this officer's plain, low-browed face bespoke limited intellectual ability, but it also reflected a certain sober-mindedness, honesty and inclination towards tidiness. He was of poor build – long-legged, awkward and somewhat diffident in his movements. He wore a smart new cap, a thin summer greatcoat of a slightly peculiar lilac shade, from beneath the breast of which a gold watch-chain peeped; his trousers had foot-straps, and he was shod in a pair of calf leather boots that were clean and shiny, though slightly worn at the heels in several places. It was, however, less from these items, which are not commonly encountered upon the person of an infantry officer, than from the man's general bearing that an experienced military eye was at once able to perceive that this was no ordinary infantry officer, but someone a little higher up in rank. He might have passed for a German, if his facial features had not belied his purely Russian origins; or he might have been an adjutant, or a regimental quartermaster (but then he would have worn spurs), or an officer who had been transferred from the cavalry, or possibly the guard, for the duration of the campaign. In fact he had been transferred from the cavalry, and at this moment, as he made his way up to the Boulevard, he was thinking about a letter he had just received from an old military friend and colleague, now retired, a land-owner in the province of T—, and his wife, the pale, blue-eyed Natasha, who was a great friend of the officer's. He was thinking in particular about one passage in the letter, where his comrade had written:

> When our copies of the *Veteran*[23] are delivered, Pupka [such was the pet name the retired Uhlan had given his wife] rushes headlong into the hallway, seizes the newspapers and runs off with them *to the S-shaped seat in the arbour, or the drawing-room* (in which, you'll remember, we whiled away the winter evenings so gloriously when your regiment was stationed in our town), and you simply can't imagine the excitement with which she reads about *your* noble exploits. She often says of you: 'That Mikhailov,' she says, 'such a *darling* man, I feel like smothering him with kisses whenever I set eyes on him, he's *fighting in the bastions*; he's sure to get the St George Cross and be written about in the newspapers', and so on and so forth, with the result that I'm definitely beginning to feel jealous.

At another point in the letter he had written:

> The newspapers are terribly late in arriving, and although a lot of the news gets around by word of mouth, you can't believe it all. For example, those *musical young ladies* you're familiar with were claiming yesterday that Napoleon[24] has been taken prisoner by our Cossacks and sent off to St Petersburg, but you can imagine how much of that I believe. One visitor from St Petersburg (he works for a government minister on special assignments, a really capital fellow, such a *risource* for us now that there's hardly anybody left in town, you've simply no idea) was stating it to us as a fact that our chaps have taken Eupatoria, that *the French have lost their line of communication to Balaclava*,[25] and that while we only lost two hundred men in the assault, the French lost as many as fifteen thousand. Pupka was so overjoyed that she *went on the spree* all night, and she says she's had a sort of premonition that you probably took part in that assault and distinguished yourself . . .

In spite of the words and expressions I have purposely marked in italics, and notwithstanding the whole tone of the letter, from which the high-minded reader will doubtless form a correct and negative impression concerning the respectability of Lieutenant-Captain Mikhailov with his own down-at-heel boots, and of his friend who writes 'risource' and has such strange notions of geography, concerning the pale friend on the *S-shaped seat* (he may, not without justification, imagine this Natasha with dirty fingernails), and in general concerning the whole of this dirty, idle, provincial milieu, so contemptible to him – in spite of all this, Lieutenant-Captain Mikhailov remembered his pale, provincial lady friend with an inexpressibly sweet sadness, recalling how he had used to sit with her in the arbour discussing *sentiments*. He remembered his good-natured Uhlan friend who would lose his temper and end up having to pay fines when they played cards for copeck stakes in the study, and how his wife would laugh at him; he remembered the friendly feelings these people entertained in his regard (possibly it seemed to him that there was even more than this where his pale friend was concerned): these people and their surroundings flickered in his mind's eye, suffused in a wonderfully sweet, comfortingly rosy light, and, smiling at his memories, he patted the pocket which contained the letter that was so *dear* to him. These memories were lent an even greater aura of charm for Lieutenant-Captain Mikhailov by the fact that the milieu in which he was now constrained to live – that of an infantry regiment – was far more lowly than the one in which, as a cavalryman and knight of the ladies, he had previously moved in the town of T—, being everywhere well received.

So much more elevated were the circles in which he had previously moved than those in which he presently found himself, that when in moments of candour he happened to tell his fellow infantrymen that he had driven his own droshky, had attended balls at the house of the provincial governor and had played cards with a government service general, they would listen to him with a kind of sceptical indifference, as though all that mattered was that they should not contradict him or demonstrate that none of this had in fact been the case – 'Let him talk', they would say, implying that if he showed no obvious contempt for the vodka-swilling of his fellows, for their quarter-copeck-stake games with old packs of cards and for the general vulgarity of the life they led, then this must be attributable to the unusually modest, easy-going and discreet quality of his disposition.

From memories, Lieutenant-Captain Mikhailov found himself passing to hopes and dreams. 'How astonished and delighted Natasha will be,' he thought as he strode along a narrow lane in his down-at-heel boots, 'when she suddenly comes across a report in the *Veteran* of how I was the first man to climb up on the cannon and receive the St George Cross. I ought to be made a captain on account of that decoration, in any case. It's quite likely that I'll be made a battalion commander this year, because a lot of men have already been killed in this campaign, and a lot more are going to die before it's over. There'll be another battle and I, as a famous man, will be given a regiment to lead . . . I'll be made a lieutenant-colonel . . . I'll get the St Anne Ribbon . . . then I'll be a colonel . . .' – and in no time he was a general, deigning to visit Natasha, the widow of his comrade (who in his dreams was dead by now). Just then, however, the playing of the regimental band came more clearly to his ears, the crowds of people burst upon his sight and he found himself on the Boulevard, a lieutenant-captain as before, awkward, timid and of no significance.

—3—

First he went over to the pavilion, beside which the bandsmen were standing, together with other soldiers from the same regiment who were holding the band parts open in front of them for them to read; they in turn were surrounded by a little circle of clerks, cadets, nannies with young children and officers in *old* greatcoats, observing rather than listening. The people round the pavilion, either standing, sitting or strolling about, were for the most part naval officers, adjutants and army officers in white gloves and *new* greatcoats. Along the broad avenue of the Boulevard strolled officers of all classes and women of all classes; a few of the women were dressed in hats, but most of them wore kerchiefs (there were also some who wore neither kerchiefs nor hats), and it was a striking fact that there was not an old woman among them – indeed, they were all of them young. Below, in the shady, scented alleys of acacia, individual groups sat or wandered.

No one seemed unusually pleased to meet Lieutenant-Captain Mikhailov, with the possible exception of Captains Obzhogov and Suslikov, both of whom were members of his regiment and both of whom warmly shook hands with him; but the former was dressed in camelhair trousers and a frayed greatcoat, wore no gloves, and had a face that was red and streaming with perspiration, while the latter shouted his remarks so loudly and in such an over-familiar manner that it was embarrassing to walk in his company, particularly under the gaze of the officers in white gloves, with one of whom – an adjutant – Mikhailov exchanged bows, and with another of whom – a field officer – it would have been permissible for him to exchange bows, since he had twice encountered the man at the house of a mutual acquaintance. Moreover, what possible enjoyment could be had from walking with Messrs Obzhogov and Suslikov when he already met them and shook hands with them six times a day as it was? It was not for the sake of this that he had come *to hear the band.*

He would dearly have liked to have gone up to the adjutant with whom he exchanged bows and talked to those gentlemen for a while, not at all in order that Captains Obzhogov and Suslikov, Lieutenant Pashtetsky and the rest should see him talking to them, but simply because they were nice people, who were acquainted with all the latest news, what was more, and might be able to tell him a thing or two . . .

But why is Lieutenant-Captain Mikhailov afraid, unable to bring himself to go up to them? 'What if they should suddenly decide they're not going to bow back to me,' he thinks, 'or what if they bow and then just carry on talking to one another as though I weren't there; or turn their backs on me completely, leaving me there all on my own among the *aristocrats*?' The word *aristocrats* (used to designate the highest select circle of any social order) has for some time now enjoyed considerable popularity among us here in Russia, where one might have supposed it ought not really to exist at all, and has found its way into every region of the country and every social stratum where vanity has managed to penetrate (and into what areas of occasion and circumstance does this vile peccadillo not reach?) – among merchants, among civil servants, government clerks and officers, to Saratov, to Mamadysh, to Vinnitsa – everywhere where there are people, in fact. And since there are a great many people in the besieged town of Sebastopol, there is also a great deal of vanity to be found; there are, in other words, *aristocrats*, even though death hangs above the heads of *aristocrat* and *non-aristocrat* alike, ready to strike at any moment.

In the eyes of Captain Obzhogov, Lieutenant-Captain Mikhailov is an *aristocrat* because he is wearing a clean greatcoat and gloves, and for this reason he finds him insufferable, even though he has a slight respect for the man; in the eyes of Lieutenant-Captain Mikhailov, Adjutant Kalugin is an *aristocrat* simply because he is an adjutant and is on 'thou' terms with another adjutant, and for this reason he is not entirely well disposed towards him, even though he fears him. In the eyes of Adjutant Kalugin, Count Nordov is an *aristocrat*, and he is forever cursing him in silence and inwardly despising him because he is an aide-de-camp to the Tsar. It is a formidable word, this *aristocrat*. Why does Second Lieutenant Zobov laugh such a forced laugh – even though there is nothing to laugh at – as he walks past his companion who is sitting there with a field officer? In order to show that even though he may not be an *aristocrat*, he is in no way inferior to him. Why is the field officer talking in such a faint, indolently mournful and affected voice? In order to demonstrate to the man with whom he is talking that he, the field officer, is an *aristocrat* and is really being extremely gracious in deigning to talk to a second lieutenant. Why is the cadet volunteer[26] waving his arms about and winking like that as he follows a lady he has only just set eyes on for the first time and would never dare accost for anything in the world? Why has the captain of artillery been so rude to the good-natured orderly? In order to demonstrate to all the men present that he never curries favour and has no need of *aristocrats*, and so on and so forth, *ad nauseam*.

Vanity, vanity, all is vanity – even on the brink of the grave, and among men who are ready to die for the sake of a lofty conviction. Vanity! It must be the distinguishing characteristic and special malady of our age. Why is it that in the records of peoples of earlier times not a mention is made of this vice, any more than there is mention of smallpox or cholera? Why, in the age we live in, are there only three kinds of people: those who accept vanity as a fact that is unavoidable and therefore justified, and who freely abandon themselves to it; those who accept it as an unfortunate but insuperable condition of human existence; and those who slavishly and unconsciously act under its influence? Why did authors such as Homer and Shakespeare write of love, glory and suffering, while the literature of our own age is merely an endless sequel to *The Book of Snobs* and *Vanity Fair*?[27]

Twice, in his inability to pluck up enough courage, Lieutenant-Captain Mikhailov walked past the little circle of 'his' *aristocrats*, but on the third attempt he managed to pull himself together and approached them. The circle was made up of four officers: Adjutant Prince Galtsin, who was something of an aristocrat even in Kalugin's eyes; Lieutenant-Colonel Neferdov, one of the so-called 'Hundred and Twenty-two' men of society who had come out of retirement and back into active service partly under the influence of patriotism, partly out of ambition, and partly because 'everyone else' was doing it; an old bachelor Moscow clubman who, while he had been here, had joined the number of those malcontents who never did anything, had no idea of what was what, and condemned every decree the authorities made; and cavalry Captain Praskukhin, who was also one of the 'Hundred and Twenty-two' heroes. Luckily for Mikhailov, Kalugin was in an excellent mood (the general had just had a highly confidential word in his ear, and Prince Galtsin, who had come all the way from St Petersburg, was putting up at his quarters), and did not consider it beneath his dignity to shake hands with the lieutenant-captain. This was more than could be said of Praskukhin, who had run across Mikhailov quite a few times in the bastion, had drunk his wine and vodka on more than one occasion, and was even in debt to him to the tune of twelve and a half roubles, lost at preference. Since Praskukhin did not really know Prince Galtsin, he was reluctant to betray to him the fact of his acquaintance with a mere infantry lieutenant-captain, so he made a slight bow in Mikhailov's direction.

'Well now, Captain,' said Kalugin. 'When are we going to see you in the bastion again, eh? Remember that time we met at the Schwartz redoubt?[28] Pretty hot, wasn't it?'

'Yes, it was,' said Mikhailov, ruefully calling to mind the pathetic figure he had cut that night when, picking his way bent double along the trench towards the bastion, he had run into Kalugin, who was striding along fearlessly, briskly rattling his sabre.

'I'm really supposed to go there tomorrow night,' Mikhailov

continued, 'but one of our officers is ill, so . . .' He began to explain that it was not really his turn tonight, but that since the commander of the 8th Regiment was indisposed, with only an ensign looking after things, he felt it his duty to offer himself in Lieutenant Nieprzysiecki's stead, and so would be going to the bastion that night after all. Kalugin did not wait for him to finish.

'I have a feeling something's going to happen in the next couple of days,' he said to Prince Galtsin.

'But, er, don't you think something might happen tonight?' asked Mikhailov, timidly, looking now at Kalugin and now at Prince Galtsin. Neither man replied. Prince Galtsin merely frowned somewhat, directed his gaze somewhere beyond Mikhailov's cap and, after a brief silence, said: 'That's a nice-looking girl over there, the one in the red kerchief. Perhaps you know her, Captain?'

'Yes, sir, she's the daughter of a sailor who lives near my quarters,' the lieutenant-captain replied.

'Let's go and take a proper look at her.'

And Prince Galtsin took Kalugin by one arm and the lieutenant-captain by the other, knowing full well that this could not but afford the latter great satisfaction, which was indeed the case.

The lieutenant-captain was a superstitious man, and he considered it a grave error to have anything to do with women before an action; now, however, he pretended to be a regular ladykiller, a performance which evidently neither Prince Galtsin nor Kalugin found very convincing, and which thoroughly astonished the girl in the red kerchief, who on several occasions had noticed the lieutenant-captain blush as he passed her window. Praskukhin walked behind them, continually nudging Prince Galtsin by the arm and making various remarks in French; but since there was not room enough for four people to walk along the path abreast of one another, he had to bring up the rear on his own, and it was only on the second round of the path that he succeeded in taking the arm of Sevryagin, a naval officer famed for his bravery, who also wished to join the company of the *aristocrats*. And the famous hero delightedly thrust his honest, muscular arm through the elbow of Praskukhin, whom everyone, even Sevryagin himself, knew was no saint. But when Praskukhin, in the process of explaining how it was that he knew 'this' naval officer, whispered to him that the man was a famous hero, Prince Galtsin, who the day before had been in the 4th bastion, had observed a shell explode twenty paces from him and considered himself no less of a hero than the other gentleman, surmising that rather too many reputations are obtained for nothing very much in particular, paid Sevryagin not the slightest attention.

So much did Lieutenant-Captain Mikhailov enjoy strolling around in this company that he forgot all about his *dear* letter from T—, the gloomy thoughts that had beset him at the prospect of his forthcoming spell of duty on the bastion and, most importantly, the fact that he was supposed to be back at his quarters by seven o'clock. He stayed with the officers until they began to address themselves exclusively to one another, avoiding his gaze and thereby letting him know that he might depart, and finally walking away from him altogether. But the lieutenant-captain was none the worse satisfied for this, and as he passed Baron Pest, a cadet volunteer who had been full of himself ever since the previous night, which he had spent in the casemate[29] of the 5th bastion – the first time he had been there – and who now as a result considered himself a hero, he was not in the least put out by the suspicious and haughty manner in which the cadet stood to attention and removed his cap.

—4—

Hardly had the lieutenant-captain crossed the threshold of his quarters, however, than thoughts of a very different kind began to preoccupy him. He saw his little room with its bumpy floor of packed earth and crooked windows stuck with strips of paper; his old bedstead with, above it, the wall-hanging depicting an Amazon on horseback, and the pair of Tula pistols nailed above that; his room-mate's, the cadet's, grubby bed with its calico print bedspread. He saw his manservant Nikita, with dishevelled, greasy hair, getting up from the floor, scratching himself; he saw his old greatcoat, his civilian boots and a cloth bundle, from which protruded the butt end of a soapy cheese and the neck of a porter bottle containing vodka, and which had been prepared for him to take with him to the bastion; and then, with a dawning sense of horror, he suddenly remembered that he was to take his company to the lodgments[30] and stay there all night.

'I expect I'll be killed tonight,' thought the lieutenant-captain. 'I've got that kind of feeling. It's even more likely because I volunteered to go, though it wasn't my turn. It's always those who go asking for trouble who are killed. What's the matter with that miserable Nieprzysiecki, anyway? The likelihood is that he's not ill at all, and yet here's a man going to be killed, bound to be killed, and all because of Nieprzysiecki! Oh well, I suppose if I'm not killed I'll get a medal. I saw how pleased the regimental commander was when I asked to be allowed to go since Lieutenant Nieprzysiecki was ill. Even if I'm not made a battalion commander I'll probably be given the Order of St Vladimir. After all, this'll be my thirteenth time on the bastion. Damn! Thirteen's an unlucky number! I'm going to be killed, I just know it, I'm bound to be killed. Yet someone has to go, a company can't just go off to fight with only an ensign in charge of it – if anything were to go wrong the honour of the whole regiment, the whole army, would be at stake. It's my *duty* to go . . . yes, that's right, it's my *duty*. But I've got a kind of premonition . . .' The lieutenant-captain had forgotten that he was visited by a more or less severe form of this premonition every time he had to go to the bastion, and was unaware that it is one experienced to a greater or lesser degree by every man before he goes into battle. When he had managed to calm his nerves a little by means of this notion of duty, which was highly developed in him as in all persons of limited intellect, the lieutenant-captain sat down at the table and began to write a farewell letter to his father, with whom his relations had of late been somewhat strained because of various money matters. After a space of some ten minutes, having finished this letter, he rose from the table, his eyes wet with tears, and, mentally reciting to himself all the prayers he knew (he was too ashamed to pray out loud in front of his manservant), began to get changed. He also had a strong desire to kiss the miniature icon of St Metrophanes which had been given to him by his mother (who was dead now) in blessing, and in which he placed an especial faith; but, being too embarrassed to do this with Nikita looking on, he decided to let all his icons hang down on the outside of his frock-coat, so he would be able to take them in his hand once he was out on the street without having to undo his coat buttons. His drunken and ill-mannered servant lethargically held up his new frock-coat for him to put on (the old one, which the lieutenant-captain usually wore to the bastion, had not been mended).

'Why has my old coat not been mended? All you ever do is sleep,' said Mikhailov, angrily.

'When do I ever get any sleep, sir?' grumbled Nikita. 'All day long I run around like a dog, wearing myself out, and still I'm not allowed to sleep.'

'You're drunk again, I see.'

'Well, if I am, it's not on your money, so don't go on about it.'

'Silence, you brute!' shouted the lieutenant-captain, on the point of striking his servant. Where before he had merely felt put out, now he finally lost all patience, vexed and exasperated by the oafish rudeness of Nikita, whom he was fond of, had even spoiled, and in whose company he had lived for twelve years now.

'Brute, brute,' the servant repeated. 'Why are you calling me a brute, master? Is this the right time for it? You shouldn't be calling me names like that.'

Mikhailov remembered where he was about to go, and felt ashamed of himself.

'Oh, Nikita, it's just that you'd try the patience of a saint,' he said, gently. 'Look, you see this letter I've written to my father? Please leave it where it is, on the table, and don't touch it,' he added, blushing.

'I shall obey, master,' said Nikita, his voice heavily emotional from the vodka he had drunk, vodka bought, as he liked to say, 'on his own money'. He showed not the slightest sign of having taken in the precise nature of his master's request, and had every appearance of being about to break down in tears.

Finally, when the lieutenant-captain reached the porch and said, 'Farewell, Nikita!', Nikita suddenly burst into torrents of affected sobbing and threw himself upon his master's hands in order to kiss them. 'Farewell, master,' he said, snuffling and moaning.

The landlady, an old sailor's widow, who was standing in the porch and could not, as a woman, remain aloof from this touching scene, began to rub her eyes with her dirty sleeve and utter words to the effect that if this was what the gentry were reduced to, what must be the sufferings of the rest, and that she, poor woman, had been left a widow; for the hundredth time, she told the drunken Nikita of her woes: how her husband had been killed in the first bombardment and how their little house had been blown to smithereens (the house in which she now lived did not belong to her), and so on and so forth. Once his master was gone, Nikita lit his pipe, asked the landlady's daughter to go and fetch some vodka, and very soon stopped crying; instead he began to quarrel with the old woman about a pail he said she had squashed.

'Perhaps I'll only be wounded,' the lieutenant-captain thought to himself as he drew near to the bastion with his company at dusk. 'But where will I be wounded? And how? Here? – or here?' he wondered, his thoughts moving from his stomach to his chest. 'What if I'm hit there,' he winced, thinking of the upper part of his leg, 'and it only grazes me? Well . . . but if a splinter gets me there it'll all be over with me!'

All this notwithstanding, the lieutenant-captain, ducking down, managed to pass along the trenches to the lodgments in relative safety. In the darkness, which by now was total, he helped a sapper officer assign the men to their various duties, and then got into a dugout underneath the parapet. There was not much gunfire; only from time to time was there a flash, now from our side, now from *his*, and the incandescent fuse of a mortar shell would describe a fiery arc in the dark, starry sky. But all the shells were landing away to the right, far short of the lodgment where the lieutenant sat crouching in his dugout, and so he calmed down somewhat, took a swig of vodka, had a few nibbles of the soapy cheese, lit a cigarette and, after saying his prayers, tried to sleep for a while.

—5—

Prince Galtsin, Lieutenant-Colonel Neferdov, cadet volunteer Baron Pest, who had run into the others by chance, and Praskukhin, whom no one had invited and to whom no one spoke but who had tagged along none the less, had all gone down the Boulevard together in order to have tea at Kalugin's quarters.

'I say, you never finished telling me about Vaska Mendel,' said Kalugin, who had taken off his greatcoat and was sitting in a soft, comfortable armchair by the window, unbuttoning the collar of his clean, starched linen shirt. 'How did he get married?'

'My dear fellow, you'd simply die laughing! *Je vous dis, il y avait un temps où on ne parlait que de ça à Pétersbourg*,' said Prince Galtsin, laughing and jumping up from the piano at which he had been sitting. He resettled himself on the window-seat, next to Kalugin. 'You'd die laughing! I know the whole story.' And he quickly launched, with much wit and humour, into an account of a love affair which we shall omit as it is of no interest to us.

What was remarkable, however, was that not only Prince Galtsin, but all these gentlemen who had made themselves comfortable in various parts of the room – one in the window, another in a chair with his legs drawn up, yet another at the piano – seemed quite different from the way they had appeared out on the Boulevard: they seemed to have lost all the absurd haughtiness and snobbery with which they addressed the infantry officers; here they were among their own kind, and they revealed themselves as thoroughly charming, high-spirited and good-hearted young men, Kalugin and Prince Galtsin especially so.

'How's Maslovsky these days?'

'Which one? The one in the Leib Uhlans or the one in the Horse Guards?'

'I know them both. I knew the one in the Horse Guards when he was still a lad and had only just left school. But how's the older one getting on – is he a captain yet?'

'Oh yes, he's been one for ages.'

'Still carrying on with that gypsy girl of his, eh?'

'No, he gave her up.' And so it went on.

Then Prince Galtsin sat down at the piano and gave everyone a marvellous rendering of a gypsy song. Although no one had asked him to, Praskukhin began to put in a second part, and did it so well that he was actually *asked* to do it again, which pleased him no end.

A servant came in with a silver tray bearing tea with cream and *krendelki*.

'Serve the Prince first,' said Kalugin.

'It's a strange thought,' said Galtsin, when he had taken his glass and was on his way back to the window-seat again. 'Here we are in a town that's under siege, tickling the ivories and having tea and cream in the sort of flat I for one would be proud to own in St Petersburg.'

'Well, all I can say is it's just as well,' said the old lieutenant-colonel, who was never satisfied with anything. 'Otherwise this constant waiting about for something to happen would be intolerable . . . Just think what it would be like if we had to live surrounded by this never-ending slaughter day after day up to our necks in mud, without any creature comforts.'[31]

'But what about our infantry officers?' said Kalugin. 'They have to live in the bastions with the rest of the men and have to eat the same bortsch they're given in the casemates. What about them?'

'There's something I don't understand,' said Prince Galtsin. 'I have to confess, I really don't see how men in dirty underwear, suffering from lice and not even able to wash their hands, can possibly be capable of bravery. You know what I mean, *cette belle bravoure de gentilhomme* – it's simply not on.'

'Well, they don't understand *that* kind of bravery,' said Praskukhin.

'Don't talk such nonsense,' said Kalugin, breaking in angrily. 'I've more experience of those men than you have, and I can tell you one thing: our infantry officers may have lice and go without changing their underwear for ten days at a time, but they're heroes, wonderful people.'

Just at that moment an infantry officer actually walked into the room.

'I . . . I've got orders . . . May I have a word with Gen . . . with

His Excellency? It's from General X., sir,' he said, bowing timidly.

Kalugin rose to his feet; without returning the officer's bow he asked him, with insulting politeness and a forced, official smile, to be so good as to wait. Then, not even asking him to sit down and indeed paying no further attention to him, he turned to Galtsin and proceeded to talk to the latter in French. The poor officer, who had been left standing in the middle of the room, was really at a loss as to what he should do – his gloveless hands dangled limply in front of him.

'It's extremely urgent, sir,' said the officer, after a moment's silence.

'Really? Then please come this way,' said Kalugin with the same insulting smile, putting on his greatcoat and escorting the man to the door.

'*Eh bien, messieurs, je crois que cela chauffera cette nuit,*' said Kalugin, when he emerged from the general's quarters.

'What's up, then? Come on, tell us, is it a sortie?' everyone began to ask.

'I really don't know, you'll have to wait and see for yourselves,' replied Kalugin, with an enigmatic smile.

'Look, old man, do tell me,' said Baron Pest. 'If there's going to be an action, I've got to join the T— regiment for the first sortie.'

'Well, off you go, then!'

'My boss is on the bastion too,' said Praskukhin, fastening on his sabre, 'so I suppose this means I'd better go as well.' No one made any reply to this, however – it was up to Praskukhin to know whether he had to go or not.

'I bet it's a false alarm,' said Baron Pest, contemplating the impending action with sinking heart, but managing none the less to don his cap at a rakish angle and march out of the room with loud, firm steps in the company of Praskukhin and Neferdov, who were also hurrying off to their posts with a sense of fear weighing on them. 'Cheerio, chaps!' 'Cheerio, chaps, see you later on tonight,' Kalugin shouted, leaning out of the window, as Praskukhin and Pest set off at a trot down the road on their horses, bending forward over the pommels of their Cossack saddles, for all the world like genuine Cossacks.

'Yes, a bit!' shouted Pest, his inconsequential reply showing that he had not been able to make out what Kalugin had said. The clatter of the small Cossack horses' hooves quickly faded along the dark street.

'*Non, dites-moi, est-ce qu'il y aura véritablement quelque chose cette nuit?*' inquired Galtsin, who was lounging in the window-seat beside Kalugin, watching the shells rising and falling over the bastions.

'I suppose I can tell you. After all, you've been in the bastions, haven't you?' Galtsin made a sign that this was so, although in fact he had been in the 4th bastion only once. 'Well, then: in front of our lunette there used to be a trench . . .' And Kalugin, who was not a specialist, though he considered he had a pretty sound grasp of military matters, began to deliver a somewhat labyrinthine account – in the course of which he got all the fortificational terms mixed up – of the enemy positions and those of our forces, and of the plan for the action that lay ahead.

'Look, they're taking pot-shots at the lodgments now. Aha! Was that one of ours or one of *his*? See, there's the explosion,' they said as they lounged in the window, watching the fiery traces of the shells crossing one another in mid-air, the flashes of gunfire that momentarily lit up the dark blue sky, and the white smoke of discharged gunpowder, and listening to the sounds of the ever intensifying cannonade.

'*Quel charmant coup d'œil!* Eh?' said Kalugin, drawing his guest's attention to this spectacle, which was indeed one of great beauty. 'You know, it's sometimes impossible to tell which are shells and which are stars!'

'Yes, I thought that was a star just now, but it fell and exploded. And that large star there – what's its name again? – looks just like a shell.'

'You know, I'm so used to these shells now that I'm sure when I get back to Russia I'll see them whenever there's a starry night. That's how used to them one gets.'

'Do you think I ought to go on this sortie?' said Prince Galtsin, after a moment's pause. The very thought of being *out there* during such a terrible cannonade made him shudder, and he reflected with a sense of relief that it was quite out of the question for him to be sent there at night.

'Enough of that, man! Stop thinking about it. Anyway, I won't allow you to go,' replied Kalugin, who was perfectly well aware that wild horses would not drag Galtsin out there. 'There'll be plenty of other opportunities.'

'Are you sure? You really think I needn't go? Eh?'

At that moment a terrible crackle of small-arms fire sounded above the din of the artillery, coming from the direction in which the two men were looking: thousands of tiny, constantly flaring points could be seen blazing along the whole length of the line.

'It's really getting started now!' said Kalugin. 'You know, I can never hear that sound of muskets and rifles without reacting to it in a special way – it seems to take hold of one, somehow. There's a cheer going up,' he added, listening to the distant, protracted roar of hundreds of voices – 'ah – ah – ah – ah – ah' – which were being carried towards him from the bastion.

'Whose hurrah is that? Theirs or ours?'

'I don't know, but they must have started fighting hand-to-hand now, because the firing's stopped.'

At that moment an orderly officer and a Cossack came galloping up to the house and stopped beneath the window. The officer dismounted.

'Where are you from?'

'The bastion. I must see the general.'

'All right, come with me. What's the trouble?'

'They've launched an assault on the lodgments – and taken them . . . The French brought up massive reserves . . . they attacked our troops . . . we only had two battalions,' said the officer, panting. He was one of the men who had been there earlier that evening. Now, barely able to catch his breath, he none the less contrived to stroll up to the front door in a thoroughly nonchalant manner.

'What's happened? Have our forces retreated?'

'No,' replied the officer, angrily. 'Another battalion arrived and beat the enemy off, but the regimental commander was killed, as well as a lot of the officers, and I've been sent to ask for reinforcements . . .'

Five minutes later, Kalugin was in the saddle of his Cossack horse (he too in that distinctive quasi-Cossack position which, I have observed, all adjutants appear for some reason to find particularly agreeable), and was setting off at a fast trot towards the bastion to deliver fresh orders and await some news concerning the final outcome of the action; while Prince Galtsin, infected with that painful excitement that is commonly experienced by onlookers who are confronted by the outward manifestations of a battle at close quarters but are not taking part in it, went out on to the street and began to walk aimlessly up and down.

—6—

Crowds of soldiers were ferrying men on stretchers or helping them along by the arm. In the street it was pitch dark; lights shone only very occasionally here and there – in the windows of the hospital, or in those of a house where some officers were sitting up late. The same rumble of artillery and small-arms fire was still coming from the bastions, and lights still flared in the black sky. Now and then could be heard the thud of hooves as an orderly galloped by, the groans of a wounded man, the voices and footsteps of stretcher-bearers, or the murmur of women as the frightened inhabitants came out on to their porches to watch the cannonade.

Among these people was our friend Nikita, together with the old sailor's widow, with whom he had now made his peace, and her ten-year-old daughter.

'Lord Almighty, Mother of Jesus,' the old woman was saying to herself, in between sighs, as she watched the shells hurtling constantly back and forth like balls of fire. 'Horrible things, horrible things, aye-aye-aye! It was nothing like this during the first bombardment. Look where it's exploded, the nasty brute, over there in the village, right on top of our house.'

'No, that's further away, it's Auntie Irina's garden they're landing in,' said the girl.

'And where, where is my master at this hour?' said Nikita, who was still slightly drunk, in a sing-song voice. 'Oh, I love that master of mine more than words can tell. He beats me, oh how he beats me, but I still love him something terrible. I love him so much that if, God forbid, he were to be killed in all these carryings-on, I don't know what I'd do with myself, Auntie, honest to God I don't! Such a master he is, there's only one word for it. Can you ever see me swapping him for one of that card-playing lot – what manner of men are those? Pah! There's only one word for it,' Nikita concluded, pointing to the window of his master's lighted room where in the lieutenant-captain's absence the Polish cadet Żwadczeski had invited a couple of guests to help him celebrate the military cross he had just been awarded. These guests, who were also Poles, were Lieutenant-Colonel Ugrowicz and Lieutenant Nieprzysiecki, the very same man whose turn it was to go to the bastion that night and who was supposed to be incapacitated by a gumboil.

'Look at the stars, the stars are falling!' cried the girl, who was looking up at the sky, breaking the silence that had followed in the wake of Nikita's monologue. 'There! There's another one fallen! Why are they doing that, mother?'

'Our house'll be blowed to smithereens,' said the old woman with a sigh, leaving her daughter's question unanswered.

'And mother, when uncle and I went there today,' continued the girl, prattling on in her melodious voice, 'there was an enormous great cannonball lying in the parlour, right beside the cupboard: it must have smashed right through the passage. It was so enormous nobody could lift it.'

'The women who had husbands and money all moved away,' said the old woman, 'but here – oh misery me, the poorest house in the neighbourhood, and they've blown it up, too. Look at him blazing away, the devil! Lord, Lord!'

'And just when we were about to leave a shell came whee-eeing over and burst to pie-ie-ces and sent earth strea-eaming all over us, and a splinter nearly got uncle and me.'

'She ought to get a medal for that,' said the cadet, who had in the meantime come out on to the porch with the officers to watch the exchange of fire.

'You go in and see the general, old woman,' said Lieutenant Nieprzysiecki, patting her on the shoulder. 'I mean it.'

'*Pojdę na ulicę zobaczýc co tam nowego,*'*[32] he added, as he went down the steps.

'*A my tymczasem napijmy sie wodki, bo coś dusza w pięty ucieka,*'† said the sanguine Żwadczeski, laughing.

—7—

More and more wounded men, some on stretchers, some on foot being helped along by others, and all talking to one another in loud voices, were coming down the street in Prince Galtsin's direction.

'You should have seen the way they came running, lads,' one tall soldier, who had two muskets slung over his shoulder, was saying in a deep voice. 'You should have seen the way they came running, shouting "Allah! Allah!"‡ Climbing on top of one another, they were. You'd kill one of them, but the others would just run over him – there was nothing you could do to stop them. Millions of them, there were . . .'

Galtsin stopped the man at this point in his narrative.

'Have you come from the bastion?'

'Indeed I have, your honour.'

'All right, tell me what happened there.'

'What happened, your honour? Well, sir, their *forces* came up and stormed the rampart, and that was that. They completely overpowered us, your honour!'

'What do you mean, overpowered you? You repulsed them, didn't you?'

'How could we do that, your honour, when *he* sent the whole of his *forces* over? He slaughtered all our men, and we didn't get

* 'Go out on to the street and see what's new.'

† 'And meanwhile we'll have a nip of vodka, cos it's getting pretty scary.'

‡ So accustomed have our soldiers become to this cry in the course of their fighting with the Turks that they will now all tell you to a man that the French shout 'Allah!' too. (Tolstoy's note.)

any reinforcements.' (The soldier was mistaken, as the trench was still in Russian hands; but this is a curious phenomenon, and it is one that may be commonly observed: the soldier who has been wounded in action invariably believes the battle to have been lost with fearful carnage.)

'Then how was it they told me the assault had been repulsed?' said Galtsin, with irritation.

At that moment Lieutenant Nieprzysiecki, who had recognized Prince Galtsin in the darkness by his white cap, came up to him, anxious to take advantage of this opportunity of having a few words with such an important person.

'Are you able to inform me, sir, of what has happened?' he asked courteously, touching the peak of his cap.

'I'm trying to find out myself,' said Prince Galtsin, and he turned once more to the soldier with the two muskets: 'Is it possible that the enemy were repulsed after you'd gone? How long is it since you left the scene of the battle?'

'I've only just arrived, your honour!' replied the soldier. 'I doubt it, sir. No, sir, he must have taken the trench – completely overpowered us, he did.'

'Well, you ought to be ashamed – giving up a trench to the enemy! This is terrible!' said Galtsin, annoyed by the man's apparent indifference. 'You ought to be ashamed!' he repeated, turning away from the soldier.

'Oh! These men are dreadful. You don't know them, sir,' said Nieprzysiecki, seizing the initiative. 'But I can tell you that it's no good expecting either pride or patriotism or indeed any noble feelings at all from them. Just look at them, those crowds of them marching along there, not even one in ten of those men is wounded – oh, no, they're all "assistants" – anything, just so long as they don't have to fight. What a despicable crew! Shame on you, men, shame on you! Giving up one of *our* trenches!' he added, addressing the soldiers.

'He had his *forces* there!' muttered the one Galtsin had spoken with.

'Ah, your honour,' said a man who was being carried on a stretcher which had at that moment drawn level with them. 'If we'd had the men we'd never have surrendered, not in a million years. But what could we do? I got my bayonet into one of them, and then something hit me . . . Oh-h, easy, lads, not so rough, lads, not so rough . . . o-o-oh!' groaned the wounded man.

'You're quite right, there really do seem to be too many men coming back,' said Galtsin, and once again he stopped the tall soldier with the two muskets. 'Why are you coming back? Hey, you there, halt!'

The soldier stood still and removed his cap with his left hand.

'Where are you going, and on whose orders?' Galtsin thundered at him. 'Good-for . . .'

Just as he was about to accost the soldier at close quarters, however, he noticed that the man's right hand was inside the cuff of his coat and that his arm was soaked up to the elbow in blood.

'I've been wounded, your honour!'

'Where have you been wounded?'

'Here, your honour,' said the soldier, pointing to his arm. 'It must have been a bullet. But I don't know what it was that got my head.' And bowing his head forward, he showed the blood-smeared, matted hair at the nape of his neck.

'And who does that other musket belong to?'

'It's a carbine, your honour. I took it off a Frenchman, sir; I would never have left the fight if I hadn't had to look after this lad here – he'd fall down if I wasn't here to help him along,' he added, pointing to a soldier who was making his way along with difficulty a short distance ahead, leaning on his musket and dragging his left leg.

'And where are *you* going, you scoundrel?' shouted Lieutenant Nieprzysiecki at another soldier who happened to be coming in his direction, hoping by this show of zeal to favourably impress the important prince. This soldier also turned out to have been wounded.

Prince Galtsin suddenly felt horribly ashamed of Lieutenant Nieprzysiecki, and even more so of himself. He could feel himself blushing – something he hardly ever did. He turned away from the lieutenant and, without questioning any more of the wounded men or bothering to keep an eye on them further, set off for the dressing station.

Forcing his way with difficulty up the steps through the throngs of walking wounded and stretcher-bearers arriving with casualties and leaving with corpses, Galtsin entered the Assembly Hall, took one quick look round, and immediately found himself turning back and running out on to the street. This was too dreadful!

—8—

The large, high-ceilinged chamber, lit only by the four or five candles the surgeons used on their rounds of inspection, was literally full. Stretcher parties were constantly arriving with casualties, setting them down one beside the other on the floor – which was already so closely packed that the wretched men were jostling one another and smearing one another with their blood – and then leaving to fetch more. The pools of blood that were visible wherever there was a vacant space, the fevered breathing of the several hundreds of men and the sweating of the stretcher-bearers combined to produce a characteristic thick, heavy, stinking fetor, in which the surgeons' candles bleakly glimmered from various corners of the room. A murmur of groans, sighs and crepitations, broken now and again by a bloodcurdling scream, ran throughout the entire area. The Sisters, with their calm faces that expressed not the futile, morbidly tearful kind of sympathy that might have been expected of women, but an active, no-nonsense and practical concern, strode to and fro among the wounded men, bearing medicine, water, bandages and lint, their uniforms flashing white against the blood-stained shirts and greatcoats. Gloomy-faced surgeons in their rolled-up shirtsleeves knelt beside wounded men while an apothecary assistant held up the candle, pushing their fingers into bullet wounds and searching them, or turning over severed limbs that still hung by a thread, in spite of the terrible groans and entreaties of the sufferer. One of the surgeons sat at a small table beside the entry door; as Galtsin came in he was recording the five hundred and thirty-second admission.

'Ivan Bogayev, private, 3rd company, S— Regiment, compound fracture of the thigh!' shouted a surgeon from the far end of the chamber, as he examined a man's shattered leg. 'Turn him over for a minute.'

'Oh – oh, father in heaven, father in heaven!' cried the soldier, begging to be left alone.

'Fracture of the skull!'

'Semyon Neferdov, lieutenant-colonel, N— Infantry Regiment. Try to put a brave face on it, colonel, or else I'll have to stop,' said another surgeon, as he picked at the unfortunate lieutenant-colonel's head with a kind of hook.

'Ah! Ah! Stop it! Oh, for the love of God, be quick, be quick, for the love of . . . A-a-a-ah!'

'Perforation of the chest . . . Sevastyan Sereda, private . . . what regiment? . . . Don't bother writing it down, he'll be dead in a minute. Take him away,' said a surgeon, walking away from one soldier whose eyes had started to roll up and was already beginning to emit a death rattle . . .

A crowd of some forty soldiers, who were acting as stretcher-bearers and were waiting for patched-up casualties to take to the hospital or corpses to take to the chapel, stood at the doorway observing this scene in silence; now and then one or the other of them would heave a deep sigh . . .

—9—

On his way to the bastion Kalugin encountered a large number of wounded men. Since he knew from experience what a bad effect such a spectacle is likely to have on a man who is about to go into battle, he did not stop to question them and tried, indeed, to ignore them altogether. As he was about to climb the hill he met an orderly galloping down from the bastion at full tilt.

'Zobkin! Zobkin! Stop for a moment, will you?'

'Yes, sir, what is it?'

'Where have you just come from?'

'The lodgments, sir.'

'What's it like there? Pretty warm, eh?'

'It's hot as hell, sir. Terrible!'

And the orderly galloped on.

Although there was not much in the way of rifle and musketry fire, the cannonade had begun again with renewed ardour and ferocity.

'That doesn't sound too good,' thought Kalugin with an unpleasant sensation, and he, too, was visited by a forewarning – that is to say, by a very commonplace thought, the thought of death. But Kalugin was not Lieutenant-Captain Mikhailov; he was proud, and possessed of nerves that would withstand anything – he was, in short, what is termed 'brave'. He did not allow his initial reactions to get the better of him, and set about reassuring himself. He recalled the adjutant – it had been one of Napoleon's, he thought – who, after communicating the orders with which he had been entrusted, had galloped back to the Emperor at full tilt, his head covered in blood.

'*Vous êtes blessé?*' Napoleon had asked him.

'*Je vous demande pardon, sire, je suis tué*,' the adjutant had replied. And with these words he had fallen from his horse and had died instantly.

Kalugin thought this was a marvellous story, and for a moment he even saw himself as that adjutant; then he gave his horse a smack of the whip, assumed an even more dashing 'Cossack position', glanced back over his shoulder at the Cossack who was riding behind him at a fast trot, standing in the stirrups, and arrived at the place where he was to dismount, every inch the gallant brave. Here he encountered four soldiers who were sitting on some large boulders and were smoking their pipes.

'What are you men doing here?' he shouted to them.

'We've been carting one of the wounded, your honour, and now we've sat down to have a rest,' replied one of the soldiers, trying to conceal his pipe behind his back and taking his cap off.

'I'll give you a rest! Return to your posts at the double, or I'll inform your regimental commander this instant!'

And together with them he began to climb the hill along the trench, meeting men who had been wounded every step of the way. When he reached the top he followed the trench that forked off to the left and, walking along it a little way, found himself completely alone. A splinter hummed by within a hair's-breadth of him and slammed into the trench. A shell rose into the sky in front of him and seemed to be hurtling straight towards him. Suddenly, he felt afraid: he quickly scrambled forward a distance of some five yards, and then fell to the ground. When the shell finally exploded, a long way off, he felt thoroughly annoyed with himself; as he got up from the ground he looked to see if anyone had observed his fall, but there was no one nearby.

Once fear has found its way into the soul, it does not readily give way to any other emotion. He, who had always boasted that he never ducked, now found himself scurrying along the trench practically on all fours. 'Ah! This is bad!' he thought, as he stumbled along, 'I'm sure to be killed' – and, feeling his breathing constrict and the sweat break out all over his body, he marvelled at himself, but no longer tried to overcome the feeling that had taken hold of him.

All at once he heard footsteps somewhere up ahead. He quickly straightened himself, lifted his head, and, briskly rattling his sabre, walked on rather more slowly than before. Now he could hardly recognize himself. When an engineer officer and a sailor appeared coming in his direction, and the officer shouted to him: 'Get down!', pointing to the bright pinhead of a shell which, growing every brighter and faster in its descent, finally slapped into the earth beside the trench, he merely inclined his head slightly, startled by the man's frightened cry, and continued on his way.

'There's a brave one for ye,' said the sailor, who had observed the falling shell with utter equanimity, his experienced eye telling him at once that none of its fragments would hit the trench. 'He didn't even bother to lie down.'

Kalugin had only a few yards still to go across the open area to the casemate where the bastion commander had his headquarters, when once again his mind went blank and he was overtaken by the same unreasoning terror; his heart began to beat faster, the blood rushed to his head, and he really had to force himself in order to reach the casemate at all.

'Why are you so out of breath?' said the general, after Kalugin had delivered the orders he had been sent with.

'I came here at the double, your excellency!'

'How about a glass of wine?'

Kalugin accepted a glass of wine and lit a cigarette. The action was now over, and only a heavy cannonade continued from both sides. In the casemate sat General X., the bastion commander, and five or six officers, one of whom was Praskukhin, discussing various details of the action. Sitting in this snug little den, the walls of which were covered with blue wallpaper and which contained a bed, a sofa, a table, a clock and an icon with a vigil lamp burning in front of it; looking at these signs of habitation and at the thick, solid beams which formed the ceiling; and listening to the detonations of the cannon, which here in the casemate seemed muffled and remote, Kalugin was decidedly at a loss to understand how he could twice have allowed himself to be overcome by such unpardonable weakness. He felt angry with himself, and longed for fresh danger in order to put himself to the test once more.

'I'm glad you're here too, captain,' he said to a naval officer who sported a moustache and was wearing a field officer's greatcoat to which was pinned the ribbon of a St George Cross. The naval officer had only just entered the casemate and was asking the general for some labourers to help clear two of his battery's embrasures which had become blocked by flying earth. 'The general asked me to ascertain,' Kalugin went on, when the battery commander had finished talking to General X., 'whether your guns are capable of firing grape into the enemy trenches.'

'There's only one that could do it,' replied the captain, morosely.

'Even so, let's go and have a look.'

The captain frowned and gave an angry grunt.

'I've been standing out there all night, and I've come in in order to get a little rest,' he said. 'Can't you go on your own? My assistant, Lieutenant Karz, is up there – he'll show you round.'

The captain had been in charge of this battery, which was one of the most dangerous, for the past six months; he had been here even before the casemates had been constructed, had lived on the bastion from the outset of the siege and had a reputation for bravery among the other naval officers. It was for this reason that Kalugin found the man's refusal particularly surprising and shocking.

'So much for reputations,' he thought.

'Well, all right then, I'll go on my own, if you'll permit me,' he said in a slightly mocking tone of voice. The captain was not, however, paying the slightest attention.

But Kalugin was not taking into account the fact that while he had, on various occasions, spent at the very most perhaps fifty hours on the bastions, the captain had been living on this one continuously for six months. Kalugin was still at the stage of being driven on by personal vanity – the desire to excel, the hope of receiving military honours, of winning a reputation, the fascination of risk. The captain, on the other hand, had already been through all that – at first he had indulged in vanity, had pretended to be brave, run foolish risks, hoped for honours and reputation, and even acquired them. But now all these incentives had lost their hold over him and he viewed the whole business rather differently: he still carried out his duties to the letter, but, understanding very well how small were the chances of survival left to him after his six months of duty in the bastion, he did not risk those chances except in dire necessity. The result of this was that the young lieutenant, who had joined the battery only a week previously and was now showing Kalugin over it (both men were rather needlessly leaning out of the embrasures and climbing up on to the banquettes), appeared ten times braver than the captain.

When he had finished looking over the battery and was on his way back to the casemate, Kalugin stumbled into the general, who was going to the watchtower with his orderlies.

'Captain Praskukhin,' said the general. 'Please go to the right lodgment and tell the second battalion of the M— Regiment who are working there to down tools immediately, withdraw without making a sound and rejoin their regiment, which is stationed at the foot of the hill in reserve. Have you got that? You'll take them to their regiment yourself.'

'Yes, sir.'

And Praskukhin set off for the lodgment at the double.

The sounds of gunfire were now growing less frequent.

—10—

'Is this the second battalion of the M— Regiment?' asked Praskukhin, arriving at his destination and nearly running into a soldier who was carrying sacks of earth.

'Yes, sir.'

'Where's your commander?'

Mikhailov, supposing it was the company commander whose presence was requested, climbed from his dugout and, taking Praskukhin for a member of the general staff, approached him with one hand touching the peak of his cap.

'The general has ordered . . . you . . . you're to go . . . immediately . . . and above all as quietly as possible . . . back, no forward, to join the reserves,' said Praskukhin, keeping a wary eye on the direction of the enemy's fire.

Recognizing Praskukhin and becoming aware of the true situation, Mikhailov let his arm drop and passed on the order. The battalion bustled into action; each man reached for his musket, put on his greatcoat and set off.

Those who have never experienced it themselves cannot imagine the sense of relief experienced by a man when, after a three hours' bombardment, he leaves a place as dangerous as the lodgments. Mikhailov, who several times during those three hours believed his end had come and who had smothered with kisses, several times over, all the icons he had with him, had towards the end grown somewhat calmer, certain that he was about to be killed and that he no longer belonged to this world. Even in spite of this, however, it cost him no little effort to prevent his legs running away with him when, with Praskukhin at his side, he emerged from the lodgments at the head of the company.

'Goodbye,' a major said to him. This was the commander of another battalion, who was remaining in the lodgments and with whom Mikhailov had shared his soapy cheese as they had crouched together in the dugout near the parapet. 'I wish you a safe journey.'

'And I wish you a safe stay; things seem to have quietened down now.'

No sooner had he said this, however, than the enemy, who had doubtless observed the activity on the lodgments, began to blaze away with an artillery fire that grew heavier and heavier. The Russian guns began an answering fire, and once again an intense cannonade set in. The stars gleamed high but faintly in the heavens. The night was so dark that you could hardly see your hand in front of your face; only the flashes of the gunfire and the bursting of the shells momentarily lit up surrounding objects. The soldiers walked quickly, in silence, overtaking one another without meaning to; all that could be heard above the incessant rolling of the guns was the measured sound of their footsteps on the dry road, the clank of bayonets or the sighed prayer of a frightened soldier: 'Lord, Lord, whatever's that?' From time to time the groaning of a wounded man could be heard, and voices shouting: 'Stretchers!' (In the company of which Mikhailov was commander, twenty-six men were killed that night by artillery fire alone.) Lightning would flare on the far-off, murky horizon, the sentry on the bastion would shout: 'Ca-a-nnon!', and a cannonball would come rapidly humming over the heads of the company, throwing up a shower of earth and stones as it landed.

'God, they're moving slowly,' thought Praskukhin, who kept looking back over his shoulder as he strode along beside Mikhailov. 'Why don't I just hurry on ahead? After all, I have delivered the order now . . . But no, I'd better not, or else this brute will tell everyone afterwards what a coward I was, more or less the way I spoke about him to the others yesterday. What will be, will be. I'll stay alongside him.'

'Why does he never leave my side,' Mikhailov was thinking meanwhile. 'I've noticed it so many times now – he always brings me bad luck: I bet that one's heading straight this way.'

When they had gone a few hundred paces further they ran into Kalugin, who was making his way to the lodgments, briskly rattling his sabre. He had been instructed by the general to find out how the building of the earthworks there was proceeding. When he met Mikhailov, however, it struck him that instead of going there in person under this terrible hail of fire – something he had not been ordered to do – he might just as well make some detailed enquiries of an officer who had been there and would know all about the situation. And, indeed, Mikhailov was able to give him a detailed report on the present state of the earthworks, although as he did so he provided Kalugin – who seemed totally oblivious to all the firing – with considerable amusement by cowering down every time a shell exploded (often quite far away), ducking his head and stating with conviction that 'that one's heading straight this way'.

'Look, captain, that one's heading straight this way,' said Kalugin, teasing him, and giving him a nudge. Continuing with them for a short distance, Kalugin at length turned off into the trench that led to the casemate. 'It would be impossible to describe that captain as being very brave,' he thought, as he passed through its doorway.

'Well, what's the latest?' asked an officer who was eating his supper and was the only person in the room.

'Oh, there's nothing, really. I think it's all going to be over in a minute or two.'

'All over? But the general's just gone up to the watchtower again. Another regiment's arrived. There, hear that? That's musketry fire again. I wouldn't go out there if I were you. Why should you, anyway?' added the officer, observing the direction Kalugin was about to take.

'I really ought to be out there,' thought Kalugin. 'But I think I've run enough risks for one day. I hope I can serve for something better than cannon fodder.'

'You're probably right, I'd better just wait for them here,' he said.

And indeed, some twenty minutes later the general returned, together with the officers who had been accompanying him. One of these was the cadet volunteer, Baron Pest; but of Praskukhin there was no sign. The lodgments had been recaptured from the enemy and occupied by the Russian forces.

When he had heard a detailed account of the action, Kalugin left the casemate together with Pest.

—11—

'There's blood all over your greatcoat: you weren't in the hand-to-hand fighting, were you?' Kalugin asked Pest.

'Oh, my dear fellow, it was dreadful! Can you imagine . . .' And Pest proceeded to describe how he had ended up in command of his entire company, how his company commander had been killed, how he, Pest, had bayoneted a Frenchman and how, had it not been for him, the day would have been lost, and so on, and so forth.

The principal elements of this story – that the company commander had been killed and that Pest had slain a Frenchman – were factually true; in recounting its details, however, the cadet boasted and made things up. He found himself boasting in spite of himself, and the reason for this was that during the whole of the action he had been lost in a fog of oblivion, to such a degree that all that had happened had seemed to be taking place somewhere else, at some other time and to some other person. It was, therefore, natural that he should now attempt to reproduce these details so that he came out of the affair with some credit. The following, however, is what really occurred.

The battalion to which Pest had been assigned for the sortie waited under fire for nearly two hours behind the defensive wall until the battalion commander gave a signal, the company commanders stirred into action, the battalion started to move, emerged from behind the parapet, and, having advanced a hundred yards or so, halted and formed itself into columns, each of which represented a company. Pest was ordered to join the right flank of the 2nd company.

Completely at a loss as to where he was and what he was doing there, the cadet took up his post and, finding his breathing strangely constricted and feeling cold shivers run up and down his spine, peered into the expanse of darkness ahead of him in expectation of something terrible. He was, however, beset less by fear – the guns were silent – as by a sense of the abnormal: it was strange to find himself on the outside of the fortress, out here in the open. Again the battalion commander gave a signal. Again the officers began to talk in whispers as they passed the orders along, and the black wall of the 1st company suddenly collapsed. Their orders had been to lie down. The 2nd company also lay down, and Pest pricked his hand on something sharp. The commander of the 2nd company alone remained standing. His stocky figure moved backwards and forwards in front of the company as, brandishing his sword in the air, he kept up a constant stream of talk.

'All right, men! Come on now, my fine fellows! We'll save our bullets and take the riff-raff with our bayonets. When I shout "hurrah" I want to see you follow me – let no man lag behind . . . You must stay together, that's most important . . . let's show them what we're made of and not get dirt on our faces, all right, men? For our father, the Tsar!' he cried. These words were sprinkled with curses, and he waved his arms about in the most alarming fashion.

'Who's our company commander?' Pest asked the cadet who was lying next to him. 'He's a bit of a daredevil, isn't he?'

'Yes, whenever there's a battle he always gets dead drunk,' the cadet replied. 'His name's Lisinkovsky.'

At that moment a sheet of flame leapt up in front of the company, followed by the most tremendous explosion, which made everyone deaf and sent a rustling hiss of stones and shell-fragments high into the air (at least fifty seconds later a stone fell from the sky, smashing a soldier's foot). This was a shell from a 'high angle' mortar, and the fact that it had hit the company was proof that the French had observed the column.

'Shells, is it? The swine . . . Just wait till we get to you, then you can try our three-edged Russian bayonets for size, you hellhounds!' said the company commander in such a loud voice that the commander of the battalion had to tell him to be quiet and stop making such a noise.

Thereupon the 1st company rose to its feet, followed by the 2nd – the order was given to slope muskets, and the battalion advanced. Pest was in such a state of funk that he lost all sense of the passage of time, of where they were going, who they were and what the purpose of their action was. He staggered along like one intoxicated. Suddenly, however, a million lights seemed to flash on at once, and there was a fearsome whistling and crackling; he gave a sudden shout, and found himself running in an unknown direction, simply because everyone else seemed to be running and shouting. Then he stumbled and fell over something – it turned out to be the company commander, who had been wounded at his post at the head of the company, had taken Pest in his red uniform for a Frenchman, and had seized him by the leg. Pulling his leg free, he stood up, but someone collided with him from behind in the darkness, nearly knocking him off his feet again, and another shouted: '*Run him through! What are you waiting for?*' Someone took hold of his musket and rammed it, bayonet first, into something soft. '*Ah! Dieu!*' someone shouted in a horrible, strident voice, and it was only then that Pest realized he had bayoneted a Frenchman.

A cold sweat broke out all over his body, as though in a fever, and he threw his musket to the ground. This state of affairs lasted only for a second, however; it suddenly occurred to him that he was a hero. Snatching up his musket and shouting 'Hurrah!' with the rest of the men, he ran away from the body of the slain Frenchman, whose boots were already being removed by a Russian soldier. Some twenty yards further on he came to a trench that was being held by Russian forces and where he found the battalion commander.

'I got one of them, sir!' he told the battalion commander.

'Well done, Baron . . .'

—12—

'Praskukhin was killed, you know,' said Pest, as he was seeing off Kalugin, who was returning to his quarters.

'Surely not!'

'He was, I saw it with my own eyes.'

'Well, goodbye. I'm afraid I'm in a bit of a hurry.'

'I really feel quite pleased,' thought Kalugin, as he arrived back at his billet. 'That's the first time we've struck lucky when I've been on duty. It was a fine battle – I'm alive and well, and I should get a first-class decoration, probably even a golden sabre. And, I must say, I've deserved it.'

When he had finished reporting all the necessary details to the general he went to his room, where he found Prince Galtsin, who had already been sitting there waiting for him for quite a long time, reading a copy of *Splendeurs et misères des courtisanes** which he had found on Kalugin's table.

It was with a quite astonishing degree of satisfaction that Kalugin, feeling himself to be back home and out of danger, put on his nightshirt, got into bed and told Galtsin the details of the action, recounting them in a perfectly natural manner and from a point of view that made them illustrate what a thoroughly courageous and efficient officer he, Kalugin, was, a circumstance he felt it hardly necessary to allude to directly since everyone knew it to be so and had no reason to doubt it, with the possible exception of Captain Praskukhin, who was now deceased. Praskukhin, although he had deemed it an honour to walk arm-in-arm with Kalugin, had only the day before confidentially informed one of his closest friends that Kalugin was a very fine man, but that, 'strictly between ourselves', he appeared to have a terrible aversion to visiting the bastions.

What had happened was that Praskukhin, who had been walking beside Mikhailov and had only just parted company with Kalugin, had begun to recover his spirits somewhat, having reached a less dangerous stretch of terrain, when he suddenly saw a brilliant flash that seemed to come from somewhere behind him, heard a sentry shout: '*Mortar!*' and one of the soldiers beside him say: 'That one's going to land on the battalion!'

Mikhailov had looked round: the bright pinpoint of a shell seemed to have stopped at its zenith in a position that made it quite impossible to determine its future trajectory. But this illusion only lasted a moment: the shell had begun to descend faster and faster, coming nearer until the sparks of its fuse were clearly visible, as it headed straight for the centre of the battalion with a deadly whistling sound.

* One of those enchanting books of which there has recently appeared such an inordinate quantity, and which for some reason enjoy an exceptional popularity among our young people. (Tolstoy's note; the novel is by Balzac.)

'Get down!' someone had shouted in a frightened voice.

Mikhailov had fallen forward on his stomach. Praskukhin found himself bending double and covering his eyes: all he heard was the sound of the shell thudding into the hard earth somewhere close by. A second elapsed. It had seemed like an hour, and still the shell hadn't gone off. Praskukhin had been afraid his panic was groundless – perhaps the shell had really landed a long way off and it was only in his imagination that he could hear its fuse hissing right next to him. He had opened his eyes and seen to his vain satisfaction that Mikhailov, whom he still owed twelve and a half roubles, was lying right at his feet and nearer the ground than he was, flat on his belly, in fact. In that same moment, however, his eyes registered the glowing fuse of the shell which was spinning on the ground only a few feet away from him.

A sense of horror – a cold sense of horror which shut out all other thoughts and feelings – seized hold of his entire being. He covered his face with his hands and fell to his knees.

Another second passed, one during which a whole world of feelings, thoughts, hopes and memories flooded through his mind.

'Who's it going to kill? Mikhailov or me? Or both of us? And if it's to be me, where will it get me? If it gets me in the head, then I'm done for; but if it's one of my legs they'll have to amputate it and I shall most certainly ask to be given chloroform and then perhaps I'll survive. But perhaps it will only be Mikhailov who's killed. Then I'll be able to tell the story of how we were walking side by side when he was suddenly killed and spurted blood all over me. No, it's closer to me – I'm the one who's for it.'

It was at this point that he remembered the twelve roubles he owed Mikhailov, as well as another debt he owed to someone in St Petersburg, one he should have paid a long time ago; the gypsy melody he had sung earlier that evening came into his head; the woman he loved appeared in his thoughts, wearing a hood adorned with lilac ribbons; he remembered a man who five years earlier had insulted him and on whom he had never got his own back. Running parallel with these and thousands of other memories, however, was an awareness of the present – an expectation of death and honour – which did not abandon him for one moment. 'Anyhow, it may not explode,' he thought, and with desperate determination he made an effort to open his eyes. But at that moment a red light struck his still-closed eyelids, and something shoved him, with a terrible crack, in the centre of his chest; he started to run blindly, but tripped over his sword, which had slid down under his feet, and fell over on his side.

'Thank God, I'm only contused,' was his first thought, and he tried to touch his chest with his hands – but his arms seemed to be bound fast, and his head felt as though it were caught in some kind of vice. Soldiers flickered past his gaze – and he found himself unconsciously counting them: 'One, two, three – ah, that one in the tucked-up greatcoat is an officer,' he thought; then there was a flash, and he wondered if it had been a mortar or a cannon; a cannon, more likely; and now there was some more firing, more soldiers going past – five, six, seven. He was suddenly afraid he might be trampled on; he wanted to shout that he was only contused, but his mouth was so dry that his tongue stuck to his palate, and he was racked by a terrible thirst. He could feel something wet in the region of his chest – this wet sensation made him think of water, and he would even have drunk whatever it was his chest was wet with. 'I must be bleeding from that fall,' he thought and, becoming more and more obsessed with the fear that the soldiers who were continuing to flicker past were about to trample on him, he mustered all his strength and tried to shout: 'Take me with you!' Instead, however, he began to groan so horribly that he grew terrified at the sounds he was making. Then red lights began to dance in front of his eyes – and he had an impression that the soldiers were piling stones on top of him. The lights grew more and more sparse, and the stones being placed on top of him seemed to weigh more and more heavily on him. He made an effort to heave them aside, straightened himself up, and then neither saw nor heard nor thought nor felt anything more. He had been killed on the spot by a shell-splinter that had struck him in the middle of the chest.[33]

—13—

When Mikhailov caught sight of the shell, he dived to the ground, screwed up his eyes, and then opened and closed them again twice. Just as Praskukhin had done, in those two seconds during which the shell lay on the ground before it went off, he experienced an ineffable multitude of thoughts and emotions. He prayed in silence, repeating over and over to himself: 'Thy will be done!', and thinking as he did so: 'Why on earth did I ever join the army? And to think I even got a transfer to an infantry division so I could take part in this campaign! I'd have done better to have stayed put in T— with the Uhlans and spent the time with my friend Natasha . . . instead, look at the mess I'm in!' And he began to count: one, two, three, four, making a silent wager that if the shell went off on an even number he would live, but that if it went off on an odd number he would be killed. 'It's all over!' he thought, when the shell finally exploded (he had no idea of whether it was on an odd or an even number), and he felt a blow and a fierce pain in his head. 'O Lord, forgive me my sins,' he said, clasping his hands, trying to sit up, and then falling back unconscious.

The first sensation he had on regaining consciousness was of the blood that was trickling down his nose and the pain in his head, which was much less fierce now. 'That must be my soul leaving my body,' he thought. 'What will it be like *there*? Lord, receive my soul in peace. The only thing that's a bit strange,' he reflected, 'is to be dying and yet to be able to hear the footsteps of the soldiers and the sounds of the firing so clearly.'

'Bring a stretcher over here – hey! The company commander's been killed!' shouted a voice somewhere above his head. It was a voice he realized he knew – it belonged to a drummer named Ignatiev.

Someone took hold of him by the shoulders. He made an effort to open his eyes and saw above him the dark blue sky, the groupings of the stars, and two shells which appeared to be chasing one another far away up there; he saw Ignatiev, some soldiers carrying muskets and a stretcher; then he saw the earth bank of the trench, and suddenly decided he was not in the next world yet, at any rate.

He had received a slight head wound from a flying stone. His first reaction to this knowledge was one almost of regret: so thoroughly and peacefully had he made himself ready for his passage *there* that this return to reality with its shells, trenches, soldiers and blood seemed most unwelcome; his second reaction was one of unconscious joy at being alive, and his third was a sense of fear and a desire to get away from the bastion as soon as possible. The drummer bandaged up his commander's head with a handkerchief and, taking him by the arm, led him in the direction of the dressing station.

'Just a moment, where am I going, and for what purpose?' thought the lieutenant-captain when he had recovered his wits slightly. 'My duty's to remain with my company and not go on ahead, particularly since we'll soon be out of firing range anyway,' whispered a voice inside him. 'And if I stay at my post even though I'm wounded, I'll be certain to get a decoration.'

'Look here, old chap, this isn't necessary,' he said, pulling his arm free of the obliging drummer, who was really only concerned to get away from this spot as quickly as possible. 'I don't want to go to the dressing station, I'm going to remain here with the company.'

And he turned back.

'You really ought to have your wound properly bandaged up, your honour,' said the battle-shy Ignatiev. 'It's only now, in the heat of battle, that you think it's not worth bothering about. It'll only get worse if you don't have it seen to. And anyway, just look at the way things are warming up. Honest to God, your honour.'

Mikhailov paused for a moment in indecision, and would doubtless have followed Ignatiev's advice had he not suddenly recalled a scene he had witnessed at the dressing station a few days previously. An officer who had a tiny scratch on his hand had come to have it bandaged up, and the surgeons had viewed it with amusement. One of them – a man with large sidewhiskers[34] – had even gone so far as to tell the officer that no one could possibly die of such a slight graze, and that one could do more damage to oneself with a dinner fork.

'Perhaps they won't take my wound seriously either, and will make rude remarks about it,' thought the lieutenant–captain. His mind made up now, he ignored all the drummer's arguments and returned to his company.

'Where's that orderly officer, Praskukhin, who was walking with me?' he asked the ensign who had been in temporary command, when they met.

'I don't know, sir. Er, I think he was killed,' the ensign replied, reluctantly. He was, to tell the truth, rather annoyed that the lieutenant-captain had come back, thereby depriving him of the satisfaction of being able to say that he had been the only officer who had remained with the company.

'Well, was he killed or was he wounded? You ought to know, after all– the fellow was with our company. Anyway, why hasn't he been brought along with the rest of the men?'

'We couldn't very well have brought him along with us the way things have been warming up, sir.'

'Oh, how could you ever have done such a thing, Mikhal[35] Ivanovich?' said Mikhailov, angrily. 'How could you leave him lying there if he was alive? And even if he was dead, you ought still to have brought his body along. Well, on your own head be it. He's the general's orderly, you know, and he may still be alive.'

'How can he be alive? I tell you, I went right up to him and saw him with my own two eyes,' said the ensign. 'For heaven's sake, sir, we're being hard enough put to it to get our own men out of here. There he goes again, it's cannonballs this time, the swine,' he added, ducking. Mikhailov ducked too, but immediately clutched at his head, which hurt horribly from the sudden movement.

'No, we absolutely must go and get him: he may still be alive,' said Mikhailov. 'It's our *duty*, Mikhailo Ivanych!'

Mikhailo Ivanych made no reply.

Mikhailov thought: 'If he was a good officer, he'd have brought the man along at the time. As it is now, we're going to have to send some men out on their own, and how are we ever going to get them to go? With all this shelling going on they could easily be killed for nothing.'

'Men! Some of you will have to go back to fetch an officer who's been left lying wounded in the ditch over there,' he said, trying not to raise his voice or sound imperious, aware of how reluctant the soldiers would be to carry out his order. And indeed, since he had addressed the order to no one in particular, no one came forward to execute it.

'Sergeant! Come over here!' he shouted.

But the sergeant merely kept on marching along as though he had not heard.

'That's just it, he may be dead, and it *isn't worth* exposing the men to danger for no reason. I'm the one who's to blame, I should have taken care of it myself. I'll go there and see if he's alive or not. It's my *duty* to,' Mikhailov told himself.

'Mikhal Ivanych, take command of the company while I'm gone. I'll catch you up later,' he said. Then, tucking up his greatcoat with one hand and passing the other over his icon of St Metrophanes the Devout, in whom he had such an especial faith, trembling with fear and practically crawling on all fours, he scrambled off down the trench.

When he had ascertained that his comrade had in fact been killed, Mikhailov, still panting, ducking, and holding on with one hand the bandage that had slipped from his head, which was really beginning to hurt again now, dragged himself back. The battalion was already at the foot of the hill and more or less out of range of the enemy's fire when he finally managed to catch up with it once more. I say 'more or less' because every so often stray shells landed even here (that very same night a splinter from one of them had carried off a certain captain who had been spending the battle in one of the sailors' dugouts).

'I think I'd better go to the dressing station tomorrow after all and have myself registered,' thought the lieutenant-captain, as an apothecary assistant, who had just arrived, bandaged him up. 'It'll help me get a medal.'

—14—

Hundreds of fresh, bloody corpses – the bodies of men who two hours earlier had been filled with all manner of hopes and desires, from the lofty to the trivial – lay with stiffened limbs on the floor of the dew-covered, flowering valley which separated the bastion from the trench, and on the smooth flagstones of the Mortuary Chapel in Sebastopol; hundreds of men, with curses and prayers on their parched lips, tossed and groaned, some among the corpses in the flowering valley, others on stretchers, on camp beds, or on the bloody floorboards of the dressing station; yet, just as on earlier days, the summer lightning flashed above the Sapun-gora, the glimmering stars grew pale, the white mist drifted in off the dark, thundering sea, the vermilion dawn flared in the east, long purple cloudlets trailed across the light blue horizon, and again, as on earlier days, promising joy, love and happiness to the whole of the quickening world, the sun's mighty, resplendent orb arose from the waves.

—15—

On the following evening the military band again played on the Boulevard, and again the officers, cadets, privates and young women strolled festively near the pavilion and along the lower avenues of white, flowering, scented acacias.

Kalugin, Prince Galtsin and a colonel were walking arm-in-arm in the area of the pavilion, discussing the action of the previous night. The principal connecting thread of their conversation, as is always the case on such occasions, was not the battle itself, but the part each man had played in it and the degree of bravery he had shown. Their facial expressions and tone of voice were serious, almost melancholy, as though yesterday's losses had affected each one of them deeply and personally. The truth was, however, that since none of them had lost anyone to whom he was particularly close (is anyone particularly close in army life?), this air of melancholy had something of an official nature about it – it was an air they considered it their obligation to display. On the other hand, Kalugin and the colonel would have been perfectly prepared to endure battles of the kind they had just witnessed every day of their lives, as long as on each occasion they were to receive a golden sabre and a major-general's star – and this in spite of the fact that they were both men of excellent character. It always gives me pleasure to hear some conqueror, who has destroyed millions of people for the sake of his own personal ambition, described as a monster. But I would ask you to inquire what is really on the minds of ensign Petrushov, Second Lieutenant Antonov, and the rest of them: you will discover that each is a little Napoleon, a little monster ready to start a conflict and kill a hundred or so men simply in order to obtain another star or an increase of a third in his pay.

'No, I'm afraid you're wrong,' the colonel was saying. 'It started on the left flank. I was there, after all.'

'Well, that may be,' replied Kalugin. '*I spent more time over on the right flank myself; I went there twice, once to look for the general, and once just to see how things were going in the lodgments. That was where the real action was, I can tell you.*'

'I expect Kalugin knows what he's talking about,' said Prince Galtsin to the colonel. 'You know, V. was telling *me* about you today; he says you're a brave fellow.'

'But the losses, such terrible losses,' said the colonel, in his tone of official melancholy. '*Four hundred of my regiment were knocked out of action. It's a miracle I got out of there alive.*'

Just then the lilac-coated figure of Mikhailov, with his worn-down boots and bandaged head, came into view at the other end of the Boulevard, heading in the direction of these gentlemen. The sight of them completely took him aback: he recalled how the night before he had ducked while Kalugin had been talking to him, and it also occurred to him that they might think his wound was merely a pretence. Indeed, if these gentlemen had not been looking towards him, he would have run down to the lower level and gone home, and would not have ventured out again until he was able to take the bandage off.

'*Il fallait voir dans quel état je l'ai rencontré hier sous le feu,*' said Kalugin, with a smile, as they met. 'I say, what's this, are you wounded, captain?' he added, with another smile, which meant:

'Well, did you see me last night? In pretty good form, wasn't I?'

'Yes, slightly. I was hit by a stone,' Mikhailov replied, blushing, and with a look on his face that said: 'Yes, I saw you, and I have to admit you're a brave man and I'm a terrible, terrible coward.'

'*Est-ce que le pavillon est baissé déjà?*' enquired Prince Galtsin, who had resumed his customary haughty manner, surveying the lieutenant-captain's cap and addressing no one in particular.

'*Non pas encore*,' replied Mikhailov, anxious to show that he too could speak French.

'Is the truce really still on?' said Galtsin, considerately addressing him in Russian and thereby implying – or so it appeared to the lieutenant-captain, at any rate – that since it must be a dreadful effort for him to speak French, why didn't they simply . . . And at this the adjutants left his side.

Just as he had done the previous day, the lieutenant-captain felt extremely lonely, and when he had finished exchanging bows with various gentlemen – some of whom he did not want to talk to and others whom he could not summon up the courage to approach – he sat down near the Kazarsky[36] Monument and lit a cigarette.

Baron Pest had also come up to the Boulevard. He was telling a long story about how he had been present when the truce was signed, and had spoken with the French officers, one of whom had apparently said to him: '*S'il n'avait pas fait clair encore pendant une demi-heure, les embuscades auraient été reprises*', and how he had replied: '*Monsieur! Je ne dis pas non, pour ne pas vous donner un démenti*', and what a good rejoinder that had been, and so forth.

While it was true that he had been present at the signing of the truce, he had not managed to say anything particularly clever, though he had wanted terribly to exchange a few words with the Frenchmen (it is, after all, not every day that one has the chance to talk to Frenchmen). Cadet volunteer Baron Pest had spent a long time walking up and down the lines, asking any Frenchman who happened to be standing nearby: '*De quel régiment êtes-vous?*' They had told him, and that had been the end of the conversation. When, however, he had begun to stray too far across the lines, a

French sentry, unaware that this soldier knew French, had started swearing at him in no uncertain terms, saying: '*Il vint regarder nos travaux, ce sacré c—*' As a consequence of which, finding nothing of further interest in the truce, Baron Pest had set off back to his quarters. It had only been later, on his way to the Boulevard, that he had thought up the French ripostes with which he was now entertaining everyone.

Captain Zobov was also there on the Boulevard, talking to everyone in a loud voice; there, too, was Captain Obzhogov, who was looking his usual dishevelled self; there were the artillery captain who curried favour with no man, the moonstruck cadet, and all the others of the day before, all of them driven by the same unaltering stimuli of falsehood, vanity, and sheer plain silliness. Only Praskukhin and Neferdov were missing – along with one or two others whom hardly anyone here ever gave a thought to or remembered now, even though their corpses had not been washed, laid out and buried yet, and whose fathers, mothers, wives and children, if they had any, would also forget about them within a month or two, had they not already done so.

'I nearly didn't recognize him, the old blighter,' said a soldier who was clearing away dead bodies, lifting by the shoulders a corpse with a stove-in chest, an enormous, bloated head, a black, glistening face and eyes with rolled-up pupils. 'Put your arms round his back, Morozka, or else he'll fall apart. Cor, what a godawful stink!'

'Cor, what a godawful stink!' That was all that remained of this man in the land of the living.

—16—

White flags have been raised both on the Russian bastion and along the trench on the French fortifications, and in between them, lying spread in little groups across the flowering valley, still dressed in their uniforms, some grey, others blue, but all without their boots, are mutilated corpses which are being gathered together by work parties and piled on to carts. A terrible cloying stench of dead bodies fills the air. Crowds of men have come straying out of Sebastopol and the French encampment in order to view this spectacle, rushing to join one another with an avid and benevolent curiosity.

Listen to what these men are saying to one another.

Here, in a circle of Russians and Frenchmen who have gathered around him, a young officer whose French, although poor, is none the less sufficient for him to be comprehensible, is examining a French guardsman's pouch.

'*Et ceci pourquoi ce oiseau ici?*' the officer asks.

'*Parce-que c'est une giberne d'un régiment de la garde, monsieur, qui porte l'aigle impérial.*'

'*Est vous de la garde?*'

'*Pardon, monsieur, du sixième de ligne.*'

'*Et ceci où acheté?*' asks the officer, pointing to the yellow wooden cigarette-holder in which the Frenchman is smoking a Russian cigarette.

'*À Balaclave, monsieur! C'est tout simple – en bois de palme.*'

'*Joli!*' says the officer, who in this conversation is directed less by his own volition than by the words and phrases at his command.

'*Si vous voulez bien garder cela comme souvenir de cette rencontre, vous m'obligerez.*' And the courteous Frenchman, taking out the cigarette, offers him the holder with a little bow. The officer gives the Frenchman his own holder in exchange, and all those present, both French and Russian, look very pleased, and smile.

Here an infantryman, smartly turned out in a pink shirt, his greatcoat draped over his shoulders, is standing in the company of some other soldiers who have their hands behind their backs and whose faces are cheerful and inquisitive. The smartly dressed man goes up to one of the French soldiers and asks him for a light for his pipe. The Frenchman sucks at his own pipe, gives its red-hot contents a poke, and then pours some of them into the Russian's pipe.

'Tobacco *bong*,' says the soldier in the pink shirt, and his audience smiles.

'*Oui, bon tabac, tabac turc*,' says the Frenchman. '*Et chez vous tabac russe? bon?*'

'Rooss bong,' says the soldier in the pink shirt, at which point his audience falls about with laughter. 'Frongsay no bong, bongzhoor mongsewer,' says the soldier in the pink shirt, thereby firing off his entire French vocabulary in one go, digging the Frenchman in the ribs, and laughing. The French soldiers are also laughing.

'*Ils ne sont pas jolis ces bêtes de russes*,' says a Zouave who is standing among the crowd of Frenchmen.

'*De quoi de ce qu'ils rient donc?*' asks another dark-featured man in an Italian accent, moving over towards the Russians.

'Caftan bong,' says the smartly dressed soldier, as he examines the embroidered skirts of the Zouave's oriental costume, and again they all laugh.

'*Ne sortez pas de la ligne, à vos places, sacré nom . . .*' A French corporal shouts, and with evident unwillingness the soldiers disperse.

And here, surrounded by a ring of French officers, is one of our young Russian cavalry officers fairly showering his listeners with French barber's slang. They are talking about a certain '*comte Sazonoff, que j'ai beaucoup connu, monsieur*', whom a French officer with one epaulette has just mentioned. '*C'est un de ces vrais comtes russes, comme nous les aimons*,' he says.

'*Il y a un Sazonoff que j'ai connu*,' says the cavalry officer. '*Mais il n'est pas un comte, à moins que je sache, un petit brun de votre âge à peu près.*'

'*C'est ça, monsieur, c'est lui. Oh, que je voudrais le voir, ce cher comte. Si vous le voyez, je vous prie bien de lui faire mes compliments. Capitaine Latour*,' says the Frenchman, bowing.

'*N'est-ce pas terrible la triste besogne, que nous faisons? Ça chauffait cette nuit, n'est-ce pas?*' says the cavalry officer, anxious to keep the conversation going, pointing in the direction of the corpses.

'*Oh, monsieur, c'est affreux! Mais quels gaillards vos soldats, quels gaillards! C'est un plaisir que de se battre contre des gaillards comme eux.*'

'*Il faut avouer que les vôtres ne se mouchent pas du pied non plus*,' says the cavalry officer, bowing, and thinking he was being extraordinarily kind. But enough of this.[37]

Let us look instead at this ten-year-old boy; at the very beginning of the truce he had come out from behind the ramparts wearing an old cap that had probably once belonged to his father, shoes with no socks, and a pair of nankeen breeches held up by a single suspender. He had spent a while walking up and down the hollow, gazing with dull curiosity at the French soldiers and the corpses that lay on the ground, and then started to pick some of the wild blue flowers with which this valley of death was carpeted. Returning homeward with a large bouquet, and holding his nose because of the smell which the wind was driving in his direction, he stopped beside one of the groups of bodies that had been gathered together, staring for a long time at the one nearest to him, a terrible, headless thing. After a little he had moved nearer and touched one of the corpse's rigid, outstretched arms with his foot. The arm gave a slight jump. He placed his foot on it again, harder this time. The arm sprang upright and then fell back into place again. The boy suddenly screamed, hid his face in his flowers and ran off to the fortress as fast as he could.

Yes, white flags have been raised on the bastion and all along the trench, the flowering valley is filled with stinking corpses, the resplendent sun is descending towards the dark blue sea, and the sea's blue swell is gleaming in the sun's golden rays. Thousands of men are crowding together, studying one another, speaking to one another, smiling at one another. It might be supposed that when these men – Christians, recognizing the same great law of love – see what they have done, they will instantly fall to their knees in order to repent before Him who, when He gave them life, placed in the soul of each, together with the fear of death, a love of the good and the beautiful, and that they will embrace one another with tears of joy and happiness, like brothers. Not a bit of it! The scraps of white cloth will be put away – and once again the engines of death and suffering will start their whistling; once again the blood of the innocent will flow and the air will be filled with their groans and cursing.

Now I have said all that I wished to say on this occasion. I am, however, beset by a painful thought. Perhaps I ought not to have said it. Perhaps what I have said belongs to the category of those harmful truths each of us carries around in his subconscious, truths we must not utter aloud lest they cause active damage, like the lees of wine which must not be shaken up if the wine is not to be spoiled.

Where in this narrative is there any illustration of evil that is to be avoided? Where is there any illustration of good that is to be emulated? Who is the villain of the piece, and who its hero? All the characters are equally blameless and equally wicked.

Neither Kalugin with his gentleman's bravado (*bravoure de gentilhomme*) and personal vanity – the motive force of all his actions – not Praskukhin who, in spite of the fact that he falls in battle for 'Church, Tsar and Fatherland' is really nothing more than a shallow, harmless individual, nor Mikhailov with his cowardice and blinkered view of life, nor Pest – a child with no steadfast convictions or principles – are capable of being either the villains or the heroes of my story.

No, the hero of my story, whom I love with all my heart and soul, whom I have attempted to portray in all his beauty and who has always been, is now and will always be supremely magnificent, is truth.

26 June 1855

SEBASTOPOL IN AUGUST 1855

—1—

Slowly trundling, at the end of August, through the thick, hot dust of the main road that leads along a series of gorges to Sebastopol, in the stretch between Duvankóy* and Bakhchisaray, was an officer's waggon (that peculiar form of transport, encountered nowhere else, and representing a cross between a Jew's *britzka*, a Russian cart and a wicker basket).

In the front of the waggon, dressed in a nankeen frock-coat and a cap that had once belonged to an officer but was now worn completely limp, an orderly squatted on his heels, tugging at the reins; in the rear, an infantry officer in a summer greatcoat sat on a heap cf packs and bundles which were covered by a horsecloth. The officer, in so far as it was possible to judge from his sedentary position, was not particularly tall, this showing less in his shoulders than in his chest and back. These had a wide, compact appearance; his neck and occiput were very well developed and resilient, and he entirely lacked the inflexion of the trunk that is called a 'waist'. Neither, however, did he have a paunch, and indeed elsewhere in his physique he was rather on the thin side, especially around his face, which bore an unhealthy, yellowish tan. It was a face that would have been handsome had it not been for a certain puffiness and the presence of large, soft wrinkles (not of the kind associated with age) which enlarged his features and

* The last posthouse before Sebastopol. (Tolstoy's note.)

made them flow into one another, giving the whole a coarse, unfresh appearance. His eyes were small and hazel-coloured, extremely lively, even insolent; he had a moustache which was very thick but small in size and somewhat chewed at the ends. His chin, and more particularly his cheekbones, were covered by an extremely dense, black and stubbly growth of beard, some two days old. On the tenth of May this officer had received a wound from a shell-splinter which had struck his head, on which he still wore a bandage. For the past week, however, he had been feeling completely recovered, and was now on his way from hospital in Simferopol back to his regiment, which was stationed somewhere over yonder, where the sounds of firing were coming from – but whether it was at Sebastopol itself, or over on the North Side, or at Inkerman, he had not so far been able to ascertain from anyone. The sounds of the firing could already be heard quite clearly, particularly on the odd occasion when there were no mountains in the way, and the wind was blowing in the right direction; they were quite frequent, and seemed near at hand. At one moment an explosion would seem to give the air a jolt, making one tremble involuntarily; at the next, a rapid series of fainter sounds, like the noise of a drum being beaten, would follow, punctuated now and then by a startling boom; at other times this would all merge into a sort of rolling crackle, similar to the peals of thunder one hears when a storm is at its height and the rain has just started. Everyone was saying – and it was indeed plain enough to hear – that there was a terrible bombardment under way. The officer hurried his orderly on, evidently anxious to rejoin his regiment as soon as possible. Coming towards them was a long train of Russian muzhiks' carts which had brought provisions to Sebastopol, and were now leaving it again filled with sick and wounded soldiers in grey greatcoats, sailors in black overcoats, Greek volunteers wearing red fez caps, and bearded militiamen. The waggon was forced to stop, and the officer, blinking and frowning because of the dust which had risen up in a thick, motionless cloud above the road, getting into his eyes and sticking to his sweaty face, surveyed with sour dispassion the faces of the sick and wounded who were being trundled past.

'Look, sir, that weakling of a soldier there's from our company,' said the orderly, turning to his master and pointing to the cart filled with wounded which had just drawn level with them.

Seated sideways in the front of the cart was a grey-bearded Russian peasant in a wool felt hat; as he rode along he was binding the leather ends of a knout, holding the knout-handle against him by the pressure of his elbow. Behind him, jolting this way and that with the movement of the cart, sat five or six soldiers in various postures. One of them, his arm held in a sling made of rope, his greatcoat draped across his shoulders over a shirt that was thoroughly dirty, sat looking cheerful, if somewhat thin and pale, in the middle of the cart; at the sight of the officer he made as though to remove his cap, but then, probably remembering that he was wounded, pretended that he had been merely about to scratch his head. Beside him, in the bottom of the cart, lay another man. The only parts of him that were visible were the two wasted hands with which he held on to the sides of the cart, and his raised knees, which flopped from side to side like wisps of bast. A third soldier, with a swollen face and bandaged head, on top of which a private's cap was firmly stuck, was sitting on one of the sides of the cart with his legs hanging down over the wheel, and seemed to have nodded off with his elbows propped on his knees. It was to this man that the itinerant officer addressed himself.

'Dolzhnikov!' he shouted.

'Er, present, sir,' replied the soldier, opening his eyes and taking his cap off. He spoke in a thick, jerky bass voice that sounded like twenty soldiers chorusing in unison.

'When were you wounded, old fellow?'

The soldier's swollen, pewter-coloured eyes came to life: he had evidently recognized his military superior.

'Your health, your honour!' he exclaimed, in the same jerky bass voice.

'Where is the regiment stationed at present?'

'It was in Sebastopol, sir; they were going to transfer it on Wednesday.'

'Where to?'

'They didn't say . . . Probably the North Side, sir! You know, today, sir,' he added in an expansive tone, putting his cap back on again, 'he's started blazing away all over the shop; nearly all shells, it is, he's even landing them in the bay; he's killed that many men, it's bloody disgusting . . .'

It was not possible to hear any more of what this soldier was saying; but from the expression on his face and from his posture, that of one who was suffering with a certain rancour of spirit, it could be guessed that nothing he said would bring anyone much comfort.

The itinerant officer, a certain Lieutenant Kozeltsov, was, for an army man, something rather out of the ordinary. He was not one of those people who live and act in a predetermined way, and who refrain from taking certain actions because they do not conform with the way others live their lives: he did everything he had a mind to do, and others tended to follow his example, convinced they were doing the right thing. His temperament was a many-sided one: he was a good singer, could play the guitar, spoke with great ease and had a talent for writing, particularly the writing of official documents, at which in his capacity of regimental adjutant he had developed into something of a dab hand. Most remarkable of all, however, was his quality of personal energy which, though it rested largely on these secondary endowments, was in itself a forceful and striking characteristic. His pride was of the kind most frequently encountered among exclusively male, especially military, circles; so thoroughly was it identified with life itself that he could see before him no other choice than either to excel or to expire. It could even be said that his pride acted as his most important personal incentive: he liked, merely for the sake of it, to excel among the people with whom he compared himself.

'Come along now, am I going to sit here listening to Moscow* wandering on all day?' muttered the lieutenant to himself, feeling his spirits sink slightly under the burden of apathy that was weighing them down, an effect produced partly by the confusion of vague thoughts left in him by the sight of the train of wounded, and partly by the soldier's words, to which the sounds of the bombardment were lending an increased force and urgency. 'That

* In many army regiments the officers refer to the common soldiers, half contemptuously and half affectionately, as 'Moscow' or 'the oath'. (Tolstoy's note.)

absurd Moscow . . . Let's be off, Nikolayev . . . What's the matter, have you fallen asleep?' he said, somewhat peevishly, to his orderly, as he adjusted the skirts of his greatcoat.

The reins gave a jerk, Nikolayev clicked his tongue, and the waggon moved off at a swift pace.

'We'll pull up for a moment to give the horses some fodder, and then it's straight on; we're not going to wait until tomorrow,' said the officer.

—2—

As he was driving into Duvankóy along a street of Tartar stone houses which had been practically reduced to rubble, Lieutenant Kozeltsov was once again held up by a military transport, this time one of shells and cannonballs which were being ferried to Sebastopol. The carts took up the whole width of the road, and Kozeltsov's waggon was forced to stop.

In the dust at the side of the road two infantrymen were sitting on the stones of a ruined wall, eating bread and watermelon.

'Travelling far, countrymen?' said one of them, as he munched his bread. He was addressing a soldier who was carrying a small bag on his shoulder and who had stopped a short distance from them.

'We've been up in the province, and now we're on our way back to rejoin our company,' the soldier replied, trying to ignore the watermelon and repositioning the bag on his back. 'We'd been out gathering hay for our company these past three weeks, nearly, when they suddenly ordered us all back to our posts, just like that; only trouble is, we don't know where the regiment is right now. The word is that it moved to the Korabelnaya last week. Have you heard anything about that, gents?'

'It's in the town, mate, in the town,' said the man who had spoken first, an old convoy soldier, digging greedily into the unripe, whitish flesh of the watermelon with his camp knife. 'We only got out of there this afternoon. It's bloody terrible in there, mate, you'd do better to stick around here and lie low in the hay for a couple of days – far better, if you ask me.'

'How do you mean, gents?'

'Are you telling me you can't hear it? He's blazing the place to kingdom come today, there's not a blade of grass left standing. As for our boys, nobody knows how many of them he's picked off.'

And so saying, the speaker made a gesture with his arm and readjusted his cap.

The itinerant soldier shook his head thoughtfully, tut-tutted for a bit, and then took his pipe out from under his boot-flap; instead of filling it with fresh tobacco, however, he merely poked the half-burned strands it already contained, lit a spill on the pipe of his colleague, started to puff away and raised his cap.

'Nobody but God, gentlemen! Begging your pardon,' he said, and hoisting his bag into position once more, he set off down the road.

'Eh, you'd do better to wait,' said the man with the watermelon, in a tone of expansive cajolery.

'All the same,' muttered the itinerant to himself as he threaded his way among the wheels of the carts that crowded the road, 'I can see I might as well buy myself a watermelon for supper, too, the way folk are talking.'

—3—

The posthouse was full of people when Kozeltsov drew up outside it in his waggon. The first person he met, while he was still outside on the porch, was a thin man of extreme youth. This was the postmaster, and he was exchanging angry words with two officers who were following behind him.

'. . . and it won't be three days you'll have to wait, it'll be more like ten! My dear man, there are even *generals* waiting,' the postmaster was saying, in an effort to be wounding. 'And I'm certainly not going to harness myself up for you.'

'If there aren't any horses, then how did that footman with all the baggage get hold of one?' shouted the senior of the two officers, who was nursing a glass of tea in his hands. While avoiding the use of the personal pronoun, he made it clear that he might easily begin addressing the postmaster by the insultingly familiar 'thou'.

'T-try to see it from our point of view,' said the younger officer, stammering. 'It's – it's not as though we were on a pleasure trip. I mean, the fact that we've been sent for means that they need us. You know, I really think I'm going to let General Kramper know about this. It – it – what it boils down to is that you haven't any respect for the rank of officer!'

'Why do you always go and put your foot in it?' said the older officer, breaking him off in vexation. 'You do nothing but get in my way. One has to know how to talk to these people. He really has lost all respect for us now. Horses, this instant, I say!'

'Nothing would give me greater pleasure, sir, but where am I going to get them?'

The postmaster was silent for a moment. Then he suddenly flushed, and, embellishing his remarks with agitated gestures, said: 'Look, sir, I hear what you're saying and I understand it all very well – but what do you expect me to do? Just give me . . .' (at this the officers' faces lit up with hope) '. . . give me to the end of the month here without being killed, and you won't find me around any more. I'd sooner go to the Malakhov than stick around here. My God! They can damn well look after themselves if this is the way they're going to run things: there's not a decent cart left in the whole stage-post, and the horses haven't had a wisp of hay for three days now.'

And with this the postmaster slipped through the gate and disappeared off somewhere.

Kozeltsov followed the officers into the waiting-room.

'Oh well,' said the older officer to the younger in a tone of complete calm, even though only a moment before he had appeared to be in a white rage. 'We've been on the road for three months now, so I suppose it won't hurt us to wait for a bit longer. We'll get there soon enough, don't you worry!'

The smoky, dirty room was so full of officers and their trunks that Kozeltsov only barely managed to find himself a seat in the window. As he studied the men's faces and listened to their conversation, he began to roll himself a cigarette. The main group of officers was seated to the right of the door around a sagging, greasy table on which stood two samovars, the brass of which was green in places, and lump sugar in various types of paper wrapping. A young, clean-shaven officer in a short, quilted caftan, which had probably been fashioned from a woman's dressing-gown, was filling the teapot with hot water. There were four of these younger officers in different parts of the room: one of them, his head resting on a fur coat, was asleep on a sofa; another, standing at the table, was carving roast mutton for a one-armed officer who was sitting down. Two others, one in an adjutant's greatcoat and the other in an infantryman's summer coat with a cartridge-pouch slung across his shoulder, were sitting by the stove ledge; merely from the manner in which they looked at the rest of the men, and from the way in which the one with the cartridge-pouch was smoking his cigar, it was possible to tell that they were not front-line officers, and that this circumstance gave them satisfaction. Not that their bearing was in any way arrogant or contemptuous; rather, it exuded a certain complacent tranquillity, one that was founded partly on money and partly on their frequent association with generals – a consciousness of their own superiority so strong that it led them to try to conceal it. Also present were a young surgeon with thick lips, and an artillery officer who looked like a German: they were practically sitting on the legs of the young officer who was sleeping on the sofa, and were counting their money. There were, in addition, four or five orderlies – some of them taking a nap and others pottering about among the trunks and bundles over by the door. Among all these faces Kozeltsov could not find one that he knew; even so, he began to listen to the men's conversation with curiosity. The young officers who, as he at once decided just by looking at them, had only recently left cadet corps,[38] made a favourable impression on him; principally, they reminded him of the fact that his brother, who had also just left cadet corps, was due to arrive at one of the Sebastopol batteries in a few days' time. On the other hand, everything about the officer with the cartridge-pouch, whose face he thought he recognized from somewhere else, struck him as insolent and repugnant. He even left his seat for one on the stove ledge, with the thought: 'If he says anything, I'll soon cut him down to size.' As a true front-line officer and good military man he had an active loathing for staff officers, as one glance at these men was sufficient to tell him they were.

—4—

'It really is jolly annoying,' one of the young officers was saying. 'Here we are, a stone's throw away, yet we can't get through. There may easily be some action tonight, and we won't be there.'

His squeaky tone of voice and the sudden blotches of red that appeared on his young face as he spoke revealed the attractive youthful timidity of one who is constantly afraid that the words are not going to come out right.

The one-armed officer surveyed him with a smile.

'You'll get there soon enough, believe you me,' he said.

The young officer looked deferentially at the haggard face of the one-armed man, which was beaming in an unexpected smile, said nothing, and returned his attention to making the tea. And indeed, in the face of the one-armed officer, in his posture, and particularly in the empty sleeve of his greatcoat, one could read much of this man's calm equanimity, which could be summed up as an attitude that seemed to say: 'This is all very well, but I know it all already, and I'm capable of doing whatever I please.'

'Well, what are we going to do, then?' the young officer asked his companion in the quilted caftan. 'Are we going to stay the night here or try to get through with the horse we've got?'

His companion rejected this last idea.

'Can you imagine, captain,' continued the officer, who had now finished pouring out the tea, turning to the one-armed man and picking up the knife the latter had dropped, 'we were told that horses were horribly expensive in Sebastopol, so we went halves on one in Simferopol.'

'I bet they charged you a pretty sum there, too.'

'I honestly don't know, captain: with the waggon thrown in it came to ninety roubles. Is that expensive?' he asked, addressing all the men including Kozeltsov, who was watching him.

'That's not too bad, if it's a young horse,' said Kozeltsov.

'Is that so? We were told it was rather expensive . . . It's a bit lame, but they told us it would get over it. It's really quite a sturdy animal.'

'Which corps have you come from?' asked Kozeltsov, who was anxious to have some news of his brother.

'Oh, we've come straight from the Nobiliary Regiment. There are six of us here: we're all going to Sebastopol as volunteers,' replied the officer, who obviously enjoyed talking. 'The only thing is, we don't know where the batteries we've been assigned to are stationed. Some people have told us they're in Sebastopol, but others say it's Odessa.'

'But couldn't you have found out in Simferopol?' Kozeltsov asked.

'Nobody seemed to know . . .[39] Can you imagine, sir, one of us went into a local government office to ask, and they were incredibly rude to him . . . just think how we felt! I've some cigarettes already made up, would you like one?' he asked the one-armed officer, who at this moment was reaching around for his cigarette case, in a positive ecstasy of obsequiousness.

'So you've come from Sebastopol, have you, sir?' he went on. 'Goodness, how extraordinary this is! You've no idea how we've all been thinking about you in St Petersburg – and about all you heroes!' he said, turning to Kozeltsov with deferential good will.

'So what do you suppose, will you have to go back again?' the lieutenant asked.

'That's what we're afraid of. Can you imagine, I mean, we've bought a horse, and all these other things you can't do without – a spirit coffee-maker and various bits and pieces besides – and now we're practically broke,' he said in a quiet voice, exchanging glances with his companion. 'So if we do have to go back, we don't know what's going to become of us.'

'But surely you must have been given your travel expenses?' said Kozeltsov.

'No, sir,' the young officer replied in a whisper. 'All they said was that we'd be paid them here.'

'And do you have a certificate?'

'I know it's supposed to be essential to have a certificate; but when I went to see a senator in Moscow about it (he's my uncle, actually), he said they'd give me the money on demand, and he didn't need to write me out a certificate. Do you suppose they will?'

'Oh, I'm sure they will.'

'Yes, I expect so too,' said the young officer, in a tone that suggested he had asked the same question at some thirty other posthouses along the way and had received a different reply at each one of them, so that now he no longer really believed what anyone said.

—5—

'They damn well ought to,' came the sudden voice of the officer who had had the angry exchange with the postmaster on the porch, and who had come over to join in the conversation. He addressed his remarks in part to the staff officers sitting nearby, evidently considering them a worthy audience. 'I'm in the same boat as these gentlemen: I volunteered for active service, even offered to go to Sebastopol and leave behind a perfectly good position, but apart from 136 roubles' travelling expenses for my journey from St Petersburg I haven't had a kopeck paid to me. I'm already out of pocket to the tune of 150 roubles. To think of it! I've only covered a distance of 800 versts, yet I've been on the road for nearly three months now, two of them in the company of these fellows. It's just as well I brought some money of my own with me. What would I have done without it?'

'Has the journey really taken you three months?' someone asked.

'How else could I have done it?' the officer went on. 'After all, I wouldn't have given up a comfortable position like that if I hadn't actually wanted to go, would I? I didn't start living like a gipsy because I was frightened . . . It was just that there was no other way. For example, I had to put up in Perekop for two whole weeks. The postmaster there didn't want to have anything to do with me. You just want to go when it pleases you, he said, but look at all these post-haste orders I've got, and those are just for starters. Oh, I suppose it was fate, really . . . I mean, I kept wanting to get on with the journey, but fate had other ideas. It had absolutely nothing to do with there being a bombardment on at present, it just didn't seem to make any difference whether I was in a hurry or not, that's all; I really wanted to get on . . .'

At such pains was this officer to account for his slow arrival, and so great appeared to be his desire to justify himself, that it was hard not to suppose that he had, after all, been influenced by fear. This became even more noticeable when he eventually started to ask where his regiment was stationed, and whether this was a dangerous spot. When the one-armed officer, who belonged to the same regiment, told him that during these past two days they had had seventeen losses in the officer category alone, he went very pale and his voice started to break.

And such indeed was the case: at that particular moment this officer was an abject coward, though six months previously he had been very far from one. He had experienced the upheaval common to many men, both before and after him. He had lived in one of those Russian provinces in which there are cadet corps. Although he had occupied a good, quiet position in civilian life, the experience of reading, both in newspaper accounts and in letters he had received from friends, about the deeds of the heroes of Sebastopol – his former colleagues and companions – suddenly inflamed him with ambition and, even more, with patriotism.

To this emotion he had sacrificed much: his comfortable position, his flat with its upholstered furniture, acquired through ten years of effort, his friends and acquaintances, and his hopes of marrying a rich lady. All this he had thrown to the winds, and as early as February had volunteered for active service, dreaming of the laurels of immortal glory and a general's stripes. Two months after making his application he received an official letter asking whether he would require financial assistance from the government. He had replied in the negative and patiently continued to wait for a posting, even though his patriotic ardour had had time to cool significantly during those two months. At the end of another two months he received another letter enquiring whether he belonged to a Masonic lodge, and containing various other questions of a routine nature, all of which he had answered in the negative. Finally, more than four months after his initial application, his posting had come through. During this latter period he had become convinced, both by his friends and under the influence of that retrospective wisdom which in every change of circumstances is expressed in a sense of discontent with one's new situation, that in volunteering for active service in the army he had committed a most foolish error. When at length he had found himself – alone, with heartburn, his face caked with dust – at the fifth posthouse, where he had encountered a despatch rider from Sebastopol who filled him in on the horrors of war, and had had to wait twelve hours to obtain a change of horses, he had utterly repented of his thoughtless decision, contemplated what lay in store for him with ill-defined horror and completed the remainder of his journey in a kind of trance, like a lamb going to the slaughter. In the course of his three months' long wandering from posthouse to posthouse, at virtually each one of which he had found himself obliged to wait and where he had met officers on their way back from Sebastopol with horrifying tales to tell, this feeling of horror had gradually intensified, until the poor officer had been transformed from the hero ready for the most desperate deeds of valour he had imagined himself to be in P— to the wretched coward he revealed himself as in Duvankóy. When, a month earlier, he had joined forces with a company of young officers fresh from cadet corps he had tried to spin the journey out for as long as possible, regarding these as the last days of his life. At each posthouse he had assembled his camp bed, sorted out the contents of his portable larder, organized a game of preference among the officers, treated the complaints book as a form of pastime, and been genuinely pleased when his order for horses was turned down.

Had he gone straight from P— to the bastions, he really would have been a hero; now, however, he was going to have to endure much mental anguish if he was to become the man, patient and calm in toil and danger, who constitutes our generally accepted image of the Russian officer. And it was going to be no easy task to rekindle his enthusiasm.

—6—

'Who was it asked for bortsch?' sang the postmaster's wife, a fat, rather grubby woman of about forty, as she came into the postroom with a tureen of cabbage soup.

The conversation immediately died away, and everyone in the room transferred his gaze to this bearer of sustenance. The volunteer from P— even winked at the young officer when she appeared.

'I know, it was Kozeltsov,' said the young officer. 'We'll have to wake him up. Come on, wakey wakey, it's dinner-time,' he said, approaching the sleeper on the sofa and nudging his shoulder.

A young lad of about seventeen with lively black eyes and a pink flush on both cheeks sprang up energetically from the sofa and came to a halt in the middle of the room, rubbing his eyes.

'Oh, I say, I am sorry,' he said in a silvery, resonant voice to the surgeon against whom he had knocked in rising.

Lieutenant Kozeltsov at once recognized his brother, and went up to him.

'Don't you know who I am?' he said, smiling.

'Aha-a-a!' cried his younger brother. 'Well I never!' And he ran to kiss him.

They kissed three times, but at the third kiss hesitated, as though each had had the same thought: why three?

'Well, am I glad to see you,' said the older man, looking at his brother. 'Let's go out on the porch and talk for a while.'

'Yes, let's, let's! I don't want any bortsch. You can have it if you like, Federson,' he said to his companion.

'But I thought you said you were hungry?'

'I'm not any more.'

Once they were out on the porch, the younger brother kept asking the older one to tell him how things were going with him, and kept repeating how glad he was to see him, without, however, managing to say anything about himself.

After five minutes or so, when their conversation was already beginning to flag slightly, the older brother asked the younger why he had not joined the guards, as *all our people at home* had expected him to.

'Oh, that!' the younger brother replied, blushing at the mere recollection. 'That really was too killingly bad, and I certainly never thought it would turn out that way. Can you imagine, just before the finals three of us went off to have a smoke – you know, in that little room behind the porter's lodge, I should think it was the same in your day – well, what do you suppose? Even though we'd all tipped him on various occasions, that rascal of a porter saw us and ran off to tell the duty officer, who soon came snooping around. As soon as he appeared, the others threw their cigarettes away and made their escape through the side door, you know the one I mean – but I was too slow. He started to get objectionable, and of course I gave him what for. He reported me to the inspector, and that was that. That was why I got such low marks for behaviour, even though all my other marks were excellent, apart from the twelve I got in mechanics – but no, that was that. I had to enlist for active service in the regular army. They said I'd get a transfer to the guards later on, but by that time I'd stopped caring and told them I wanted to go and fight in the war.'

'You don't say!'

'Actually, you know, joking apart, everything suddenly seemed so bloody awful that I simply wanted to get to Sebastopol as quickly as I could. Anyway, if things work out right I may do better for myself here than I'd have done in the guards: with them you have to wait ten years before you can be a colonel, whereas out here Totleben[40] became a general in two. Well, perhaps I shall be killed – but what can you do about that?'

'You are a proper character,' said his brother, smiling.

'But really, you know,' the younger one went on, smiling and blushing, as if he were preparing to confess something particularly shameful, 'all that's just so much nonsense; the real reason I asked to fight in the war was that I somehow felt guilty about continuing to live in St Petersburg while out here men were dying for their country. And then, too, I wanted to be where you were,' he added, even more bashfully.

'You really are a funny chap,' said the older brother, taking out his cigarette case and avoiding the other's eyes. 'It's a pity we won't be together.'

…ell me truthfully, is it really as terrible as they say on …ons?' the younger brother asked, suddenly.

…bad at first, but one gets used to it. You'll see for yourself.'

…here's something else you can tell me, too: what do you think, are they going to take Sebastopol? I don't believe they will, ever.'

'God knows.'

'The only thing that really bothers me is this damn stroke of bad luck I've had. Can you imagine, on our way here a whole bundle of our stuff was stolen, including my shako, and now I'm in the most dreadful fix; I simply don't know how I'm going to present myself. You know, we have these new shakos now, and in fact there are a whole lot of other changes, too, all of them for the better. I can tell you all about them . . . When I was in Moscow I got about all over the place.'

The younger Kozeltsov – his Christian name was Vladimir – was very like his brother Mikhail, but in the way an opening rosebud resembles a faded briar. His hair was of the same light brown colour, but it was thick, and sprouted in curls about his temples. It stuck up on the soft, white skin at the back of his neck in a little quiff – a sign of good luck, as nurses like to say. The similarly soft, white skin of his face was not so much permeated as sporadically ignited by a healthy, full-blooded glow, which betrayed every shift of his moods and feelings. He had his brother's eyes, but in him they were rounder and brighter, an effect that was heightened by their frequently being covered in a gentle, moist brilliance. A light brown fuzz stood forth on his cheeks and above his red lips, which often spread in a shy smile that showed his white, gleaming teeth. Slender, broad-shouldered, in an unfastened greatcoat that revealed a glimpse of a red shirt with a high collar, cigarette in hand, leaning against the porch railing, his face and gestures displaying his simple-hearted joy at seeing his brother again – such a pleasant, good-looking boy was he that one could scarcely take one's eyes off him. He was delighted to be rejoined with his brother and eyed him with pride and veneration, imagining him to be a hero. In some respects, however – with regard to worldly education, for example, something which, if truth be told, he did not himself possess, or the ability to speak French, to conduct oneself correctly in the presence of important persons, or to dance well – he was rather ashamed of him, looked down on him and even hoped, if possible, to give him some instruction. His head was still full of St Petersburg, and in particular the house of a certain lady who was fond of pretty boys and who on festive occasions had invited him to visit her home, that of a Moscow senator, where he had once danced at a grand ball.

—7—

When they had talked all they wanted to, and had finally begun to feel the way close relatives often do – namely, that although each is very fond of the other, they neither of them have terribly much in common – the brothers fell silent for quite a long time.

'Right, then. Get your kit together and we'll set off at once,' said the older brother at last.

The younger brother suddenly blushed and hesitated.

'Are we going straight to Sebastopol?' he asked, after a moment's pause.

'Why not? After all, you haven't much kit with you; I think we'll manage to get it all in.'

'All right, let's go now,' said the younger brother with a sigh, and he started to make for the waiting-room.

Before he opened the door, however, he stopped in the passageway, inclining his head sadly, and began to reflect: 'Straight to Sebastopol, that hell on earth – how dreadful! But it can't be helped, it had to come sooner or later. At least now I'm with my brother . . .'

The fact was that only now, confronted with the thought that once he got into the waggon he would not get out of it again until they reached Sebastopol, and that no lucky chance was going to delay their arrival there – only now did he have a clear presentiment of the danger he himself had sought, and for a moment he lost his nerve at the thought of its proximity. Somehow managing to calm himself, he went into the waiting-room; but when a quarter of an hour had elapsed, and he still had not re-emerged, the older brother opened the door in order to tell him to hurry up. With the air of a guilty schoolboy, Kozeltsov the younger was discussing something with the officer from P—. When his brother opened the door he was completely caught off his guard.

'In a moment, I'll be out in a moment!' he said, waving to his brother. 'Wait for me out there.'

A moment later he did indeed emerge, and came over to his brother with a deep sigh.

'Do you know what, I can't come with you,' he said.

'What? Rubbish.'

'I'm telling you the truth, Misha. None of us has any money left, and we're all in debt to that lieutenant-captain from P—. It's damned embarrassing!'

The older brother frowned and for quite a long time said nothing.

'Do you owe him a lot?' he asked, giving his brother a doubtful look.

'Yes . . . well, no, not really; but I feel so ashamed of myself. He paid all my expenses at three of the posthouses we stopped at, and he provided all the sugar for the tea . . . so I don't really know . . . oh, and we played preference, too . . . I owe him a bit for that.'

'This is too bad, Volodya! I mean, what would you have done if you hadn't run into me?' he said sternly, avoiding his brother's eye.

'Well, you see, Misha, I thought I'd get my travel money in Sebastopol, and then I'd pay him back. That is allowed, after all; anyway, I'd better stay here and go along with him tomorrow.'

The older brother took out his purse and, not without some trembling of the fingers, extricated two ten-rouble notes and one three-rouble note.

'This is all the money I have,' he said. 'How much do you owe him?'

It was not quite true that this was all the money he had; he had, in addition, four gold roubles which were sewn into the cuff of his greatcoat in case of emergencies, but he had vowed to himself not to touch them.

It turned out that the younger Kozeltsov, with his sugar and games of preference, owed the officer from P— only eight roubles. His older brother gave him the money, remarking merely that if one is out of funds one should not play preference.

'What sort of stakes were you playing for, anyway?'

The younger brother kept resolutely silent. It seemed to him that the question cast aspersions on his integrity. His annoyance at himself, the shame he felt at having committed an act that could arouse such suspicions, and the wounding comments of his brother, to whom he was so deeply attached, provoked in him such an intense and painful reaction that he could not bring himself to reply, sensing that he would be unable to choke back the tearful sounds that were rising to his throat. He took the money without a glance, and went back to rejoin his companions.

—8—

Nikolayev, who had fortified himself in Duvankóy with two jars of vodka he had bought from a soldier who had been selling the stuff on the bridge there, gave the reins a tug and the little vehicle wobbled off down the stony road that nursed patches of shade here and there as it led along the course of the Belbek[41] towards Sebastopol. The brothers sat in the back, knocking legs with each other; although they never ceased to think about each other for a single moment, they both maintained a stubborn silence.

'Why did he have to insult me?' the younger brother was thinking. 'Couldn't he just have kept quiet about it? It's as if he suspected I was a thief; he still seems to be angry with me even now, so relations between us have probably been soured for good. Yet how fine it would have been, the two of us fighting together in Sebastopol. Two brothers, the closest of friends, both fighting the enemy: one already quite mature, a bit of a rough diamond, perhaps, but a brave fighter nevertheless, the other still young, but also a brave fellow . . . It'll only take me a week to show them all that I'm not as young as all that! I'll stop blushing, my face will display courage, and I'll have a moustache – not a big one, perhaps, but in a week it'll have grown to a reasonable size.' Here he tweaked the fuzz that had grown at the corners of his mouth. 'Perhaps we'll get there tonight, and I'll go into battle alongside my brother. I suppose it's just that he's a stubborn sort of fellow, and very brave – the kind of man who doesn't say much but puts up a better performance than the rest. What I'd like to know,' he continued to reflect, 'is whether he's trying to squeeze me against the edge of the waggon like this on purpose. He must realize that I'm uncomfortable. I expect he's just pretending to have forgotten I'm here. Let's suppose we get there tonight,' he mused, his body pressed against the edge of the waggon, trying not to move a muscle in case his brother noticed he was uncomfortable, 'and are sent straight to the bastion – I to help man the guns, and my brother to join his company – and we go there together. Suddenly the French attack us. I fire shell after shell, killing a vast number of them; but still they keep on coming straight at me. Finally it becomes impossible to fire any more, and it looks as though it's all over, there's no escape for me; but my brother leaps forward with his sabre, I snatch up a musket, and we rush to the defence along with the rest of the men. The French hurl themselves on Misha. I run up, killing one of them, and then another, thus saving my brother's life. I'm wounded in one arm, I seize the musket in the other and keep running; but my brother is cut down dead at my side by a bullet. I stop running for a moment, look at him sadly, get up and shout: "Follow me, men! Let us avenge his death! I loved my brother more than all else on earth," I say, "and now I have lost him. Let us take vengeance, let us destroy our enemies or else die forthwith!" They all raise a shout and rush after me. Then the entire French force appears, with Péllisier [42] himself at its head. We slaughter them all, but in the battle I'm hit a second and a third time, and I fall down at the point of death. Then everyone comes running up to me; Gorchakov[43] arrives and asks me if I have a last request. I tell him there's nothing I want except to be put to lie beside my brother, and that I want to die with him. They carry me over and put me down beside my brother's blood-stained corpse. I raise myself on one elbow and say merely: "Yes, you placed too little value on two men who truly loved their fatherland; now they have both fallen . . . may God forgive you!" – and then I die.'

Who can tell to what extent these dreams will soon be fulfilled?

'Listen, have you ever been in a hand-to-hand fight?' he asked his brother suddenly, entirely forgetting that he had resolved not to talk to him.

'No, never,' the older man replied. 'Two thousand of the men in our regiment have been killed, all of them by shells hitting the earthworks. That's how I got my wound, too. War's not at all how you think it is, Volodya!'

The younger Kozeltsov found this use of the affectionate 'Volodya' strangely touching. He wanted to clear the matter up with his older brother, who had absolutely no idea that he had offended him.

'You're not angry with me, are you, Misha?' he asked after a moment's silence.

'Why should I be angry with you?'

'Oh, I don't know – because of what we were talking about just now. Oh well, it doesn't matter.'

'Not one little bit,' replied the older man, turning to him and clapping him on the leg.

'But I am sorry, Misha, if I annoyed you.'

And the younger brother turned away in an effort to conceal the tears that had suddenly sprung to his eyes.

—9—

'Is this really Sebastopol, so soon?' asked the younger brother, when they reached the summit of the hill and before them spread the bay with all its masts, the open sea with the enemy fleet in the distance, the white shore batteries, the docks, aqueducts, barracks and other buildings of the town, and the clouds of white and lilac-tinted smoke that constantly rose along the yellow hills surrounding it. The smoke hung motionlessly in the deep blue sky, suffused by the pinkish rays of the sun which, as it sank towards the horizon, was already laying a carpet of reflected light across the dark sea.

Volodya caught his first sight of this terrible place, about which he had thought so much, without the slightest tremor; indeed, he surveyed this truly ravishing and unique spectacle with a sense of aesthetic enjoyment and a hero's satisfaction in the thought that within the space of half an hour he too would be part of it; he continued to survey it with concentrated attention right up to the very moment they arrived at the North Side and the waggon train of his brother's regiment, where they would be able to obtain reliable information concerning the regiment's whereabouts and learn which battery they were to join.

The officer in charge of the waggon train lived not far from the 'new town' – a huddle of wooden shanties built by sailors and their families – in a tent adjoining a rather large shelter which had been woven together from green oak twigs that were not yet completely dry.

The brothers found the officer sitting at a card table. On it stood a glass of cold tea with cigarette ash floating in it, and a tray on which were a vodka bottle and some crumbs of bread and dry caviare. The officer wore no uniform – he was dressed in a dirty, yellowish-coloured shirt, and trousers, and he was counting an enormous stack of banknotes with the aid of a large abacus. Before we go on, however, to discuss the personality of this officer, and his manner of discourse, let us take a closer look at the interior of his shelter and thus become a little acquainted with his work and way of life. The newly constructed shelter was very large indeed – solidly woven and comfortable, with tables and benches wattled from turf – and was of the type normally provided only for generals or regimental commanders. The walls and ceiling were covered by a series of three hangings, the purpose of which was to prevent leaves from falling to the floor; the hangings were extremely ugly, but were new and had probably cost a good deal. The iron bedstead that stood against the principal hanging (its design showed an Amazon on horseback) was covered by a bright red plush bedspread, on top of which lay a dirty, torn leather cushion and a raccoon fur coat. On the table were a mirror in a silver frame, a shockingly dirty silver hairbrush, a broken horn comb the teeth of which were congested with oily strands of hair, a silver candle-holder, a bottle of liqueur with a red and gold label, a gold watch, the face of which displayed a portrait of Peter the Great, two gold rings, a box containing some kind of capsules, a piece of a crust of bread and a scattering of old playing cards. Under the bed stood an assortment of porter bottles, both full and empty. This officer was in charge of the waggon train and was responsible for feeding the horses. With him lived a great friend of his, a Commissariat officer who was involved in shady dealings on the side. When the brothers stepped into the shelter, the Commissariat officer was asleep in the tent; the waggon train officer was doing the regimental accounts in order to have them ready before the end of the month. He was a very handsome, soldierly-looking man: tall, with a bushy moustache and a well-bred, solid physique. His only unattractive features were a certain sweaty puffiness about the face, which almost concealed his small grey eyes (making him look as though he had been pumped full of porter), and a thorough neglect of personal hygiene that displayed itself in everything from his thin, oily hair to his large, unstockinged feet in their ermine slippers.

'That's a fair bit of money you have there,' said the older Kozeltsov as he came into the shelter, greedily fastening his eyes, in spite of himself, on the stack of banknotes. 'I wouldn't say no to a loan of half that amount, Vasily Mikhailych!'

At these words, and catching sight of his visitors, the waggon train officer made a wry face, as though he had been caught in the act of stealing. Gathering the money together, and forgetting to stand up, he bowed.

'Ah, if only it were mine . . . but it belongs to the government, my dear chap. I say, who's this you've got with you?' he said, as he stuffed the money away into a box beside him, and looked Volodya straight in the face.

'This is my brother, fresh from cadet corps. Actually, the real reason we came to see you was to ask you where the regiment is.'

'Sit down, gentlemen,' said the waggon train officer, getting to his feet. Seeming to forget his guests for a moment, he wandered through into the tent. 'Are you thirsty? How about some porter?' they heard his voice enquire from within.

'That wouldn't come amiss, Vasily Mikhailych!'

Volodya was somewhat taken aback by the waggon train officer's grand manner, his air of careless negligence, and the respect accorded to him by his brother.

'This must be one of their crack officers, one all the others look up to; he's probably generous, honest and very brave,' he thought, sitting down on the sofa in a shy, self-deprecating manner.

'Well, and where is the regiment?' asked the older brother, addressing the tent.

'What's that?'

The older brother repeated the question.

'Zeyfer was here today: he said they all transferred to the 5th bastion yesterday.'

'Is that for certain?'

'If I'm telling you so, it must be; but actually, the devil only knows! It doesn't cost much to make him lie, either. What do you say, will you have a glass?' said the waggon train officer, still speaking from inside the tent.

'You know, I think I will,' said Kozeltsov.

'How about you, Osip Ignatych?' the voice from the tent continued, evidently addressing the sleeping Commissariat officer this time. 'You've slept long enough; it's nearly eight o'clock now.'

'Stop bothering me, I'm not asleep,' a lazy, thin little voice replied, pronouncing its *r*s and *l*s with a pleasantly guttural quality.

'Well, get up, then! I want you to be around.'

And the waggon train officer re-emerged to confront his guests.

'Serve us with porter! The Simferopol stuff!' he cried.

An orderly, whom Volodya thought looked rather supercilious, came into the shelter and whisked a bottle of porter out from under Volodya's legs, knocking against him as he did so.

'Yes, my dear chap,' said the waggon train officer as he poured out some glasses, 'we've a new regimental commander now. Can't get his hands on the money fast enough. Requisitioning things right, left and centre.'

'Well, I expect he's one of these types who likes to do everything their own way – one of the new generation,' said Kozeltsov, raising his glass politely.

'The new generation! He'll end up a skinflint just the same as all the others. When he was in charge of a battalion it was Figaro here, Figaro there – but from now on he'll have to sing a different tune. It won't wash with us, my dear fellow.'

'No, quite.'

The younger brother had not a clue as to what they were talking about, but he dimly sensed that his brother was not being quite candid, and was merely saying things to keep the officer happy, since it was the officer's porter he was drinking.

The bottle was already practically empty, and the conversation had been running on in the same vein for quite some time when the flaps of the tent were thrust open and there emerged a rather short, fresh-faced man who was wearing a blue satin dressing-gown with tassels, and a military cap that sported a red band and a cockade. As he came forward he gave his black moustache a twirl, and scrutinizing some indeterminate point on the carpet, returned the officers' bows with a barely noticeable movement of one shoulder.

'I'll have a glass, too!' he said, sitting down at the table. 'Well now, young man, travelling from St Petersburg, are you?' he said in a kindly sort of way, turning to Volodya.

'Yes, sir. I'm going to Sebastopol.'

'Volunteered, did you?'

'That's right, sir.'

'I don't know what gets into you gentlemen, I really don't,' the Commissariat officer went on. 'I think now that I'd even consider walking back to St Petersburg, if they'd let me. My God, this dog's life is getting me down, I can tell you.'

'What's so bad about this place?' the older Kozeltsov asked him. 'You seem to have quite a reasonable sort of life here.'

The Commissariat officer gave him a look and turned away.

'It's this constant danger we're exposed to' ('What sort of danger can he be talking about, sitting over here on the North Side?' thought Kozeltsov) '– the deprivation, the impossibility of obtaining even the simplest things,' he went on, still talking to Volodya. 'What does get into you? I really don't understand you gentlemen! If there were some advantage to be had . . . but to do it as you do . . . I mean, is it right, your being made cripples for the rest of your lives?'

'Some people may be out for profit, but there are others who are serving for the sake of honour,' said the older Kozeltsov, breaking into the conversation again, this time with irritation in his voice.

'What sort of honour is it when there's nothing to eat?' said the Commissariat officer, laughing scornfully and turning to the waggon train officer, whom Kozeltsov's last remark had also provoked to laughter. 'Come on, let's hear a bit of *Lucia*,' he said, pointing to a musical box. 'I'm so fond of it.'

'Is he to be trusted, that Vasily Mikhailych?' Volodya asked his brother when, as it was getting dark, they finally emerged from the shelter and continued their journey to Sebastopol.

'Oh, he's all right. He's just unbelievably tight-fisted, that's all. I mean, he gets at least three hundred roubles a month! Yet he lives like a pig – you saw it. No, it's that fellow from the Commissariat I can't stand; one of these days I'll beat the daylights out of him. Would you believe it, that scoundrel arrived from Turkey with twelve thousand . . .' And Kozeltsov began to wax eloquent on the subject of extortion, with a little of the animosity (if truth be told) of one whose condemnation is grounded less on the notion that extortion is wicked than on his own sense of annoyance that there are people who profit by it.

—10—

It would not have been true to say that Volodya was in a bad mood when, towards nightfall, the two brothers approached the large pontoon bridge that led across to the other side of the bay, but he did feel a certain heaviness of heart. All he had seen and heard was so little in accord with the impressions of his recent past: the light, spacious examination hall with its parqueted floors, the good-natured voices and laughter of his companions, his new uniform, his beloved Tsar, whom for seven years he had been accustomed to see in person and who, bidding them farewell with tears in his eyes, had called them his children – and so little, too, in accord with his beautiful, lavish, rainbow-coloured dreams.

'Well, here we are, then,' said the older brother, after they had driven up to the Michael battery and got out of the waggon. 'If they'll allow us on to the bridge we can go straight to the Nicholas Barracks. You can stay there overnight, and I'll go to regimental headquarters and find out which battery you're in; I'll come and fetch you tomorrow.'

'Do we have to do it that way?' said Volodya. 'Why can't we go together? And I'll go to the bastion with you, too. After all, I've got to get used to it some time, haven't I? If you can go, then so can I.'

'You'd do better not to.'

'No, really, at least I'll find out what . . .'

'My advice is for you not to come, but if you really want to . . .'

The sky was dark and cloudless; the gloom was already being vividly lit by the glimmer of the stars and the constantly moving lights of shells and gunfire. The large white structure of the battery and the start of the bridge loomed out of the darkness ahead. Literally every second the air was shaken with increasing stridor and clarity by artillery discharges and explosions that followed one another in rapid succession. Audible somewhere behind this noise, as if echoing it, was the gloomy mutter of the bay. A light wind was blowing in from the sea, and there was a smell of dampness in the air. The brothers drew near to the bridge. A militiaman clumsily knocked his musket against the ground as he raised it, with a shout of: 'Who goes there?'

'Soldiers!'

'I have orders to let nobody through.'

'Come on, we've got to.'

'You'll have to ask the officer in charge.'

The officer in charge, who was sitting on an anchor and had dozed off to sleep, rose with a start and ordered the militiaman to let the brothers through.

'It's one way only, remember; you can't turn round and come back again. Hey, where are you lot off to all at the same time?' he shouted in the direction of the regimental waggons, piled high with gabions, which were lining up at the entrance to the bridge and blocking it.

As they stepped down on to the first pontoon, the brothers ran into some soldiers who were returning from the other side, talking in loud voices to one another.

'If he got his ammunition money it means he's settled his account, that's what,' one of them was saying.

'Hey, lads!' said another voice. 'As soon as you get across to the North Side you're back in the real world again, and that's a fact! The air's completely different.'

'That's enough of that kind of talk!' said the first voice. 'One of those bloody things came flying over here only the other day and blew the legs clean off two of our sailor lads. So no more of that talk, I say.'

The brothers walked across the first pontoon, waiting for the waggon that would pick them up; when they reached the second, which was already awash in places, they halted their progress. The wind, which back on the shore had not seemed particularly strong, was violent and buffeting here; the bridge was pitching, and the waves hissed across its boarded surface as they broke against timbers, anchors and hawsers. To their right was the roaring sea, black and obscurely menacing, marked off by a black, even and unending line from the starry horizon and its blend of light and greyness; and somewhere far in the distance gleamed the lights of the enemy fleet. To their left was the dim, black mass of a Russian man-of-war, and they could hear the waves slapping against its sides; a steamboat could be seen moving rapidly and noisily away from the North Side. The flash of a shell bursting beside it lit up, momentarily, the tall piles of gabions on its deck, two men standing beside them, and the white foam and spray of the greenish waves cut by the ship as it forged ahead. By the edge of the pontoon bridge a shirtsleeved sailor sat chopping at something with an axe, his legs dangling in the water. Ahead, above Sebastopol, similar flashes came and went, and the terrible sounds drifted ever nearer, with ever-increasing volume. A wave suddenly broke against the right-hand side of the bridge, drenching Volodya's legs; two soldiers walked past him, their feet splashing in the water. A sudden flash, which was followed by a loud explosion, lit up the portion of the bridge that lay ahead of them, and they caught a glimpse of a waggon and a man on horseback; whining shell-fragments lashed the water into spray.

'Well, if it isn't Mikhail Semyonych!' said the rider, bringing his horse to a standstill in front of the older Kozeltsov. 'On your feet again, eh?'

'As you see. Where are you off to?'

'Oh, I'm going to the North Side to get some more ammunition: I'm standing in for the regimental adjutant today, you see . . . We're expecting an assault any minute now, but we've hardly five rounds per man. A fine state of affairs!'

'But where's Martsov?'

'One of his legs was blown off yesterday . . . It happened in town, he was asleep in his room . . . You might still find him, he's down at the dressing station.'

'The regiment's on the 5th bastion, is that correct?'

'Yes, we've taken over from the M—s. You should call in at the dressing station: there are quite a few of our chaps there, they'll show you the way.'

'Well, and is my room on Main Street still in one piece?'

'My dear fellow, the building was shelled to kingdom come ages ago. You won't recognize Sebastopol now; there's not a single woman left in the place, no taverns, no brass bands; the last pub closed down yesterday. It's about as cheerful as a morgue . . . Goodbye, then!'

And the officer rode off at a fast trot.

Volodya suddenly felt terribly afraid: he kept thinking that at any moment a cannonball or a shell-splinter might come hurtling over and blow his head off. The dank gloom, all the sounds – especially the querulous plashing of the waves – everything seemed to be telling him that he should go no further, that no good lay in store for him here, that his feet would never again tread Russian soil once he had crossed to the other side of the bay, that he should turn back at once and run away somewhere, as far away as possible from this terrible place of death. 'But perhaps it's too late for that now, perhaps it's all been decided already,' he thought, and he shivered, partly at this thought, and partly because the water had penetrated his boots and his feet were getting wet.

Volodya sighed deeply and left his brother's side, stopping a short distance away.

'Lord, am I really going to be killed – I, of all people? Lord, have mercy upon me!' he said in a whisper, and he crossed himself.

'Well, let's be off, Volodya,' said his older brother, as the waggon rolled on to the bridge. Did you see that shell?'

On the bridge the brothers met waggons full of wounded men; there were others carrying gabions, and one was laden with furniture and was being driven by a woman. When they reached the other side, no one tried to stop them. Edging their way by instinct along the wall of the Nicholas battery, listening as they went to the sounds of the shells that were already beginning to burst above their heads now, and to the roar of the fragments as they hurtled earthwards, they reached the place on the battery where the icon was kept. Here they learned that the 5th light battery, to which Volodya had been assigned, was stationed on the Korabelnaya.[44] They decided to ignore the risk and go straight to the 5th bastion together; there they would sleep the night at the older brother's quarters and would continue their journey to the unit on the following day. Entering a corridor and picking their way over the legs of the sleeping soldiers who lay along the entire length of the battery wall, they finally arrived at the dressing station.

—II—

As they entered the first ward, which was furnished with camp beds on which the wounded lay and was steeped in the loathsome, cloying miasma of hospitals, they met two Sisters of Mercy coming towards them.

One of these women, who was aged about fifty, with black eyes and a severe facial expression, was holding a pile of lint and bandages in her arms and giving instructions to a young lad, an apothecary assistant, who was following behind her; the other, an extremely pretty girl of around twenty, with a pale, delicate, fair-complexioned face that was somehow lent an especial sweetness and helplessness by the white nurse's headdress that surrounded it, was walking by the older woman's side, apparently afraid of being left behind, her hands in the pockets of her apron and her eyes directed at the ground.

Kozeltsov addressed them with a question: did they know where Martsov was, the man who had had his leg blown off the day previously?

'Do you mean the patient from the P— Regiment?' the older woman asked. 'Are you related to him, then?'

'No, ma'am, I'm a friend of his.'

'Hm! Very well, take them to see him,' she said to the young nurse, in French. 'He's through there.' And with that, she and the apothecary assistant went off to tend to another of the wounded men.

'Come on, what are you staring at?' said Kozeltsov to Volodya, who was looking at the wounded soldiers with a wide-eyed, agonized expression on his face, unable to tear himself away. 'Let's go.'

Volodya went off with his brother, but continued to gaze around him all the while, repeating to himself without being aware of it: 'Oh, my God! Oh, my God!'

'I suppose he hasn't been out here very long?' said the nurse to Kozeltsov, indicating Volodya who was following them along the corridor, sighing and groaning to himself.

'He's only just arrived.'

The pretty nurse took a look at Volodya and suddenly burst into tears.

'Oh God, God!' she cried, with despair in her voice. 'When is all this going to stop?'

They entered the officers' ward. Martsov was lying on his back, his sinewy arms, bare to the elbows, thrown up behind his head, and his yellowish face displaying the expression of one who is clenching his teeth so as not to cry out in pain. His undamaged leg, clad in a sock, was protruding from under the blanket, and one could see that its toes were twitching convulsively.

'Well, and how are you today?' asked the nurse, as with her delicate fingers, on one of which Volodya observed a gold ring, she raised the wounded man's slightly balding head and straightened his pillow for him. 'Here are some friends of yours who've come to see you.'

'I'm in pain, of course,' said the patient, testily. 'Leave me alone, I'm all right!' And with that, the toes in the sock began to move even faster. 'Hallo! I'm sorry, but can you tell me your name again?' he said, addressing Kozeltsov. 'I know it's bad of me, but a man forgets everything in here,' he said, when the other had told him his surname. 'We used to share the same quarters, didn't we?' he added without any evident pleasure, casting an enquiring look in Volodya's direction.

'This is my brother, he only arrived from St Petersburg today.'

'Hm! Well, I've earned a *full discharge*,' he said, screwing his features into a grimace. 'God, how it hurts! . . . I wish it could all be over.'

He gave his leg a jerk and covered his face with his hands, muttering something.

'You'd better leave now,' said the nurse in a low voice; there were tears in her eyes. 'He's in a very bad way.'

While they were still back on the North Side, the brothers had agreed to go to the 5th bastion together; but on emerging from the Nicholas battery they came, as it were, to a tacit agreement that neither should expose himself to unnecessary danger, and that each should travel separately.

'All that worries me is how you're ever going to find the place on your own,' said the older brother. 'I suppose Nikolayev can take you to the Korabelnaya, and I'll make my way alone and join you tomorrow.'

These were the last words to be spoken between the two brothers during this, their final farewell.

—12—

The thunder of the cannon continued as loudly as ever, but Catherine Street, along which Volodya was making his way, followed by a taciturn Nikolayev, was completely empty and quiet. In the gloom all he could see was the broad thoroughfare with, on either side, the white walls of large houses that had been reduced to rubble in many places, and the stone pavement along which he was walking. From time to time he met soldiers and officers. As he was passing along the left-hand side of the street, near the Admiralty building, he caught sight, by the glow of a bright lamp which was shining behind the wall, of the acacia shrubs that had been planted along the pavement, with their green supports and tired, dusty leaves. He could hear every sound quite distinctly: his own footsteps and those of Nikolayev, following behind him, and Nikolayev's stertorous breathing. He was thinking about nothing in particular: the pretty nurse, Martsov's leg and the toes moving inside the sock, the gloom, the shells and the various manifestations of death all moved dimly through his imagination. His young, impressionable soul ached and shrank in the consciousness of his own isolation, and of the fact that no one else seemed to care what happened to him in this hour of danger. 'I'll suffer in agony, I'll be killed – and no one will shed a tear!' he reflected. All this was a long way from the heroic life, filled with compassion and vitality, about which he had had such beautiful dreams. The shells came whistling and exploding nearer and nearer; Nikolayev's sighs grew more frequent, but still he uttered no word. As they were crossing the Maly Korabelny bridge, he saw a bright object hurtle past him into the bay, whistling as it went. For a second it lit the lilac-coloured waves, disappeared from view, and then rose out of the sea again in a column of spray.

'Look, sir, that one's still alight!' said Nikolayev.

'Yes,' he answered, astonished at the thin, reedy little voice in which he heard himself speaking.

They met stretcher parties ferrying wounded men, and more waggons laden with gabions; on the Korabelnaya they encountered a regiment; men on horseback were riding past. One of these was an officer, accompanied by a Cossack. The officer was riding at a fast trot, but catching sight of Volodya he brought his horse to a standstill beside him, looked searchingly into his face, turned away again and then rode off, delivering a smack of his whip to the horse's flanks. 'I'm alone, I'm alone! No one could care less whether I exist or not,' thought the poor boy in horror, and he genuinely felt like bursting into tears.

Continuing uphill past a high, white wall, he entered a street of small, devastated houses which were continuously illuminated by the flashes of exploding shells. A drunken, tormented-looking woman who was emerging from a gateway in the company of a sailor stumbled against Volodya, muttering: '. . . because if he'd been a decent sort of fellow, a gentleman . . . Oh, pardon me, officer, your honour!'

The aching in the poor boy's heart was getting worse and worse; the lightnings on the black horizon were growing ever more frequent, as were the whistling and explosions of the shells around him.

Nikolayev gave a deep sigh and suddenly began to say, in a voice that to Volodya sounded as though it were coming from beyond the grave: 'Such a hurry he was in to get here. Travelling and travelling. A fine place to hurry to. When the clever gentlemen, the ones who have any brains, go to hospital as soon as they're the slightest bit wounded and stay there. That's the only way to manage, if you ask me.'

'What do you mean? After all, my brother's completely recovered now,' replied Volodya, hoping by means of conversation to dispel the unpleasant feeling that had taken hold of him.

'Recovered! What kind of recovery is it when he's still as sick as a dog? The ones who've really recovered, and the ones who've got any sense, those fellows stay in hospital at a time like this. What joy can a man expect out here, eh? He's more likely to get his arm blown off – that's all. And he won't have to wait long before it happens, either. It's bad enough here in town – it must be purgatory up there on the bastion. You can't put a foot forward without saying a prayer to yourself. Ach, the devil, listen to it bansheeing away past!' he added, transferring his attention to a shell-fragment that was whistling by close at hand. 'Take what he's done now, for example,' Nikolayev continued. 'He's ordered me to show your honour the way. Of course, I know the score: what I'm told to do, I do. But the point is that he's gone and left the waggon with some soldier or other, and the bundle isn't tied up. Get along with you, he says, get along; but if anything goes missing you can bet your boots it'll be Nikolayev who takes the blame.'

Continuing a few paces further, they emerged on to a square. Nikolayev sighed and said nothing.

'That's your artillery over there, your honour,' he said, suddenly. 'Ask the sentry: he'll show you where to go.'

When Volodya had gone a few yards and no longer heard the

sounds of Nikolayev's sighing behind him, he suddenly felt completely and utterly alone. This consciousness of his own isolation and of the danger he was in – in the jaws of death, he thought – lay on his heart like some cold and unspeakably heavy stone. He stood still in the middle of the square and looked round to see if anyone was watching him, clutched at his head and thought out loud, with a sense of horror: 'Lord! Am I really a coward – a base, vile, worthless coward? Am I really incapable of dying an honourable death for the fatherland and for the Tsar, for whom so recently I dreamed with joy of dying? Yes! I'm a wretched, pathetic creature!' And with a genuine sense of despair and disenchantment with himself he asked the sentry which was the house of the battery commander, and walked up to it.

—13—

The battery commander had his quarters in a small, two-storeyed house which one entered from the yard; the sentry pointed the building out to Volodya. In one of the windows, which had been pasted over with strips of paper, the dim light of a candle burned. An orderly was sitting in the porch, smoking his pipe. He went inside to announce Volodya's arrival, then came back and showed Volodya into one of the rooms. The room contained a writing-table piled high with official documents, placed between two of the windows and underneath a broken mirror; there were one or two chairs and an iron bedstead with a mattress and clean linen, with a small hanging on the wall beside it.

In the doorway stood a handsome man with a large moustache – a sergeant-major; at his side he wore a broadsword, and he was dressed in a military greatcoat that displayed the ribbons of the St George Cross and the Hungarian Medal. In the middle of the room a short staff officer, aged about forty, was strolling to and fro; one of his cheeks was swollen and tied up in a handkerchief, and he was wearing a thin, shabby old greatcoat.

'Ensign Kozeltsov II, attached to the 5th light battery, reporting for duty, sir,' said Volodya, trotting out the phrase he had learnt at cadet corps, as he entered the room.

The battery commander drily returned his bow and, without offering his hand, asked him to sit down.

Volodya sat down shyly on a chair beside the writing-table and began to toy with a pair of scissors that had somehow found their way into his hands; the battery commander, meanwhile, his hands clasped together behind his back and his head lowered, cast only an occasional glance at the hands that were twiddling the scissors and, without once saying a word, continued to stroll about the room with the air of one who is in the process of remembering something.

The battery commander was a rather stout little man; on the crown of his head he had a large bald patch; he had a thick moustache which he had allowed to grow straight and which covered his mouth, and large, pleasant eyes. His hands were well proportioned, clean and plump; as he strolled about with confidence and a certain foppish air, his almost bow-legged gait advertised the fact that the battery commander was not a timid sort of fellow.

'Yes,' he said, coming to a halt beside the sergeant-major. 'We'd better give those ammunition horses a bit more fodder, otherwise they'll be no good for anything. What do you think?'

'Oh, I'm sure we could give them a bit extra, your honour! Oats are getting cheaper all the time just now,' the sergeant-major replied, with a motion of his fingers, which he was keeping in line with the seam of his trousers, but which in the normal course of events he evidently liked to use in order to assist the conversation by means of gestures. 'By the way, your honour, I had a note from our forager, Franshchuk, who's up at the waggon train; he says we really ought to buy some axles there; apparently they're very cheap. Will you give him the go-ahead?'

'Yes, tell him to buy some. He's got money, hasn't he?' And the battery commander began to stroll about the room again. 'Where's your kit?' he suddenly asked Volodya, coming to a halt in front of him.

So overwhelmed had poor Volodya been by the thought that he was a coward that he now tended to detect contempt in every word and glance that came his way. He had the impression that the battery commander had already fathomed his secret and was out to tease him. Covered in confusion, he replied that his kit was on the Grafskaya, and that his brother had said he would deliver it to him the following day.

But the lieutenant-colonel did not bother to hear him out and, turning to the sergeant-major, asked: 'Where are we going to put this ensign?'

'Ensign, sir?' said the sergeant-major, causing Volodya still further embarrassment by the cursory glance with which he looked him up and down, a glance which seemed to enquire: 'What sort of an ensign is this, and is it worth putting him anywhere?' 'There's room for him downstairs, in the lieutenant-captain's quarters, your honour,' he continued, after a moment's thought. 'The lieutenant-captain's in the bastion just now, so his bed's not in use.'

'Well, there you are, will that do for now?' said the battery commander. 'I expect you're tired. We'll find you some better quarters tomorrow.'

Volodya got up and bowed.

'Would you like some tea?' the battery commander asked, as Volodya was already on his way towards the door. 'I can provide you with a samovar.'

Volodya bowed and went out. The colonel's orderly led him downstairs and showed him into a bare, dirty room that was strewn with various items of lumber and contained an iron bedstead and mattress with no sheets or blanket. A man in a pink shirt was asleep on the bed, covered by a greatcoat.

For a moment, Volodya thought the man was a common soldier.

'Pyotr Nikolaich!' said the orderly, giving the sleeping man's shoulder a hefty nudge. 'There's an ensign supposed to be sleeping here . . . This is one of our cadets,' he added, turning to Volodya.

'Oh, please don't let me disturb you!' said Volodya; but the cadet, a tall, thickset young man with a handsome but thoroughly unintelligent face, got up off the bed, threw on his greatcoat and, evidently still not properly awake, left the room.

'It's all right, I'll sleep outside,' he muttered.

—14—

When he was at last left alone with his thoughts, Volodya's first sensation was one of revulsion at the chaotic, cheerless state of his own mind. He wanted to fall asleep and forget about everything around him – including himself. He snuffed out the candle, lay down on the bed and, loosening his coat, used it to cover himself, pulling it up over his head in order to alleviate the fear of darkness from which he had suffered ever since he was a child. Then, however, he suddenly had the thought that a shell might come flying over, land on the roof and kill him. He began to listen; directly above his head he could hear the footsteps of the battery commander.

'Oh well,' he thought; 'if a shell does hit the house it'll be those who are upstairs that are killed first. At least I won't be the only one.' This thought calmed him somewhat, and he began to nod off to sleep. 'But what if the French take Sebastopol tonight and come bursting in here? What will I defend myself with?' He got up again and paced about the room. His fear of this real danger had driven away his superstitious fear of the dark. The room contained no serviceable blunt objects beyond a samovar and a saddle. 'I'm hopeless, I'm a coward, a despicable coward!' he suddenly thought, and once more experienced a painful sensation of self-contempt, even self-disgust. He lay down again and tried not to think. Then the impressions of the day that had passed began to flood into his brain, mingling with the incessant detonations of the bombardment that made the glass in the room's single window rattle, and again reminded him of the danger he was in: he dreamt, now of wounded men and blood, now of shells and shell-fragments that burst into the room, now of the pretty nurse bandaging his wounds and weeping over him as he lay dying, now of his mother seeing him off in the local town and praying with all her heart before a miracle-working icon – and again found that he could not sleep. But suddenly the thought of a benevolent, almighty God, who could bring all things about and who heard every prayer, came clearly to his mind. He got down on his knees, made the sign of the cross over himself, and placed his hands together as he had been taught to do as a child. This gesture instantly gave him a long-missed sense of relief.

'If it is necessary that I die, if my absence is required, then bring it about, O Lord,' he prayed. 'Do it swiftly. But if bravery and fortitude, which I lack, are what is needed, grant me them, but save me from shame and ignominy, which I am unable to bear, and teach me what I must do in order to carry out Your will.'

Volodya's childish, frightened, limited soul suddenly acquired a new strength and radiance, and gained a perception of new, brighter and more spacious horizons. In the brief interval of time this sensation lasted he thought and felt much else besides, but soon fell peacefully asleep, without a care in the world, to the continued crackling and booming of the bombardment, and the trembling of the windowpanes.

Great Lord in heaven! You alone have heard, You alone know the simple but impassioned, desperate prayers of ignorance, anguished repentance and suffering that have ascended towards You from this terrible place of death – from the prayers of the general, who only a second ago had been thinking of his lunch and a St George Cross around his neck, but who was suddenly brought face to face with Your proximity, to those of the exhausted, hungry and louse-ridden private lying sprawled on the bare floor of the Nicholas battery, imploring You to grant him the reward he instinctively anticipates, the one that will compensate him for all these undeserved sufferings. Verily, You never weary of hearing the prayers of Your children, and in every time and in every place You send down a ministering angel to instil patience, a sense of duty and the comfort of hope into their souls.

—15—

The older Kozeltsov, meeting a private from his own regiment out on the street, set off with him directly to the 5th bastion.

'Keep close to the wall, your honour,' said the private.

'Why should I do that?'

'It's dangerous here, your honour; look, get your head down, here's one coming now,' said the private, listening to a cannonball which came whistling over and slammed into the dry surface of the roadway on the other side of the street.

Paying no heed to the man, Kozeltsov walked off briskly down the centre of the road.

The streets were just the same as when he had visited Sebastopol back in the spring; so, too – though perhaps more frequent now – were the flashes, the explosions, the groans and the encounters with wounded men; so were the batteries, parapets and trenches. Now, however, it all for some reason appeared at once more melancholy and more in earnest – there were more shot-holes in the buildings, and there were no lights in the windows at all now, except for those in Kushchin House (the hospital); not one woman was to be seen anywhere; the former atmosphere of long-established habit and freedom from care had been replaced by one of gloomy expectation, of weariness and tension.

But here was the last trench, and here, too, was the voice of a private of the P— Regiment who had recognized his old company commander; here, in darkness, was the 3rd battalion, huddled up against a wall, briefly and sporadically illuminated by salvoes of gunfire and betraying its presence by the muffled talk of the men and the clacking of their muskets.

'Where's the regimental commander?' Kozeltsov asked.

'He's in the naval casemate, your honour,' replied the private, eager to oblige. 'Come on, sir, I'll take you there myself.'

The soldier led Kozeltsov from trench to trench until, in one of them, they came to a small ditch. In the ditch sat a sailor, smoking his pipe; a door was visible, and behind it cracks of light could be seen.

'Is it all right to go in?'

'Just a moment, sir, I'll tell them you're here,' said the sailor, and he went inside.

On the other side of the door two voices could be heard in conversation.

'If Prussia insists on maintaining her neutrality,' one of the voices was saying, 'then Austria will do the same . . .'

'Never mind about Austria,' said the other voice. 'What about the Slavic lands? . . . Well, find out what he wants.'

Kozeltsov had never been in this casemate before. He was struck by the decorative appearance of its interior. The floor was parqueted, and the door was closed off by little screens. Two beds stood against the walls, and in one corner hung a large, gold-framed icon of the Virgin Mary with a pink vigil lamp burning in front of it. A naval officer lay asleep, fully clothed, on one of the beds, while on the other, facing a table on which stood two opened bottles of wine, two men – the new regimental commander and an adjutant – sat talking to each other. Although Kozeltsov was certainly no coward and had, indeed, nothing to fear either from the military authorities in general or the regimental commander in particular, at the sight of this colonel who only a short time ago had been one of his everyday companions he lost his nerve and began to shake in his shoes, so haughtily did the colonel rise to his feet and fasten him with his attention. What made matters even worse was that the adjutant also intimidated him by the way he sat there looking, as if to say: 'I'm merely a friend of your commander's. It's not me you're reporting to, and I have neither the power nor the wish to demand deference of you.'

'How strange,' thought Kozeltsov, as he looked at his commander. 'It's only seven weeks since he took the regiment over, yet everything about him – his uniform, his bearing, his gaze – displays the authority of a regimental commander, the kind of authority that's based less upon age, seniority of rank and military prowess than it is on money. It seems like only yesterday,' he thought, 'that this same Batrishchev was getting drunk with us, wearing the same dark-coloured cotton shirt week in, week out, and eating his eternal meatballs and fruit dumplings alone by himself in his room, yet now look at him! There's a starched white shirt under that wide-sleeved overcoat he's wearing, he's smoking a ten-rouble cigar, and there's a six-rouble bottle of Lafitte on the table – all bought at sky-high prices from the quartermaster in Simferopol – and his eyes have that cold arrogance proper to an aristocrat of wealth, which says: "Being one of the new breed of regimental commanders, I'm still one of you: but don't forget that whereas all you've got is your sixty roubles – one third of your salary – tens of thousands pass through my hands, and believe me I know you'd give your right arm to be where I am." '

'It's taken you a while to get back on your feet again,' the colonel said to Kozeltsov, eyeing him coldly.

'I was quite badly injured, sir, and even now my wound hasn't completely healed.'

'Well, you shouldn't be here then,' said the colonel, casting a doubtful glance at the officer's stocky figure. 'Do you think you'll be able to carry out your duties?'

'Yes, sir, of course I will, sir.'

'Right then, I'm very glad to hear it. You'll take over from ensign Zaytsev in command of 9th company – that's the one you had before; you'll receive your orders directly.'

'Very well, sir.'

'And when you go there, please be so good as to tell the regimental adjutant I should like to have a word with him,' said the regimental commander by way of conclusion, signalling with a little bow that the audience was at an end.

As he emerged from the casemate, Kozeltsov muttered something under his breath several times, hunching his shoulders together as though in pain, embarrassment, or annoyance at something; his annoyance was, however, directed not at the regimental commander, with whom he had no complaint, but at himself and everything about himself. Discipline and its prerequisite, subordination, are only agreeable (the same is true of all relations derived from the sanction of law) in so far as they are grounded not simply in a mutual acceptance of their necessity, but on the subordinate's recognition that those placed in authority over him are possessed of a higher degree of experience, military prowess or – not to beat about the bush – moral development; as soon, however, as discipline is founded, as often happens in society, on casual fortune or the money principle, it unfailingly ends up either as overweening arrogance on the one hand, or concealed envy and irritation on the other – instead of acting beneficially to unite a mass of men into a single unit, it produces quite the opposite effect. The man who feels unable to inspire respect by virtue of his own intrinsic merits is instinctively afraid of contact with his subordinates and attempts to ward off criticism by means of superficial mannerisms. His subordinates, who see only this superficial aspect of the man, one which they find offensive, are inclined, quite often unjustly, to suppose it conceals nothing good.

—16—

Before joining his fellow officers, Kozeltsov went over to re-introduce himself to his company and see where it was stationed. The parapets constructed from gabions, the figurations of the trenches, the guns he passed, and even the shell-fragments and unexploded shells he tripped over as he walked along – all these things, constantly illuminated by the flash of gunfire, were very familiar to him. All of this had been deeply etched on his memory three months earlier during the two continuous weeks he had spent on this same bastion. Although there was much in this recollection that did not bear thinking about, it somehow merged with the fascination of the past, and he found himself recognizing familiar places and objects with pleasure, as though the two weeks he had spent here had been quite agreeable ones. The company was deployed along the wall that constituted the 6th battalion's defences.

Kozeltsov walked in at the completely unprotected entrance to a long casemate in which, he was told, the 9th company was stationed. So full of soldiers was this casemate (it was packed to the door) that there was literally nowhere to put one's feet. In one part of it a crooked tallow candle was burning, held by a soldier who was lying down. Another soldier was reading aloud from a book, spelling out the syllables one by one, and holding the text right up to the candle. In the stinking semi-darkness of the casemate, raised heads could be seen avidly listening to the reader. The book was a primer, and as he entered the casemate, Kozeltsov heard the following.

'Fear of death is an inborn sense in man.'

'Trim the wick a bit,' said a voice. 'This is a real fine book.'

When Kozeltsov asked if the sergeant-major was present, the man stopped reading and the soldiers began to stir, coughing or blowing their noses in the way an audience always does after a prolonged spell of keeping quiet. The sergeant-major, buttoning up his coat, rose from beside the group of men surrounding the reader and, stepping across the legs of some and on the legs of others who had no room to move them, came over to the officer.

'Greetings, sergeant! Well, is this the whole of our company?'

'Greetings and welcome, your honour,' replied the sergeant-major, looking at Kozeltsov in a cheerful, friendly manner. 'Are you better now, your honour? Well, thank the Lord! We'd been getting fair browned-off without you, truly we had.'

It was immediately obvious that Kozeltsov was popular with the men of the regiment.

From the interior of the casemate, voices could be heard saying: 'Our old company commander's here, the one who was wounded, you remember – Mikhail Semyonych, Kozeltsov's his last name,' and so on. Some of the men even came over to him, and the drummer said hello to him.

'Hello there, Obanchuk!' said Kozeltsov. 'Still in one piece?' Then, raising his voice, he said, addressing all the men: 'Good health, men!'

'Good health, sir!' came a dull roar from the casemate.

'How are you, men?'

'Poorly, your honour: those Frenchies are getting the better of us – they're giving us a really nasty hammering from behind those trenches of theirs. But that's all they ever do: they never come out into the open.'

'Well, perhaps I'll bring you luck and God will see to it that they do come out into the open, lads!' said Kozeltsov. 'It won't be the first time we've fought together: let's give them another thrashing!'

'We'll do our best, your honour!' several voices piped up.

'He's got a lot of guts, his honour has, he's really got a lot of guts,' said the drummer to another soldier in a voice which, though soft, was still loud enough to be audible, as if in support of what the company commander had been saying, and as if in order to persuade the soldier that there had been nothing boastful or fanciful about it.

After visiting the soldiers, Kozeltsov walked over to the defended barracks to join his fellow officers.

—17—

There was a large number of men in the big room that constituted the barracks: they were all either naval, artillery or infantry officers. Some were asleep; others had seated themselves on a packing crate and a gun carriage and were talking to one another; others yet again – these formed the largest and noisiest group – had spread out two felt cloaks on the floor beyond the central arch and were sitting on them, drinking porter and playing cards.

'Aha! Kozeltsov, Kozeltsov! Good to see you, man! . . . How's your wound?' cried voices from every side. Here, too, it was evident that Kozeltsov was well liked, and that his fellow officers were glad to see him back.

When he had finished shaking hands with men he knew, Kozeltsov joined the large group of officers who were playing cards – most of these were his friends. A lean, handsome man with dark brown hair, a long, thin nose and a bushy moustache with sideburns was dealing cards with white, shapely fingers, on one of which there was a large gold ring with a seal. He was dealing the cards rapidly and carelessly, clearly anxious about something and trying to conceal the fact by his offhand manner. Beside him, to his right, a grey-haired major who had had a considerable amount to drink was leaning his head in his elbows, punting with affected indifference for fifty-copeck pieces, and paying his debts as he went along. On his left, a small, red-complexioned officer with a perspiring face squatted on his heels, reacting with a forced smile and a strained laugh each time he lost; he kept fumbling with one hand in the empty pocket of his *sharovary*, and he played for high stakes – not, however, in ready money, a fact that was clearly jarring upon the handsome, brown-haired man. A thin, pale, clean-shaven officer with a bald head and an enormous, cruel mouth prowled up and down the room holding a wad of banknotes. Every so often he would stake the whole wad, and every time he won.

Kozeltsov took a glass of vodka and sat down near the card-players.

'Come and punt with us, Mikhail Semyonych!' the officer who was acting as banker said to him. 'I'll bet you've brought plenty of money with you.'

'Where would I get money? Actually, I spent all I had left in town.'

'I don't believe you. You must have won something in Simferopol, surely?'

'Yes, but not very much,' said Kozeltsov; evidently, though, he did not wish the others to believe him, for he undid his coat and took the old cards into his hands.

'Well, let's see what jokes the Devil can play, or perhaps it's only a gnat – you know what they're capable of. Only I'll have to have a few drinks first, to strengthen my nerve.'

After a while, having drunk another three vodkas and several glasses of porter, he felt completely in tune with the mood of the assembled company – one of a general stupefaction and oblivion of reality – and lost his three remaining roubles.

By this time the small, perspiring officer had run up a debt of 150 roubles.

'No it's not my lucky day,' he said casually, preparing a fresh card.

'Kindly pay what you owe,' said the officer who was banker, interrupting his dealing for a moment and giving him a look.

'Will you allow me to pay tomorrow?' the perspiring officer asked, getting to his feet and fumbling energetically in his empty pocket.

'Hm!' growled the banker, dealing out all the cards in the pack to right and to left. 'It's no good,' he said, when he had finished. 'I've had enough. We can't go on like this, Zakhar Ivanych,' he added. 'We're supposed to be playing for cash, not credit.'

'Do you doubt my word, then? I don't find that very amusing.'

'Who's going to pay me? That's what I'd like to know,' muttered the major, who by this time was thoroughly drunk and had won about eight roubles. 'I've paid in more than twenty roubles now, yet whenever I win I don't get a copeck.'

'How can I pay you when there's no money on the table?' said the banker.

'That's no concern of mine!' shouted the major, getting to his feet. 'It's you chaps I'm playing with, honest ones – not the likes of him.'

The perspiring officer immediately lost his temper.

'I've told you – I'll pay tomorrow. How dare you say an insolent thing like that to me?'

'I'll say whatever I like. Honest chaps don't behave like that, that's what I think!' shouted the major.

'That's enough, Fyodor Fyodorych!' they all started to say at once, restraining the major. 'Stop it!'

But the major, it seemed, had been waiting for this moment in order finally to launch himself into a furious rage. He suddenly leapt to his feet and moved unsteadily towards the perspiring officer.

'Saying insolent things, was I? I'll have you know that I'm a good deal older than you, and I've served the Tsar for twenty years. Insolent? You little ninny!' he squealed suddenly, growing more and more excited at the sound of his own voice. 'Bounder!'

But let us quickly lower the curtain on this deeply depressing scene. Tomorrow, perhaps even this very day, each one of these men will go proudly and cheerfully to his death, and will die with calm and fortitude; under these conditions, which appal even the most detached of sensibilities and are characterized by a total absence of the human and of any prospect of salvation, the only relief is that of oblivion, the annihilation of consciousness. Buried in each man's soul lies the noble spark that will make a hero of him; but this spark grows weary of burning brightly all the time – when the fateful moment arrives, however, it will leap up like a flame and illuminate great deeds.

—18—

On the following day the bombardment continued with undiminished intensity. By around eleven in the morning, Volodya Kozeltsov was sitting with a group of battery officers and, having already managed to get to know them a little, was taking a good look at these new faces – observing, asking questions and telling his own story. The modest, somewhat technical conversation of the artillery officers inspired him with respect, and appealed to him. His own shy, innocent and attractive appearance likewise won him the officers' favourable attention. The captain who was the battery's chief commanding officer, a rather short, red-haired man with a topknot and smooth temples, who had been trained according to the old artillery traditions, was something of a ladies' man and had a reputation as a scholar, chaffed him affectionately about his youth and his pretty face, and generally behaved towards him like a father towards a son, something Volodya found very agreeable. Then there was Sub-lieutenant Dyadenko, a young officer with tousled hair who went around in a tattered greatcoat and had a Ukrainian accent, pronouncing all his *o*s. Although he had a very loud voice, constantly went in search of pretexts for bitter arguments and moved in a nervous, jerky fashion, Volodya found him sympathetic, as beneath this unpolished exterior he could not help discerning a good and extremely kind human being. Dyadenko was forever offering Volodya his services, and kept trying to prove to him that the guns in Sebastopol were incorrectly positioned. Only Lieutenant Chernovitsky, a man with permanently raised eyebrows who was, however, more polite than any of the others, who wore a frock-coat that was at least reasonably clean, if not new, with neatly sewn-on patches, and who sported a gold chain across his satin waistcoat, aroused Volodya's distaste. Chernovitsky kept plying him with questions about what the Tsar and the War Minister were doing, informed him, with affected enthusiasm, about the feats of bravery that were being performed in Sebastopol, complained about how little patriotism one seemed to encounter anywhere and what senseless decrees the authorities issued, and so on and so forth. Although Chernovitsky exuded an air of knowledgeableness, intelligence and decent feeling, Volodya found the total effect somehow studied and lacking in spontaneity. In particular, he observed that the other officers hardly ever spoke to Chernovitsky. Cadet volunteer Vlang, the man Volodya had aroused from slumber the day before, was also here. Vlang did not really join in the conversation but, sitting unobtrusively in a corner, laughed whenever there was something to laugh at, remembered whenever something had been forgotten, asked for vodka to be served and rolled cigarettes for everyone. Whether it was Volodya's unassuming, polite manner – Volodya talked to him as if he were an officer and did not order him about as a junior – or his pleasant appearance that so captivated 'Vlanga', as the soldiers called him, for some reason inflecting his name as if it were a feminine noun, he never once took his large, slow eyes off the new officer's face, anticipated and forestalled all his wishes and spent the whole time in a kind of amorous ecstasy which, needless to say, aroused the attention of the officers and prompted them to laughter.

Before dinner they were joined by a lieutenant-captain who had just come off his spell of duty on the bastion. Lieutenant-Captain Kraut was a handsome, energetic officer; he was fair-haired and sported a large, reddish moustache and sideburns. He spoke excellent Russian, but too correctly and elegantly for a Russian. His bearing as a military man in general mirrored his command of the language: he was an excellent soldier and comrade, and extremely reliable where money was concerned. But precisely because all these aspects of his character were so blameless, he seemed to lack something as a human being. Like all Russian Germans – and in strange contrast to those idealistic 'German' Germans – he was extremely practical.

'Here he comes, here's our hero!' said the captain, as Kraut, swinging his arms and clanking his spurs, came breezily into the room. 'What would you like, Fridrikh Krestyanych: tea or vodka?'

'I have already asked them to bring me some tea,' he replied. 'But in the meanwhile a drop of vodka would cheer the soul and would certainly not come amiss. Very nice to meet you; I beg your most gracious favour,' he said to Volodya, who had risen to his feet and bowed. 'Lieutenant-Captain Kraut. The artillery NCO in the bastion said you only arrived yesterday.'

'I'm extremely grateful for the use of your bed, sir: I spent the night on it.'

'Did you sleep all right? One of its legs is broken, and there's no one to mend it, there being a siege; you have to place something under it.'

'Well, none the worse for your spell of duty, I take it?' asked Dyadenko.

'Oh, it was all right. Only Skvortsov was hit, and they "mended" one of our gun carriages for us. Blew the side-plate clean to pieces.'

He got up from where he was sitting and began to stroll about; it was evident that he was completely in the grip of the pleasant feeling of relief experienced by those who have escaped from danger.

'Now then, Dmitry Gavrilych,' he said, giving the captain's knee a shake. 'How are you, old fellow? What about your commission, still no word?'

'No news yet, no.'

'And there won't be any, either,' Dyadenko chipped in. 'I've already told you why.'

'Tell me again.'

'It's because your despatch wasn't worded correctly.'

'There you go, always arguing,' said Kraut, smiling merrily. 'A real, obstinate Ukrainian. Well, you'll end up a lieutenant in spite of yourself.'

'No, I won't.'

'Vlang, please fetch my pipe and fill it for me,' he said to the cadet, who at once eagerly ran off to fetch it for him.

Kraut made all the men feel more lively; he told them about the bombardment, asked what had been going on while he had been away, and had a word for everyone.

—19—

'Well, how's it going? Settled down with us yet?' Kraut asked Volodya. 'I'm sorry to have to ask, but will you tell me your Christian name and patronymic? We in the artillery generally use them, you know. Have you bought a saddle-horse yet?'

'No,' said Volodya. 'I'm not sure what to do. I told the captain I don't have a horse, nor any money either, until I get my forage and travel allowances. I was thinking of asking the battery commander if he'd lend me a horse on a temporary basis, but I'm afraid he'll say no.'

'Old Apollon Sergeich?' Kraut made a noise with his lips that expressed scepticism, and glanced at the captain. 'I don't think you'll get much joy out of him.'

'Oh well, if he does turn you down it won't be the end of the world,' said the captain. 'To tell you the truth, you don't really need a horse around here; but there's no harm in asking. I'll have a word with him today.'

'What? You don't know him,' Dyadenko cut in. 'If it was anything else, he'd turn you down. But this he won't refuse . . . Do you want to bet on it?'

'Oh, we all know you, you just like arguing!'

'I say it because I know I'm right: he's stingy about everything else, but he'll give you a horse because it's not worth his while to keep it.'

'What do you mean, not worth his while, when he's getting eight roubles back on oats for every horse he feeds?' said Kraut. 'It'll be worth this young fellow's while not to have to keep a horse he doesn't need.'

'Ask him to give you Starling, Vladimir Semyonych,' said Vlang, who had returned with Kraut's pipe. 'He's a first-rate horse.'

'He's the one that threw you into the ditch at Soroki, isn't he, Vlanga?' the lieutenant-captain laughed.

'And anyway, what if he is getting eight roubles?' said Dyadenko, pursuing the argument. 'His estimates are for ten roubles fifty.[45] Stands to reason it can't be worth his while.'

'If he didn't pocket the difference he'd have nothing left at all! I expect when you're the commander of a battery you won't even let a man have a horse to ride into town and back on!'

'When I'm battery commander all my horses will get four bags of oats a day; I won't make anything on the side, never fear.'

'Oh well, if you live, you'll learn,' said the lieutenant-captain. 'You'll take your profit, same as all the rest, and so will he,' he added, pointing to Volodya. 'When he's battery commander he'll be putting the loose change away in his pocket too.'

'Why should he want to do that, Fridrikh Kresyanovich?' said Chernovitsky, butting in. 'He's probably got a private income, so why should he want to make a profit?'

'No, sir, I . . . I'm sorry, captain, but . . .' said Volodya, blushing scarlet, '. . . I consider that remark a dishonourable one.'

'Aha! Ha! A real daredevil, isn't he?' said Kraut. 'Just wait till you've worked your way up to the rank of captain, my lad, then you won't talk to me like that.'

'I don't know anything about that; all I know is that if the money isn't mine, I have no right to take it.'

'I'll tell you this, young man,' began the lieutenant-captain in a more serious tone of voice. 'I wonder if you're aware that when you're in command of a battery you generally, if you do things right, have a surplus of five hundred roubles in peacetime, and a surplus of seven or eight thousand roubles if there's a war on – and that's only for the horses. Very well. The battery commander doesn't concern himself with the matter of the soldiers' provisions: that's been the arrangement in the artillery for as long as anyone can remember: if you're a bad manager, you won't have any surplus. Now even though it's not in the regulations, you've got to cover the following expenses out of that extra money: one' (he crooked a finger) 'you've got shoeing; two' (he crooked another finger) 'you've got medical supplies – then you've got stationery. On top of that, my friend, you've got to pay out up to five hundred roubles a head for off-horses, and remounts come in at fifty roubles a time – it's a price you'll have to pay, too – that makes four. Again, even though it says nothing about it in the regulations, you'll have to supply your soldiers with a change of collars, you'll find you spend an awful lot of money on coal, and then there's the officers' mess to be taken care of. If you're a battery commander you have to live in decent style: you'll need a carriage, and a fur greatcoat, and all kinds of things . . . it goes without saying . . .'

'But the main thing,' intervened the captain, who all this time had remained silent, 'the main thing, Vladimir Semyonych, is this: what about someone like myself who's served in the army for twenty years on a salary of two hundred roubles a month, in constant hardship? Can't he be allowed to earn himself a crust of bread for his old age after all the hard work he's put in, when those contractors are making tens of thousands every month?'

'What's that got to do with it?' said the lieutenant-captain, butting in again. 'Just don't be in too much of a hurry to pass judgement, that's all – wait till you've seen a bit more service.'

Volodya was beginning to feel terribly guilty and ashamed for having spoken so rashly, and he merely muttered something and went on listening in silence as Dyadenko, with the greatest of zeal, leapt into the argument and proceeded to attempt to prove the contrary.

The disputation was interrupted by the arrival of the colonel's orderly, who said that dinner was now served.

'Tell Apollon Sergeich to serve us some wine today,' Chernovitsky said to the captain, as he buttoned up his tunic. 'What's he saving it for? If we're killed, no one will get it!'

'Why don't you tell him yourself?' said the captain.

'No, you're the senior officer: we must do things by the regulations.'

—20—

The table in the same room where Volodya had reported to the colonel the day before had been moved away from the wall and spread with a dirty tablecloth. Today the battery commander shook his hand and asked him questions about life in St Petersburg and what sort of journey he had had.

'Well, gentlemen, those of you who drink vodka please help yourselves. Ensigns don't drink,' he added, giving Volodya a smile.

The battery commander did not seem at all as stern as he had done the previous day; indeed, he was acting like a good-natured, hospitable host and elder colleague. Even so, all the officers, from the old captain to the argumentative Dyadenko, demonstrated by the polite way in which they addressed the commander, looking him straight in the eye, and by the way they came up timidly, one by one, to take a glass of vodka, that they held him in great respect.

Dinner consisted of a large tureen of cabbage soup in which

floated fatty gobbets of beef and an enormous quantity of peppers and bay leaves, Polish *zrazy*[46] with mustard, and peppered meat pies served with butter that was not quite fresh. There were no table-napkins, the spoons were of either the tin or the wooden variety, there were only two glasses, and the only drink on the table was a grey decanter of water; the decanter's neck had been broken off. The meal was not, however, a tedious one: the conversation never flagged for one instant. It centred initially on the battle of Inkerman, in which the battery had taken part and concerning the unsuccessful outcome of which each man ventured his own ideas and suggestions, falling silent whenever the battery commander began to speak. It then moved on naturally to the question of the inadequate calibre of the light field-pieces, and to that of the new, simplified cannon, at which point Volodya was able to demonstrate his knowledge of artillery. What the conversation never really touched upon, however, was the truly dreadful situation of Sebastopol; it was as though each man had already devoted too much thought to this subject for him to wish to discuss it further. Neither, to Volodya's surprise and dismay, was there ever any mention of the duties he was to perform; it was as if he had come all the way to Sebastopol solely in order to talk about simplified cannon and have dinner with the battery commander. While they were eating, a shell landed not far from the house. The floor and walls shuddered as from an earthquake, and the windows were clouded by powder smoke.

'I don't expect you see such things in St Petersburg; but we often have little surprises like that here,' said the battery commander. 'Vlang, take a look and see where that one landed.'

Vlang went to look and said the shell had landed in the square. No one mentioned the incident again after that.

Just before dinner came to an end, an old man – the battery clerk – came into the room carrying three sealed envelopes, which he gave to the battery commander. 'This one's *extremely urgent*, sir, a Cossack's just brought it from the commander of artillery,' he said. The officers could not help watching the battery commander's fingers as, experienced in this task, they broke open the seal on the envelope and took out the *extremely urgent* document. 'What's this going to be?' each man wondered. It might be orders for a complete withdrawal from Sebastopol, or it might be a command that summoned the entire battery to the bastions.

'Not again!' said the battery commander, angrily flinging the document down on the table.

'What does it say, Apollon Sergeich?' asked a senior officer.

'They want an officer and crew for some mortar battery or other they've got over there. I've only four officers, and not one of my own crews is complete,' growled the battery commander. 'Yet here they are, at me again. Anyway, someone will have to go, gentlemen,' he said, after a moment or two's silence. 'Whoever it is must be at the Turnpike at seven . . . Get the sergeant-major over here. All right, gentlemen, make up your minds who it's to be,' he said.

'This fellow hasn't been anywhere yet,' said Chernovitsky, indicating Volodya.

The battery commander made no reply to this.

'Yes, I'd like to go,' said Volodya, feeling a cold sweat breaking out on his neck and back.

'No, why should it be him?' said the captain, intervening. 'We all know that no one's going to refuse to go, but we're not having any gatecrashers, either. And since Apollon Sergeich is leaving it up to ourselves, why don't we draw lots like we did last time?'

Everyone was in agreement: Kraut cut some strips of paper, rolled them up and placed them in his cap. The captain fooled around and even ventured to ask the colonel if on this occasion they might not have some wine, 'to give us courage', as he put it. Dyadenko sat looking gloomy, Volodya smiled to himself about something, and Chernovitsky kept telling everybody that he was the one who would have to go. Kraut alone remained absolutely calm.

Volodya was allowed to draw first. He picked up one of the longer rolls of paper, but immediately decided to exchange it for another which was shorter and fatter. Opening it out, he read the word 'Go'.

'It's me,' he said, sighing.

'Well, may God go with you. You'll get your baptism of fire without having to wait for it,' said the battery commander, watching the young ensign's embarrassed features with a good-natured smile. 'But you'd better be off at the double. And to make things more cheerful for you, Vlang will go along with you as NCO.'

—21—

Vlang was overjoyed by his assignment. He promptly ran off to get ready and, as soon as he was properly dressed, came back to give Volodya a hand, urging him to take with him his camp bed, his fur greatcoat, his old copies of *Fatherland Notes*,[47] his spirit coffee-maker and various other possessions he could not possibly need. The captain advised Volodya to read, before he did anything else, the section of the handbook* that dealt with the firing of mortars, and to copy out from it immediately the table giving angles of elevation. Volodya set to this task at once, and observed, to his surprise and joy, that although his fear of danger and his even greater fear of proving to be a coward were still causing him some uneasiness, they were almost as nothing compared with the day before. Part of the reason for this lay in the immediacy of the occasion and the activity it involved; but it was also partly (and mainly) due to the fact that fear, like every powerful emotion, is incapable of being sustained at the same high level for any appreciable length of time. In other words, he had already passed the stage of being afraid. At about seven that evening, just as the sun was beginning to dip behind the Nicholas Barracks, the sergeant-major came in to report to him that the men were ready and waiting.

'I've given the list of names to Vlanga. He'll tell you what they are if you ask him, your honour!' he said.

Some twenty artillerymen armed with broadswords at the ready were standing at the side of the house. Volodya approached them, accompanied by the cadet. 'Ought I to make a short speech, just say "Good health, men", or not say anything at all?' he wondered. 'Oh, why don't I just say "Good health, men" – I'm sure that's correct.' And, plucking up his courage, he cried, 'Good health, men!' The soldiers answered cheerfully: this fresh young voice

* *Handbook for Artillery Officers*, published by Bezak. (Tolstoy's note.)

sounded pleasantly to the ears of each of them. Volodya briskly led the way, and though his heart was hammering inside him as if he had just run several versts at full sprint, his gait was light and his face cheerful. As they approached the Malakhov on their way up the hill, he noticed that Vlang, who had never once lagged behind and who back at barracks had seemed such a valiant fellow, was constantly stepping aside and ducking his head, as though all the shells and cannonballs, which were indeed whistling past with great frequency now, were coming straight in his direction. Some of the soldiers were doing the same, and most of their faces wore an expression which, if it was not one of fear, was at least one of apprehension. Volodya found all this thoroughly reassuring and encouraging.

'So here I am on the Malakhov, and it isn't nearly as bad as I thought it would be! I'm able to keep going without ducking, and I'm far less afraid than the others. Does that mean I'm not a coward?' he pondered with delight, and even a certain rapturous self-satisfaction.

This sense of fearlessness and self-satisfaction was, however, soon shaken by the spectacle he stumbled upon in the semi-darkness at the Kornilov battery as he was looking for the bastion commander. Four sailors were holding a bloody, coatless and bootless corpse by its arms and legs, preparing to heave it over the parapet. (This was the second day of the bombardment, and already there was no time to gather up the dead bodies that lay on the bastions; instead they were being thrown into the moat so that they did not get in the way of the gun crews.) Volodya froze for a moment as he saw the corpse strike the top of the parapet and then slowly slither down into the fosse; luckily for him, however, the bastion commander happened to come along just then, gave him some orders and supplied him with a guide to take him to the battery and the casemate that had been designated for the gun crews. I shall not relate all the many further horrors, dangers and disenchantments experienced by our hero in the course of that evening; how, instead of the artillery work he had witnessed on Volkovo Polye,[48] which had been characterized by the kind of order and precision he had been hoping to find here, he found two cracked little mortars with no sights, the muzzle of one of which had been crumpled by a cannonball, while the platform of the other had been blown to splinters; how he was unable to get anyone to repair the platform until the morning; how not one of the charges was of the weight specified in the handbook; how two of the soldiers in his unit were wounded and how on at least a couple of dozen occasions he himself came within a hair's breadth of death. He was fortunate in having been given a helper, an immensely tall naval gunner who had been handling these mortars ever since the beginning of the siege. The gunner managed to persuade Volodya that they could still be made to work, showed him round the whole bastion in the darkness by the light of a lantern, as if this were his kitchen garden, and promised to have everything in proper working order by the following morning. The casemate to which Volodya's guide took him was an oblong pit excavated in the stony soil some two cubic *sazhens*[49] in dimension, and covered by large oak beams. It was here that Volodya and all his men were to accommodate themselves. Vlang, the moment he caught sight of the low entrance to the casemate, rushed through it before all the others, barely missed bruising himself on the stone floor and then hid himself away in a corner, from which he did not emerge. Volodya, on the other hand, waiting until all the soldiers had found places for themselves on the floor along the walls and some of them had lit their pipes, set up his bed in a corner, lighted a candle, lit a cigarette from it and lay down to smoke. Above the casemate there was a constant rumble of gunfire, none of it particularly loud, with the exception of a single cannon which was very near at hand and which, every time it fired, shook the casemate so violently that earth came showering down from the ceiling. In the casemate itself it was quiet: the only sounds were made by the men, still wary of the new officer, exchanging the odd remark from time to time, asking someone to move aside, or someone else for a light; by a rat, scrabbling somewhere between the stones; or by Vlang, who had not yet mastered himself and was looking wildly around him, every so often uttering a loud sigh. As he lay there on his bed in that crowded corner lit by a single candle, Volodya experienced the cosy sensation he had had as a child, when during games of hide-and-seek he had crept into a cupboard or under his mother's skirts and, almost without daring to breathe, had listened, felt a fear of the dark and yet strangely enjoyed himself. He had a slight sense of nervous glee.

—22—

After some ten minutes or so, the soldiers regained a little of their self-confidence and began talking to one another. Nearest the officer's bed and candle sat the two most important men, both artillery NCOs. One of them was old and grey-haired, and was wearing the ribbons of practically every medal and cross there was, with the exception of the St George Cross; the other was young, a Kantonist,[50] and was smoking cigarettes he had rolled by hand. The drummer, as ever, had taken upon himself the duty of serving the officer. The lance-corporals and recipients of the St George Cross also sat fairly well inside, while in the shadows near the entrance huddled the 'obedient ones'. It was among these that the conversation began. What sparked it off was the noise made by someone tumbling unceremoniously into the casemate.

'Hullo, mate, fed up with being out of doors? Or are the girls giving you trouble?' said one voice.

'They never played tunes like that in the village where I come from,' said the man who had entered the casemate, laughing.

'He's not too keen on shells, is our Vasin,' quipped one of the men from the 'elite' corner.

'Well, I mean, if it's serving a good purpose, that's one thing,' Vasin's slow voice said. Whenever he spoke, all the others were silent. 'On the twenty-fourth they were blazing away at us fit to burst; but now we're being blown to kingdom come for a load of shit, and we don't even get so much as a thank-you from the higher-ups!'

At these words of Vasin's everyone burst out laughing.

'What about Melnikov? I bet he's still out there,' someone said.

'Get him in here,' said the old NCO. 'The enemy's killing men for nothing today, and that's a fact.'

'Who's Melnikov?' asked Volodya.

'Oh, he's one of our soldiers, your honour, who's not very

bright. He isn't scared of anything, and now he just wanders around outside all the time. You want to see him; he looks just like a bear.'

'He has some magic charm he says he knows,' said Vasin's lugubrious voice from the other corner.

Melnikov entered the casemate. He was corpulent (a characteristic extremely rare among the common soldiery), with red hair and a ruddy complexion, an enormous protruding forehead, and bulging, clear blue eyes.

'Aren't you afraid of being blown up by a shell?' Volodya asked him.

'Why should I be, sir?' Melnikov replied, shrugging his shoulders and scratching himself. 'I know it won't be a shell that gets me.'

'Perhaps you'd like to live here, then?'

'Of course I would, sir. It's wonderful here!' he said, bursting into sudden peals of laughter.

'Aha, they ought to take you on a sortie! Do you want me to have a word with the general?' said Volodya, though he did not know a single general here.

'Of course I do, sir!'

And Melnikov dived for cover behind the other men.

'Let's have a game of "noses", lads! Who's got a pack of cards?' his voice could be heard hurriedly asking.

And indeed a game of cards was soon under way in the corner by the entrance – the sounds of laughter, the slapping of noses with the pack of cards and the calling of trumps could be heard. Volodya had tea made with the samovar with which the drummer had provided him; he offered some to the NCOs, joking and talking with them in an effort to make himself popular, and delighted with the respect they showed him. The common soldiers, too, when they saw that the 'master' was 'on the level', started to enter into conversation with him. One man aired his view that the state of siege in Sebastopol could not last much longer, and said a reliable friend of his in the navy had told him that Constantine, the Tsar's brother, would soon be coming to our rescue with the aid of the American fleet; the same friend had also said that there was soon to be a two-week long ceasefire in order to let everyone have a rest, and that if anyone did any firing they would receive a fine of seventy-five copecks per round.

Vasin, who as Volodya had now had time to observe, was a small, sidewhiskered man with large, good-natured eyes, told first amid universal silence, and then to the accompaniment of laughter, how when he had arrived home on leave everyone had initially been delighted to see him; subsequently, however, his father had begun sending him out into the fields to work, and his wife had kept being asked for by the chief forester's lieutenant, who would send his droshky over to their house in order to collect her. Volodya found all this hugely entertaining. Not only did he not feel the slightest twinge of fear or distaste associated with the crowding and foul smell in the casemate, he felt positively light-hearted, and thought it all most agreeable.

Many of the soldiers were already snoring. Vlang, too, had stretched out on the floor, and the old NCO, having spread out his greatcoat to lie on, was crossing himself and muttering his bedtime prayers, when Volodya suddenly conceived a desire to get out of the casemate and see what was going on outside.

'Legs in!' the soldiers shouted to one another, as soon as he stood up; and legs were drawn in to let him pass.

Vlang, who had appeared to be asleep, suddenly raised his head and grabbed the side of Volodya's greatcoat.

'No, please don't go out there, how can you even think of it?' he said, in a tearful, wheedling tone of voice. 'Listen, you don't know what it's like yet; there's constant firing out there; you're better in here . . .'

In spite of Vlang's pleading, Volodya managed to struggle his way out of the casemate and sat down on the step outside, where he found Melnikov changing his boots.

The air was clean and fresh – especially after the casemate; the night was clear and quiet. Behind the rolling of the gunfire could be heard the sound made by the wheels of carts which were delivering loads of gabions, and the voices of the men working in the powder magazine. High above their heads stretched the starry heavens, perpetually criss-crossed by the fiery trails of shells; to their left, a small, narrow opening led into another casemate, and in it one could see the legs of the sailors who lived there, and hear their drunken voices. In the foreground loomed the elevation of the powder magazine, around which flitted the shadowy figures of stooping men, and on the very top of which, under the hail of shells and bullets that constantly whistled by this spot, stood a tall, black-coated figure, who, hands in pockets, was trampling down the earth the other men were carrying in sacks. Shells frequently hurtled past and exploded in the close vicinity of the magazine. The soldiers who were carrying the sacks would duck down or jump aside; but the black figure never once moved from the spot and calmly went on trampling down the earth, maintaining a steady posture.

'Who's this fellow in black?' Volodya asked Melnikov.

'No idea, sir; I'll go and take a look.'

'No, don't go, there's no need for you to.'

But Melnikov, who was not listening to him, stood up, went over to the man in black and spent some considerable time standing beside him, likewise indifferent and immovable.

'He's the powder storesman, your honour,' he said, when he came back. 'The magazine was holed by a shell, so the infantrymen are bringing in earth to repair the damage.'

Every so often a shell would seem to head straight for the casemate.

At such moments Volodya would duck around the corner and then poke his nose out again, looking up at the sky to see if any more shells were headed their way. Although Vlang came out of the casemate several times, begging him to go back inside, Volodya continued to sit on the step for about another three hours, finding this test of fortune and observation of shell trajectories strangely enjoyable. By the end of the evening he knew the positions of a good number of the enemy guns and was able to predict where their shells would land.

—23—

Early on the morning of the following day – the 27th – Volodya, feeling rested and cheerful after ten hours' sleep, emerged once more on to the step of the casemate. This time, Vlang was about to clamber out after him, but at the first sound of a bullet he rushed back inside, falling head over heels, much to the general amusement of the soldiers, most of whom had ventured out for a while to take a breath of air. Only Vasin, the old artillery NCO and a few of the others made a point of rarely coming out into the open trench; the rest could not be restrained: they all came pouring out of the stinking casemate into the fresh morning air, and in spite of the firing, which was just as intense as it had been the evening before, settled themselves down either in the neighbourhood of the step or beneath the parapet. Melnikov, indeed, had been roaming around the batteries since the crack of dawn, every so often casting a phlegmatic glance up at the sky.

Near the step sat two old soldiers and one young curly-headed one – of the Jewish race, to judge by his appearance. This young soldier had picked up one of the stray bullets that lay scattered about and, having flattened it against a stone by hammering it with a shell-splinter was carving from it a cross in the manner of the St George; as they talked among themselves, the other men watched his work develop. The cross was really turning out very handsomely.

'You know, if we stay here much longer,' one of the older men was saying, 'when the war's over we'll all get our discharge.'

'That's right! I only had four years to go until my discharge, and now I've been in Sebastopol five months.'

'Just being here doesn't count for discharge,' said another man.

At that moment a cannonball whistled above the heads of the conversationalists in close proximity to Melnikov, who was making his way along the trench towards them.

'That one nearly killed Melnikov,' one of the men said.

'No, it didn't,' Melnikov replied.

'Look, here's a cross for your bravery,' said the young soldier who had made it, giving it to Melnikov.

'No, my friend, a month in this place counts as a year in the service – there was an imperial decree about it,' one of the older men said, continuing the conversation.

'Well, whichever way you look at it, when this lot's all over the

Tsar'll hold a review in Warsaw and even if we don't get our discharge we'll be put into the reserves.'

Just then a bullet whined, dangerously close, above their heads and struck a stone.

'Watch out, or you'll be getting your final discharge before the day's out,' one of the men said.

Everyone laughed.

They did not have to wait for the day to be out; a couple of hours later, two of them had indeed received their 'final discharge', and five of them had been wounded; but the rest of the men went on cracking jokes as though nothing had happened.

The naval gunner was as good as his word: by the following morning the pair of mortars had been restored to a usable condition. At about ten o'clock, following an order from the bastion commander, Volodya summoned his unit together and led it up to the battery.

As soon as the men sprang into action they lost all trace of the fear they had shown on the previous day. Only Vlang was unable to gain control of himself: he kept dodging and ducking as before, and, as a result of watching him, Vasin lost his composure and started to get into a fuss, cowering down every now and then. But Volodya was in a transport of enthusiasm: the thought of danger simply did not enter his mind. His delight in the fact that he was doing his duty well, that not merely was he not a coward but was even brave, his sense of being in command, and the presence of twenty men who, he was aware, were eyeing him with curiosity, had turned him into a swashbuckling warrior. His bravery made him conceited; he played the dandy in front of the other men, climbing up on to the banquette and unfastening his greatcoat to make himself more noticeable. The bastion commander, who in the course of eight months' service had had time to get used to most forms of bravery, and who happened at that moment to be making the rounds of his 'estate', as he liked to call it, could not help admiring this pretty boy in the unfastened greatcoat, under which a red shirt, whose collar encircled a soft, white neck, was visible, and who, his face and eyes on fire, kept clapping his hands and shouting 'Mortar one! Mortar two!' in a resonant, commanding voice, merrily running up on to the parapet to see where his last shell had landed. At half past eleven the firing abated on both sides, and at exactly twelve noon the assault on the 2nd, 3rd and 5th bastions of the Malakhov Hill[51] began.

—24—

At around noon two naval officers had taken up positions at the top of the Telegraph Hill on the Russian-held side of the bay, between Inkerman and the northern fortification. One of them was scanning Sebastopol through a mounted field-glass, while the other, a naval hussar on horseback accompanied by a mounted Cossack, had just ridden up to the large signal post.

The sun was shining high and brilliant above the bay, which glittered warmly and cheerfully, studded with motionless ships and moving sailboats and skiffs. A light breeze was barely rustling the withered leaves of the scrub oaks near the Telegraph, filling the sails of the small boats and raising a gentle swell. On the other side of the bay one could see Sebastopol, looking just as it always did, with its unfinished church, its column, its seafront, its green boulevard stretching along the side of the hill and its elegantly proportioned library building; with its little azure coves filled with masts, its aqueducts with their picturesque arches, and its clouds of blue powder smoke, lit up from time to time by a crimson blaze of gunfire; still the same, beautiful, festive, proud Sebastopol, surrounded on the one hand by yellow, misty hills and on the other by the bright blue sea, sparkling in the sun. Out there on the horizon, along which a smudge of black smoke from a steamship trailed, long white clouds were creeping landwards, promising wind. Along the whole line of the fortifications, especially among the hills on the left, balls of dense, compressed white smoke kept suddenly materializing, several at a time, accompanied by flashes that were sometimes visible even in the midday glare – burgeoning out, assuming varied forms, and turning darker as they rose into the sky. These puffs of smoke appeared now here, now there: on the enemy batteries, among the hills, in the town and high up in the sky. The sounds of the explosions succeeded one another without a break, merging into one another and making the air vibrate . . .

By twelve o'clock the puffs of smoke had begun to appear more rarely, and the air shook less from the roar.

'The 2nd bastion's stopped returning fire altogether now,' said the hussar on horseback. 'They've been blown to pieces. It's terrible!'

'Yes, and those fellows on the Malakhov have only been sending one round for every three of theirs,' replied the officer who was looking through the field-glass. 'It really makes my blood boil, their not replying like that. There's another – it's hit the Kornilov battery, but they haven't fired back.'

'Well, it's as I told you: they always stop firing when it gets around to twelve,' said the other. 'We might as well go and have lunch . . . they'll be expecting us . . . there's nothing much to see now anyway.'

'Wait, don't distract me!' said the officer with the field-glass, which he was now training on Sebastopol with avid concentration.

'What can you see? What is it?'

'There's movement in the trenches, dense columns of men are on the move.'

'Yes, I can see them,' said the naval officer. 'They're marching in columns. We'd better send a signal.'

'Look, look! They've come out of the trenches!'

Indeed, even the naked eye could now make out what looked like dark stains spreading downhill through the gully from the French batteries towards the bastions. Ahead of these stains several dark strips could be seen quite close to the Russian lines. White puffs of smoke leapt up at various points on the bastions, appearing to run along them. The wind bore across the rapid patter of rifle and musketry fire, a sound like that of rain beating on a windowpane. The black strips were moving through the smoke, drawing nearer and nearer. The sounds of the firing, growing louder and louder, merged into a continuous rolling thunder. The puffs of smoke, which were rising more and more frequently, soon spread along the lines and at last fused into a single, lilac-coloured, smoking and developing cloud in which flashes of light and black dots briefly appeared here and there.

Then, finally, all the sounds united into one earth-shattering detonation.

'It's an assault!' said the officer, his face pale, letting the other man look through the field-glass.

Some Cossacks came charging along the road at full gallop; officers rode by, followed by the commander-in-chief in a carriage, accompanied by his suite. Gloomy excitement and an anticipation of something terrible could be read on every face.

'They can't have taken it!' said the officer on horseback.

'My God, a flag! Look! Look!' said the other in a strangled voice, moving away from the field-glass. 'The French colours are flying on the Malakhov!'

'It's impossible!'

—25—

The older Kozeltsov, who in the course of the night had managed to win back all his money and then lose it again – this time even including the gold roubles he had sewn into his cuff – was still sunk in an unhealthy, heavy but deep slumber in the defended barracks of the 5th bastion when the fateful cry, repeated by various voices, went up:

'Battle alarm . . . !'

'Wake up, Mikhailo Semyonych! There's an assault on!' he heard a voice shout.

'Must be one of those boys from training school,' he muttered, opening his eyes but not yet taking anything in.

Suddenly, however, he saw an officer running from one corner of the room to another for no apparent purpose, and with such a pale and frightened face that he took in the situation at once. The thought that he might be taken for a coward who was trying to get out of joining his company at the critical moment had a galvanizing effect on him. He ran off to join his company as fast as he could. The firing of the artillery had stopped; but the crackle of rifle fire was raging furiously. The bullets were whistling over not one by one, like the balls from carbines, but in teeming formations, the way flocks of birds fly above one's head in autumn.

The whole of the area Kozeltsov's battalion had occupied the day before was now shrouded in smoke, and hostile shouts and exclamations could be heard. Soldiers, wounded and unscathed alike, were coming towards him in droves. Running forwards another thirty yards or so, he glimpsed his company, pressed up against the wall, and the familiar face of one of his men, pale as death now, and marked by fear. The faces of the other men were also pale and frightened.

Kozeltsov found himself affected, in spite of himself, by the men's sense of terror. A chill ran down his spine.

'They've taken the Schwartz redoubt,' said a young officer, his teeth chattering. 'We're all done for.'

'Nonsense!' Kozeltsov said angrily and, since he wanted to raise his own spirits by means of a gesture, he drew his small, blunt iron sabre and shouted: 'Forward, lads! Hurra-ah!'

So loud and resonant was his voice that it produced on him the effect he desired. He raced forward along the traverse; with a shout, some fifty soldiers rushed after him. When at the far end of the traverse they emerged on to an open area, the bullets came lashing down, quite literally, like hail; two of them struck him, but where they had hit and what damage they had done – whether he had merely been contused or had in fact been wounded – he had no time to find out. In the smoke ahead of him he could make out the figures of men in blue coats and red trousers and hear cries that sounded distinctly Russian. One of the French soldiers was standing on the parapet, waving his cap and shouting something. Kozeltsov thought his last hour had come; yet this same thought emboldened him. On and on he ran. He was overtaken by a few soldiers who were running even faster; others appeared from somewhere at his side, also running. The blue-coated men kept their distance, retreating to their trenches, but he kept stepping on the bodies of dead and wounded. By the time he had run as far as the outer fosse, all these human figures mingled together in his eyes; feeling a pain in his chest, he sat down on the banquette and, looking through one of the embrasures, saw to his satisfaction that crowds of the blue-coated men were running in confusion back to their trenches, and that the entire field was strewn with motionless dead and crawling wounded, all of them in red trousers and blue coats.

Half an hour later, lying on a stretcher outside the Nicholas Barracks, he knew that he had been wounded, but could feel hardly any pain; all he wanted was a rest and something cool to drink.

A small, fat surgeon with large black sideburns came over to him and unfastened his greatcoat. Looking down over his chin, Kozeltsov watched what the surgeon was doing to his wound, and studied the surgeon's face, but felt no pain whatsoever. The surgeon pulled Kozeltsov's shirt back into place over the wound, wiped his fingers on the skirts of his coat and silently, without looking at him, went on to the next patient. Kozeltsov observed with a detached gaze all that was taking place around him. As he ran through in his mind what had taken place on the 5th bastion, he reflected with profound relief and self-satisfaction that he had discharged his duty well, that for the first time in his army career he had done the best he could have been expected to do, and had nothing to reproach himself for. The surgeon, who was now changing the dressing of another wounded officer, pointed to Kozeltsov and said something to a priest with a large, red beard, who was standing nearby holding a cross.

'What's the matter, am I going to die?' Kozeltsov asked the priest when he came over.

The priest made no reply, but said a prayer and gave him the cross to hold. Kozeltsov felt no fear of death.

He took the cross in his enfeebled hands, pressed it to his lips and wept.

'Well, have the French been dislodged at all points?' he asked the priest in a firm tone of voice.

'Yes, victory is ours at all points,' the priest replied in a Ukrainian accent, pronouncing all his *o*s; in order not to cause further distress to the wounded man, he was concealing from him the fact that the French colours were already flying on the Malakhov.

'God be praised, God be praised,' said the wounded man, unaware of the tears that were flowing down his cheeks, and experiencing a sense of ecstasy as he realized he had performed a heroic deed.

For a fleeting moment he remembered his brother. 'God grant him a similar happiness,' he thought.

—26—

But such was not the lot that awaited Volodya. As he was listening to a story Vasin was telling him, a shout of 'The French are coming!' went up. For a moment, Volodya felt the blood drain from his head, and his cheeks turned cold and pale.

In that second, he remained motionless; on looking round, however, he saw that the soldiers were doing up their greatcoats in relative calm and were clambering out of the casemate one by one; one of them – he thought it looked like Melnikov – even said, jokingly: 'Don't forget the bread and salt, lads!'

Together with Vlanga, who stuck close behind him all the way, Volodya hauled himself out of the casemate and ran towards the battery. There was a complete absence of artillery fire on both sides. Volodya felt his spirits raised, less by the sight of the men's calm than by this cadet's pathetic, undisguised cowardice. 'I'm not really like him, am I?' he thought, as he ran cheerfully towards the parapet, beside which stood his mortars. He had a clear view of the French soldiers running across the open field towards the bastion, and could see crowds of them stirring in the trenches that lay nearest, their bayonets glinting in the sun. One of them, a little broad-shouldered man in a zouave's uniform, was running ahead of the rest, sword in hand, leaping over the shell-holes as he went. 'Fire grape!' Volodya shouted, running down from the banquette; but his men had already taken the matter into their own hands, and the metallic hiss of grapeshot being fired, first from one mortar and then from the other, sounded in the air overhead. 'Mortar one! Mortar two!' came Volodya's shouted orders, as he ran through the smoke from one mortar to the other, having completely forgotten the reality of danger. From the side sounded the loud crackle of the Russian covering fire, and the men's hasty shouts.

Suddenly a cry of despair, echoed by several voices, came from the left: 'They're getting through! They're getting through!' Volodya looked round. Some two dozen French soldiers had appeared from behind them. One of them, a handsome black-bearded man in a red fez cap, was coming on ahead of the others, but when he was about a dozen yards from the battery he stopped, aimed his rifle, fired, and then continued to walk towards them. For a second

Volodya stood still as though he had been turned to stone, unable to believe his eyes. By the time he had recovered his wits and started to look around him, the men in blue coats were up on the parapet; one of them had even climbed down again and was spiking one of the guns. There was no one left near Volodya except Melnikov, who had seized hold of a handspike[52] and was rushing forward with an expression of fury on his face, showing the whites of his eyes. 'Follow me, Vladimir Semyonych! Follow me! We're done for!' he cried in a voice of despair, brandishing the handspike in the direction of the French soldiers who were approaching from the rear. The cadet's violent appearance had clearly taken them aback. Melnikov brought the handspike down on the head of the man in front, and the others came to a halt, uncertain of what to do next. Continuing to look about him, and shouting 'Follow me, Vladimir Semyonych! Don't stay here! Run!' Melnikov ran towards the trench from which the Russian infantry were firing at the French forces. Having jumped into the trench, he leaned out of it to see what his beloved ensign was doing. Something wrapped in a greatcoat was lying face down in the place where Volodya had been standing, and the entire area was now occupied by French soldiers, who were firing at the Russians.

—27—

Vlang found his battery on the second line of the defences. Of the twenty soldiers who had made up the mortar brigade, only eight had escaped with their lives.

By nine that evening Vlang and his battery were on board a steamer which was ferrying a cargo of soldiers, cannon, horses and wounded over to the North Side. There was no firing anywhere now. The stars shone brightly in the sky, just as they had done the previous night, but a strong wind was creating a swell at sea. Without warning, a series of flashes leapt along the ground between the 1st and 2nd bastions; explosions shook the air, illuminating strange black objects and flying stones. Down by the docks something was on fire, and the red flames were reflected in the water. The pontoon bridge, packed with people, was lit up by the glare from the Nicholas battery. On the distant headland where the Alexander battery was situated, a great sheet of flame seemed to be hanging above the water, illuminating the base of the smoke-cloud that had formed above it; just as they had done the night before, the calm, insolent lights of the enemy fleet gleamed far out at sea. The fresh wind chopped the surface of the bay. By the light of the glow from the various fires one could see the masts of the sunken Russian ships, which were slowly slipping deeper and deeper beneath the waves. There was no talking on deck; above the even hiss of escaping steam and keel-cut waves one could hear the horses stamping and snorting in the tow-barge, the words of command spoken by the captain, and the groans of the men who were wounded. Vlang, who had had nothing to eat all day, took a piece of bread from his pocket and began to chew it; suddenly, however, remembering Volodya, he started to weep so loudly that the soldiers near him grew curious.

'Strewth! He's eating a bit of bread and crying at the same time, our Vlang,' said Vasin.

'That lad's not right in the head, if you ask me,' another man said. 'Christ, they've set fire to our barracks and all,' he continued, sighing. 'Think of all the lads who've bought it over there; and now those Frenchies have taken it, easy as winking.'

'Well, at least we got out of there alive, thank the Lord,' said Vasin.

'It's a shame, though.'

'What's a shame? Do you think he's going to have the place all to himself? Not on your life! Just you wait and see, our lads'll take it back again. Won't matter how many of them will have to die, you can bet your boots the Tsar will give the command and we'll take it back again! You think we'll just leave it to him? Never! Here you are,' he said, addressing the French now. 'Here's the bare walls, but we've blown up all the trenches. All right, so you've got your flag up on the Malakhov. But you'll never dare poke your noses into the town. You wait, we'll settle your hash, just give us time.'

'That's right, we will,' said the other man, with conviction.

Along the whole line of the Sebastopol bastions, which for so many months now had been seething with an unusually active life, had seen heroes released one by one into the arms of death, and had aroused the fear, hatred and, latterly, the admiration of the enemy forces, there was now not a soul to be seen. The whole place was dead, laid waste, uncanny – but not quiet: the destruction was still continuing. The ground, churned up and displaced here and there by fresh explosions, was everywhere covered in twisted gun carriages with the corpses of Russian and enemy soldiers crushed beneath them, heavy cast-iron cannon which by dint of dreadful force had been buried into shell-holes and half buried under mounds of earth, shells, cannonballs, more corpses, craters, split beams, casemates, and yet more silent corpses in grey and blue greatcoats. This entire landscape frequently shuddered and gleamed in the crimson glare of the explosions that continued to make the air vibrate.

The enemy forces could see that something incomprehensible was taking place in grim Sebastopol. These explosions, coupled with the dead silence that hung over the bastions, made them shudder; but, with the calm and mighty resistance they had met still fresh in their memories, they did not yet dare believe that their unflinching antagonist had disappeared, and in silence, without moving, they waited anxiously for this murky night to end.

Surging together and ebbing apart like the waves of the sea on this gloomy, swell-rocked night, uneasily shuddering with all its massive volume, swaying out along the bridge and over on the North Side by the bay, the Sebastopol force slowly moved in a dense, impenetrable crush away from the place where it had left behind so many brave men, the place that was entirely saturated in its blood; the place which for eleven months it had held against an enemy twice as powerful, and which it had now been instructed to abandon without a struggle.

The first reaction of every Russian soldier on hearing this order was one of bitterness and incomprehension. This was succeeded by a fear of pursuit. As soon as they had abandoned the positions they had grown used to defending, the men felt exposed and unprotected, and crowded anxiously in the darkness by the entrance to the bridge, which was pitching in the high wind. Their bayonets clashing, the infantry huddled together in jostling throngs of regiments, carriages and militia; officers on horseback bearing fresh orders forced their way through; townsfolk and officers' orderlies stood weeping and begging beside loads of personal belongings, which were not being allowed through; with a rumble of wheels the artillery cut its way towards the bay shore, in a hurry to embark. Countless immediate and practical concerns took second place to what was uppermost in everyone's mood: a general instinct for self-preservation and a common desire to escape from this terrible place of death as quickly as possible. This feeling was shared equally by the soldier lying fatally wounded among five hundred other men similarly at their last gasp on the stone surface of the Paul Quay, praying God for deliverance; by the militiaman who with the last of his strength was pushing into the densely packed crowd in order to make way for a general to get through on horseback; by the general himself, who was firmly in command of the crossing-point and was restraining the hasty energies of his men; by the sailor who had become caught up in the ranks of an advancing battalion and was having the last breath crushed out of him by the fluctuating mass; by the wounded officer being carried on a stretcher by four others who, forced to stop outside the Nicholas battery having likewise had the breath knocked out of them by the crowd, were compelled to stop and put the stretcher down; by the artilleryman who had served by his gun for sixteen years and was now, in compliance with a bewildering order from the supreme command, heaving it, with the assistance of his comrades, off the steep escarpment and into the bay; and by the sailors who had just finished opening the scuttles in their ships and were now rowing briskly away from them in long-boats. Each man, on arriving at the other side of the bridge, took off his cap and crossed himself. But this feeling concealed another – draining, agonizing, and infinitely more profound: a sense of something that was a blend of remorse, shame and violent hatred. Nearly every man, as he looked across from the North Side at abandoned Sebastopol, sighed with a bitterness that could find no words, and shook his fist at the enemy forces.

St Petersburg
27 December 1855

NOTES

1. *the Sapun-gora*: called 'Mont Sapouné' by the French, and 'Sapoun Hill' or 'Mount Sapoune' by the British – the high ground south-east of Sebastopol.

2. *the North Side*: district on the north shore of the Great Bay (called 'the Roadstead' by the British) of Sebastopol.

3. *muskets*: the Russian infantry were equipped only with muskets, while the French and British had rifles. Tolstoy makes no distinction using the Russian word *ruzh'yo* ('gun') to denote both.

4. *the Grafskaya*: quay on the Town Side of Sebastopol near the opening of Sebastopol Harbour (called the 'Southern Bay' by the Russians) into the Great Bay.

5. *the sunken ships*: during the intensive building of defences that went on in the autumn of 1854, part of the Russian fleet was sunk in the Great Bay to protect the town against attack from the sea.

6. *all her guns*: ships' guns were widely commandeered for use on land batteries during the fighting.

7. *Kornilov*: Vice-Admiral Vladimir Alekseyevich Kornilov (1806–54), an outstanding Russian commander during the Crimean War and, with Totleben, one of the principal organizers of the Sebastopol defences. He was fatally wounded during the first allied bombardment.

8. sbitén: a drink made with honey and spices.

9. *a handsome building with Roman numerals carved on its pediment*: the hall of the Sebastopol Assembly of Nobles. It was here that the great

Russian surgeon N. I. Pirogov set up and ran a field hospital or dressing station (*perevyazochny punkt*).

10. *the 5th bastion*: the western fortification of the Sebastopol defence line.

11. *the first bombardment*: this took place on 5 October 1854.

12. *a sailor*: 'As the bombardment continued, the supply of powder ran low. In large part this was caused by the naval gunners manning many of the batteries, who fired furiously and with little regard for aim.' (J. S. Curtiss, *The Russian Army Under Nicholas I, 1825–1855*, Duke University Press, Durham, North Carolina (1965), p. 334.)

13. *the Grand Dukes*: Nikolai Nikolayevich and Mikhail Nikolayevich, the two sons of Nicholas I, who had arrived at the front during the autumn to bolster the morale of the troops, and who seemed to Tolstoy 'to have the air of excessively well-behaved children, but were very fine fellows, both of them'.

14. *the fifth*: 5 October 1854.

15. *the 24th*: 24 October 1854 – the date of the battle of Inkerman.

16. *the 4th bastion*: the southernmost fortification of the Sebastopol defence line, situated on the Boulevard Heights between the Town Ravine and the Boulevard Dell.

17. *the battle of the Alma*: the battle along the banks of the River Alma on 8 September 1854; this was the first engagement with the allies, and it ended in defeat for the Russians.

18. *carbines*: the Russian word is *shtutser*, the term used for the Minié rifle and the British threaded rifle.

19. *the Yazon redoubt*: this was situated behind the 4th bastion, and was formed either at the end of November or the beginning of December 1854 by connecting the 20th, 23rd, 53rd and 62nd batteries. The redoubt got its name from the brig *Yazon*, whose crew worked on its construction.

20. sukhar': a rusk of dried bread.

21. *feigned, anticipatory look of suffering*: Nikolai Rostov, in *War and Peace*, makes a similar observation on the field of Austerlitz.

22. *the Green Hill*: the 'Mamelon Vert', on which the British had their batteries.

23. *the* Veteran: *The Russian Veteran*, the official Russian army newspaper.

24. *Napoleon*: the reference is to Napoleon III of France (1808–73).

25. *the French have lost their line of communication to Balaclava*: the 'comrade', here revealing his ignorance, means the British, who had a cable railway connecting them with their base at Balaclava.

26. *cadet volunteer*: 'cadet volunteer' is offered as a translation of the Russian *yunker*.

'. . . while the cadet schools furnished most of the noted officers in the Russian army, who entered service with a fair military education and a fine knowledge of marching, riding, and formation drill, by far the greatest number of officers began their careers as volunteers who served as sergeants or yunkers in army regiments. Probably the most numerous were those entering with noble status. They might qualify for commissions after serving as sergeants for two years if vacancies developed, although if no vacancy occurred they had to wait longer. Those who qualified as university graduates could obtain commissions after three months' service as sergeants, and university students without degrees needed only six months to qualify. The students received their commissions promptly even if no vacancies existed. Volunteers from middle-class and intellectual families needed four months of service to qualify for commissions, while déclassé nobles (*odnodvortsy*) had to serve six years as sergeants. A special limitation on the promotion of yunkers in the cavalry regiments required them to present "definite proof that they have the means to maintain themselves in those regiments in proper manner".

'Most of the yunkers came to the regiments without proper schooling. Many were students dismissed from the gymnasia for poor work, or who had had to leave because of lack of funds. Others had had some sort of home education from tutors or other instructors. Many of them were pampered youngsters unfit for any career or spoiled sons of generals and other officers. The army at least offered them a livelihood, while those with ability could make good careers.' (Curtiss, op. cit., pp. 186–7.)

27. *Why did authors . . .* Vanity Fair*?*: in his study of Tolstoy published in 1890, the Russian thinker Konstantin Leontiev made an interesting reply to this passage, and it may bear quoting in part:

'First, in the times of Homer and Shakespeare, people probably found nothing contemptible or wrong with a person's thinking about how he is looked upon by those who are superior, stronger, more eminent, more lustrous, et cetera. It seemed so natural and so simple that there was no reason here to be disturbed.

'Second, the desire to please and to make a favourable impression on others appears in people at the sight of more than just their superiors. For example, in our "democratic" times, the desire to ingratiate oneself with the lower classes, the mob, the common man, has grown stronger and more harmful than the ancient, everlasting, and natural desire to equal one's superiors in at least something or other (even while remaining in one's own place), to be liked by them, to obtain access to their society, et cetera . . .

'If some petty impulse of pride were to make a person betray his duty, his love, a true feeling, or some other noble matter, one could censure him for it. But if people do their work, do their duty, as more or less all the Russian officers in Tolstoy's stories do, what harm is there if they amuse themselves a little, even by aspiring to that which is superior, a practice which the young (at the time) author called especially vain?

It is special, and it is incorrect, for one can be vain about anything at all – about the most diverse things: a luxurious and a spartan way of life; tidiness and slovenliness; an illustrious and a base origin; pride and humility, et cetera.

'Moreover, we might ask how Count Tolstoy knew for certain in 1855 what the various officers felt?

'Of course, this is nothing more than suspicious conjecture by a mind still immature and driven in one direction by the morbid negation characteristic of the fifties. Finally – and forgive me for being personal – if Count Tolstoy was inwardly unsettled in youth and like this himself, we are not obliged to believe that through it, he thoroughly and accurately knew the soul of everyone else. I might furthermore add, by the way, that at that time Count Tolstoy found all these proud and vain impulses in people of the educated class only. He is silent everywhere about the pride and vanity of soldiers and peasants . . .

'The point is that in the days of Homer and Shakespeare there prevailed a world outlook that was religious and aristocratic, or heroic and consequently more aesthetic than today's. But today, there prevails a world outlook that is utilitarian and moral, with a tendency towards egalitarianism. Therefore, all these suspicions and captious objections have also multiplied so awkwardly in our literature since the forties . . .' (*The Novels of Count Tolstoy*, trans. Spencer Roberts.)

28. *the Schwartz redoubt*: the 1st Schwartz redoubt was a fortification situated between the 4th and 5th bastions.

29. *the casemate*: a defended room in a fortress, designed for protection against bombs and shells.

30. *the lodgments*: a military term used in fortification to denote weak entrenchments.

31. *creature comforts*: 'Cavalry officers especially had a tradition of wild and frivolous conduct suitable to the cornets and subalterns from the *jeunesse dorée*. When Prince A. I. Baryatinsky joined a cuirassier regiment as a cornet in 1833, his tour of duty "was, in keeping with the current cavalry mores, a series of carousels, pranks, of idle civil life". Far from regarding this as a serious defect, the higher military authorities looked on it with amusement, "as consequences of youth and *élan* characteristic of a military man in general and of a cavalryman in particular". Even if they did not misbehave, the young hussars and uhlan officers rarely paid much attention to their military roles – from which, indeed, their squadron commanders willingly excused them – but spent much of their time at the estates of hospitable landowners.' (Curtiss, op. cit., p. 197.)

32. Pojdę na ulicę . . ., *etc.*: the inclusion of dialogue in the original language is an important feature of the second sketch, and it is a device which Tolstoy developed to full effect in *War and Peace*.

33. *He had been killed . . . chest*: In the work already quoted, Leontiev gives a perceptive commentary on the death of Praskukhin, comparing it with the deaths of Prince Andrey and Ivan Ilyich:

 'In these three depictions of death the author observes excellently and with all possible precision available to the human mind those nuances and differences, some of which depend on the nature of the illness or on injury to the organism in general, and others on the nature of the dying man himself and the ideals by which he lived.

 'Praskukhin is not sick. His death is sudden, in the tumult and confusion of battle. Of course, the thought of death is constantly in his mind, because men are being killed all around him, but there is no preparation whatsoever of his emotions for separation from life. Moreover, Praskukhin is by no means ideal – not in any sense; he is not even religious, not Orthodox in his feelings, as in the case of Mikhailov, the other officer whom Tolstoy describes in the same sketch. When Mikhailov suffers a bloody gash in the head from a rock, he thinks he has been killed . . . Praskukhin, on the contrary, imagines that he is merely contused, and gives no thought whatsoever to God or his soul.

'One can more or less successfully imagine the confusion of thought and emotion during combat in an ordinary man, who, while being no coward, is not particularly brave either, and who cherishes no lofty ideal in his heart. It is possible to experience this in time of combat danger, quite independently of how the battle may end for one: in death, a wound, or no harm whatsoever.

'But we definitely do not know what a person thinks or feels upon crossing that elusive boundary called death. To depict the change of thoughts and emotions in a contused or wounded man is artistic courage; but to depict the postmortal state of the soul is no longer courage – it is feeble pretence, and nothing more.

'I find, for example, that the depiction of Prince Andrey's last days and minutes contains not only more poetry, but also more truth than the death of Praskukhin or Ivan Ilyich, because in these latter two deaths Count Tolstoy permits himself to look more boldly behind that fearful and mysterious veil which separates earthly life from the life beyond the grave; in the description of Prince Andrey's death, he very skilfully avoids this.

'Praskukhin is killed: "He neither saw nor heard nor felt anything more," et cetera.

'Ivan Ilyich, on the contrary, experiences no fear whatsoever in his very last minutes, because there is no death.

'In place of death, there was light . . . " 'Death is finished,' he said to himself. 'It is no more.' He drew in a breath, stopped in the middle of a sigh, stretched out, and died."

'Of course, such an expedient is incomparably more clever, profound, and subtle in an artistic sense than the flat assertion that Praskukhin thought or saw no more . . .

'. . . from the standpoint of semi-scientific, or even of completely scientific accuracy, Ivan Ilyich's death is better and truer than Praskukhin's. (Leontiev, op. cit.)

34. *sidewhiskers*: during the reign of Nicholas I, sidewhiskers and moustaches could *only* be worn by members of the armed forces. They seem to have been particularly popular among the medical corps.

35. *Mikhal, Mikhailo*: Ukrainian forms of the name 'Michael' (Russian 'Mikhail').

36. *Kazarsky*: Aleksandr Ivanovich Kazarsky (1797–1844), the commander of the brig *Merkuriy*, whose crew distinguished itself in a battle with two Turkish warships on 14 May 1829.

37. *enough of this*: this scene is based on the encounters Tolstoy had with members of the allied forces during the occasional truces and cease-fires that were arranged to make possible the clearing away of the dead bodies. There is also an echo here of his encounter with French and British prisoners of war during 1854. These face-to-face meetings with the citizens of Western nations made a profound impression on Tolstoy. On 5 November 1854, he noted in his diary: 'Saw French and British prisoners . . . the very appearance and gait of these men somehow filled me with a sad conviction that they are far superior to our troops.' Subsequent conversations with these foreign nationals made Tolstoy anxious to visit the West, and may have largely been at the root of his decision to visit Paris in 1857.

38. *cadet corps*: 'In 1855 there were twenty-three of these, with 8,300 students and 1,400 instructors . . . Once enrolled, the cadets took a general course of four years, with great stress on mathematics, along with history and geography, Russian grammar and literature, and French and German . . .' (Curtiss, op. cit.) In the two upper years of these military educational establishments the cadets took military subjects: tactics, fortification, gunnery, topographic sketching and military history, and also physics, chemistry and higher mathematics. They also did much drilling – posture, marching, and the study of the manual of arms.

39. *Nobody seemed to know . . .*: 'One of the chief reasons for Menshikov's failings as an administrator was his lack of a staff capable of handling the necessary routine work, which led to general disorder. One officer who was in Sebastopol reported: "His whole staff consisted of Colonel Wunsch, chief of staff, and several clerks: the army had no Quarter-master General, no intendant, no director of hospitals. In the clerical section . . . there was such chaos that sometimes they did not know where a certain regiment was . . ." According to a Colonel Batezatul who served in the Crimea, Colonel Wunsch "concentrated in his person all the functions: chief of staff, general on duty, Quartermaster General, intendant, director of the chancellery, hospitals and posts, general police master, and so on." Thus from the beginning of operations in the Crimea, great disorder existed in the administration of the army.' (Curtiss, op. cit., pp. 328–9.)

40. *Totleben*: Eduard Ivanovich Totleben (1818–84), the Russian general

and military engineer who supervised the building of the fortifications around Sebastopol. Author of *A Description of the Defence of Sebastopol*, the two volumes of which appeared, in both French and Russian, in St Petersburg in 1863 and 1868.

41. *the Belbek*: river running parallel to the Great Bay of Sebastopol.

42. *Péllisier*: Jean-Jacques Péllisier (1794–1865), commander-in-chief of the French force from May 1855 onwards.

43. *Gorchakov*: Mikhail Dmitriyevich Gorchakov (1793–1861) commander-in-chief of the Russian Crimean army from February 1855 onwards.

44. *the Korabelnaya*: the eastern district of the South Side of Sebastopol, on the opposite side of the harbour from the North Side.

45. *his estimates are for ten roubles fifty*: see Introduction, pp. 23–5.

46. *Polish* zrazy: meat pies stuffed with rice, buckwheat porridge, etc.

47. Fatherland Notes: a journal which was published in St Petersburg from 1839 until 1884.

48. *Volkovo Polye*: an artillery range in St Petersburg.

49. *two cubic* sazhens: a *sazhen*, or *sagene*, was equivalent to 134 metres.

50. *a Kantonist*: the son of a soldier, trained for lifelong military service in a special army school.

51. *the Malakhov Hill*: *Malakhov kurgan*, 'the Malakoff' – one of the principal fortifications of Sebastopol, situated on the eastern side of the defence line between the 2nd and 3rd bastions; it was considered the key to the whole Sebastopol position. A suburb of Paris is named after the hill.

52. *a handspike*: an instrument used for turning guns and lifting heavy weights. 'Maj. Mordecai in his report remarked . . . that the Russians had ingenious devices for pointing the guns without exposing the men to enemy fire' (Curtiss, op. cit., p. 150).